ALONG THE JOURNEY RIVER

ALSO BY CAROLE LAFAVOR

Evil Dead Center

ALONG THE JOURNEY RIVER

A Mystery

CAROLE LAFAVOR

Foreword by LISA TATONETTI

Afterword by THERESA LAFAVOR

University of Minnesota Press
Minneapolis
London

Published by the University of Minnesota Press
111 Third Avenue South, Suite 290
Minneapolis, MN 55401-2520
http://www.upress.umn.edu

The University of Minnesota is an equal-opportunity educator and employer.

Library of Congress Cataloging-in-Publication Data
Names: LaFavor, Carole, author. | Tatonetti, Lisa, writer of foreword.| Lafavor, Theresa, writer of afterword.
Title: Along the Journey River : a mystery / Carole laFavor ; foreword by Lisa Tatonetti ; afterword by Theresa Lafavor.
Description: Minneapolis : University of Minnesota Press, [2017]
Identifiers: LCCN 2017052711| ISBN 978-1-5179-0355-8 (pb)
Subjects: LCSH: Ojibwa Indians–Fiction. | Indian reservations–Minnesota–Fiction. | Ethnic relations–Fiction. | Lesbians–Fiction. | Mystery fiction. | BISAC: FICTION / Mystery & Detective / General. | FICTION / Lesbian.
Classification: LCC PS3562.A274 A76 2017 | DDC 813/.54–dc23
LC record available at https://lccn.loc.gov/2017052711

To my black cocker spaniel, Athabaska,
for fifteen years of listening and unconditional love.
I'll see you again in the Spirit World.

FOREWORD

Lisa Tatonetti

Carole laFavor (1948–2011), a Two-Spirit Ojibwa, was a nurse, author, and activist who directly engaged the intersectional nature of sexuality, gender, Indigeneity, and HIV/AIDS at a time when few people were acknowledging these connections. Her life and her writing deserve careful attention because of their rich contributions to the field of health advocacy as well as to the literary tradition of Minnesota, to Native American and Indigenous literary studies, and to queer Indigenous literature.

In every sense of the word, laFavor was a pathbreaker. She was a member of the first out lesbian softball team in Minnesota, the Wilder Ones, and was an American Indian Movement member who took part in sending medical supplies to Wounded Knee during the 1973 standoff between Indigenous activists and the U.S. government. She testified at the 1983 Pornography Civil Rights Hearings in Minnesota, where she spoke about her own personal experience of assault as well as the pattern of violence against Indigenous women.[1] At key moments, laFavor stepped up and spoke out when critical issues faced by Native peoples were not being addressed.

Carole laFavor's social justice work is perhaps most significant in her HIV/AIDS activism during the late 1980s and 1990s. The only Indigenous person appointed to the first Presidential Advisory Council on HIV/AIDS (PACHA), which was formed by U.S. President Bill Clinton in 1995, laFavor worked toward what we now would term health sovereignty by using her 1986 diagnosis as a spring-board to social and political engagement on behalf of HIV-positive Indigenous peoples.

An important and now little known aspect of laFavor's activism is her work to help the Centers for Disease Control and Prevention (CDC) educate the public about the then-growing epidemic: she was featured in "Understanding AIDS," the first public informational pamphlet the U.S. Secretary of Health and CDC produced for widespread public distribution. In May and June 1988, the CDC attempted the unprecedented task of contacting every U.S. citizen by mail. As a result, laFavor's picture and first name—accompanied by the text "Obviously women can get AIDS. I'm here to witness to that. AIDS is not a 'we,' 'they' disease, it's an 'us' disease"—was included in a mailer sent to more than 107 million households and reprinted in national publications with vast reading audiences, such as *TIME* and *People*. That same year, the CDC also featured laFavor in televised public service announcements (PSAs) that were essential to late 1980s HIV/AIDS education. While the CDC intentionally elided laFavor's race and sexual orientation in its campaign to raise mainstream awareness and gain broad funding support for the rapidly spreading disease, laFavor foregrounded her identity as well as her diagnosis in her interviews, videos, and innumerable public speaking engagements for tribal nations, colleges, community centers, and health organizations across the United States and Canada.

As this history demonstrates, laFavor was never content to simply point out problems; instead she was committed to enacting productive change. She helped found Positively Native, a national organization for Native Americans with HIV/AIDS and subsequently edited the periodical of the same name. During this pivotal historical time she also was a founding member of the Minnesota American Indian AIDS Task Force (now the Indigenous Peoples Task Force), a landmark organization that began as a volunteer-led effort in 1987. Sharon M. Day (Bois Forte Band of Ojibwe) headed the creation of the task force and became the organization's executive director in 1990. Day and laFavor's commitment to serving Indigenous peoples and, importantly, to making the needs and presence of queer Native peoples visible shaped the educational response and essential materials the organization produced. As Day notes, "So much of the work then . . . really ignored women and . . . still does to a great extent today. But our first two clients were Native lesbians and I believe we, the task force, put out the first lesbian brochure in the country." She continues, "We created some posters by Native artists that were targeted to gay and bisexual men. And when we did training, we decided that we weren't going to sort of soft shoe around the whole issue of sexuality. . . . And so what we did was [to start with] the conversation around sexuality."[2]

The Minnesota American Indian AIDS Task Force and laFavor, in particular, gained international exposure with *Her Giveaway: A Spiritual Journey with AIDS* (1987), directed by noted Sisseton Wahpeton Dakota filmmaker Mona Smith.[3] Smith's film, which is part public service announcement and part biography, focuses on laFavor's experiences as an Indigenous woman living with HIV/AIDS. *Her Giveaway,* the first film on Native American people and HIV, quickly became one of the most widely used resources in the country. Smith explains, "Within two months after it was released, it was in Sweden and Brazil and other places around the world. So it found a market because of the AIDS epidemic and because Carole's story was one that people of all kinds could connect with."[4]

The feminist and activist interventions laFavor made through the American Indian Movement and the Minnesota American Indian AIDS Task Force were paralleled by her contributions to the literary world. Thus the publication of *Along the Journey River* in 1996 represented, on one hand, a unique intervention into mainstream detective fiction, while on another, an important contribution to the growing body of queer Indigenous literature. As the first detective novel by an out Indigenous lesbian, *Along the Journey River* takes the settler project of the private investigator, which most often highlights urban locales and the entangled laws of the U.S. nation-state, and repurposes it with an eye toward reservation spaces and Indigenous justice. In doing so, laFavor joined an increasing number of LGBTQ/Two-Spirit Native writers who were reclaiming historical traditions and recognizing queerness as part of the very fabric of Indigeneity.

Before highlighting laFavor's notable place among out Indigenous writers of the 1980s and 1990s, I turn first to the term "Two-Spirit," which she uses in both *Along the Journey River* and her second novel, *Evil Dead Center* (1997). Just like the author, the protagonist Renee LaRoche employs the term as a way to gesture toward the complex gender traditions that existed in most Indigenous nations before invasion and colonization. The violence visited on alternatively gendered Native peoples by conquistadors, Christian missionaries, and settlers—who murdered, beat, derided, and isolated nonheteronormative Indigenous peoples—drove these gender traditions underground. For hundreds of years such Indigenous gender traditions were suppressed but not erased by ongoing settler colonial practices; not until the 1970s and 1980s were these multiple gender practices publicly invoked by Indigenous peoples who identified as bisexual, gay, and/or lesbian. The rise of the Red Power movement in the late 1960s and early 1970s included the formation of groups like the Gay American Indians (GAI), which was started by Barbara Cameron (Lakota) and Randy Burns (Northern Paiute) in 1975. These groups recalled and purposefully reclaimed the complexity of Native genders and sexualities. By the late 1980s, Indigenous activists and Native anthropologists began using "Two-Spirit"; in 1990, these activists, scholars, and their non-Native allies formally brought the term to anthropologists as a replacement for *berdache,* a word with marked negative connotations that anthropologists had long used to refer to multiply gendered Native peoples. Like her HIV/AIDS activism, laFavor's use of "Two-Spirit" for herself and her protagonist speaks to her intention to reclaim queer desire and gender diversity as a space of productive understanding for Native peoples.

This recognition of the healing power of the erotic was taken up by queer Indigenous writers like Paula Gunn Allen (Laguna Pueblo), Beth Brant (Bay of Quinte Mohawk), Chrystos (Menominee), Janice Gould (Koyangk'auwi Maidu), Maurice Kenny (Mohawk descendant), and Vickie Sears (Cherokee). Through poetry and fiction that spanned an array of topics—from explicitly naming and reclaiming third-gender roles, to celebrating the gender bending of trickster narratives, to exploring the lives of contemporary queer Native people—these Native authors were among the first group of writers to overtly claim lesbian, gay, and/or Two-Spirit identities in public spaces and to directly address queer Indigeneity in their texts. Carole laFavor's novels followed and added to an important literary tradition that by this time included single-authored texts like Kenny's *Only as Far as Brooklyn* (1979), Brant's *Mohawk Trail* (1985) and *Food and Spirits* (1991), Chrystos's *Not Vanishing* (1989) and *Dream On* (1991), Gould's *Beneath My Heart* (1990), and Sears's *Simple Songs* (1990), as well as edited collections like Brant's *A Gathering of Spirit: A Collec-*

tion by North American Indian Women (1988) and the Gay American Indians' *Living the Spirit: A Gay American Indian Anthology* (1988).[5]

In terms of situating laFavor's writing within the tradition of queer Indigenous literature, *Along the Journey River* was only the second novel with a queer Indigenous protagonist. Both novels are groundbreaking, but laFavor's Renee LaRoche offers readers a very different sense of queer Indigeneity than does Paula Gunn Allen's Ephanie Atencio from *The Woman Who Owned the Shadows* (1983). Ephanie, as is common for this period in Native American literature, presents readers with a character painfully caught between Native and non-Native traditions who never overtly names herself a lesbian; by contrast, in Renee, laFavor depicts a tribally grounded woman who fully embraces both her sexuality and her Indigeneity. *Along the Journey River* therefore represents a significant contribution to Native American literature on multiple levels.

Throughout *Along the Journey River* and *Evil Dead Center*, Renee embraces and draws strength from a Two-Spirit erotics that ties her to family and, through her detective work, helps her support her tribal community (the fictional Red Earth reservation) from instances of racism, abuse, and injustice. When we first meet Renee in *Along the Journey River*, we encounter a strong, centered Native woman who is secure in her Two-Spirit identity and accepted by both her immediate family and her larger reservation community. As the narrator notes, her grandmother's "attitude about her being a lesbian wrapped Renee with the love she needed" (page 11). That reciprocal relationship forms the basis of Renee's calling to undertake investigative work for her nation.

Carole laFavor depicts Renee's investigative skills as having a spiritual impetus. For example, Renee's grandmother places her detective work within the clan responsibilities of her people and, when sacred items are stolen from the tribe, those items call out to Renee in dreams. In *Along the Journey River* and *Evil Dead Center*, laFavor builds on the project of groups like the GAI by explicitly referring to the history of Anishinaabeg gender traditions while also envisioning Two-Spirit people's present-day potential to support the ongoing health and welfare of Indigenous communities: sexuality, spirituality, and nationhood are intimately entwined in laFavor's fiction.

Ultimately these new editions of Carole laFavor's novels underscore the significance of her writing to the Indigenous literary canon, remind us of the power of her activism for HIV-positive Native peoples, and return her important claims for the centrality of Two-Spirit peoples, bodies, and histories to the public eye.

NOTES

1. See Catharine A. MacKinnon and Andrea Dworkin, editors, *In Harm's Way: The Pornography Civil Rights Hearings* (Cambridge, Mass.: Harvard University Press, 1998).

2. Sharon M. Day, personal interview with author, January 2016.

3. Skyman-Smith (producer) and Mona Smith (director), *Her Giveaway: A Spiritual Journey with AIDS* (New York: Women Make Movies, 1987).

4. Quoted in J. A. Machiorlatti, "Video As Community Ally and Dakota Sense of Place: An Interview with Mona Smith," in *Native Americans on Film*, ed. M. E. Marubbio and E. L. Buffalohead (Lexington: University Press of Kentucky, 2013), 324.

5. Maurice Kenny, *Only as Far as Brooklyn* (Boston: Good Gay Poets Press, 1979); Beth Brant, *Mohawk Trail* (New York: Firebrand Books, 1985) and *Food and Spirits* (New York: Firebrand Books, 1991); Chrystos, *Not Vanishing* (Vancouver: Press Gang Publishers, 1989) and *Dream On* (Vancouver: Press Gang Publishers, 1991); Janice Gould, *Beneath My Heart* (New York: Firebrand Books, 1990); and Vickie Sears, *Simple Songs* (New York: Firebrand Books, 1990); Beth Brant, editor, *A Gathering of Spirit: A Collection by North American Indian Women* (New York: Firebrand Books, 1988); Gay American Indians and Will Roscoe, editors, *Living the Spirit: A Gay American Indian Anthology* (New York: St. Martin's Press, 1988). Discussed in the next paragraph is Paula Gunn Allen, *The Woman Who Owned the Shadows* (San Francisco: Spinsters Ink, 1983).

ALONG THE JOURNEY RIVER

1

Renee eased her jeep around the last curve, pulling in tight next to the giant eastern pine. She wished she hadn't agreed to come by with news on the robbery. It had been one hell of a day, and the image of home and Sam's loving arms called to her. It wasn't supposed to have taken so long at the tribal police station, but how'd Lydia put it? "Whenever you get two or more Indians together, it takes the whole damn day!"

She looked around the family land that government rhetoric labeled "without improvements," land the Coon family left to its natural state. The cabin seemed as if it had grown there right along with the trees and bushes. A wood fire and fresh fry bread smell drifted across the yard. "Mm, that helps, eh Mukie? Friday's smells," Renee murmured to the black cocker next to her.

Gram and Aunt Lydia's yard chickens had already gone to roost, subscribers, like the elders, to the early-to-bed-early-to-rise philosophy. Ren could hear their soft clucking in the distance. *Telling each other bedtime stories again.* She smiled.

"*Boozho!*" Coming through the kitchen, Renee grabbed a piece of warm fry bread, swabbing it generously with butter and tossing a chunk to Mukwa. "Gram? Auntie?" She slid her fingers along the nickel handles on the old wood stove's door, worn shiny from all the use.

"*Anin,* my girl." Ren heard Gram's willowy voice calling from where she always sat, in front of the cabin's bay window facing the head of Gi sina Nibi Lake, in the rocker Gramps made seventy-seven years ago—for her puberty ceremony and their wedding. Rounding the corner, Renee saw Gram leaning back, her eyes closed, listening to her grandson Tony Coon on KAIO, Red Earth's tribal radio. The twisted diamond willow cane Ren had carved for her lay on the floor next to the rocker.

"Auntie tell ya 'bout the robbery at Elko?" Kissing her gram's forehead, Renee collapsed into the overstuffed chair next to the stone fireplace. As always, she glanced at the sepia-tinted Coon family photo propped on the mantel, a gift seventy years ago from an interviewer at the Minnesota Historical Society.

"A little. You know your auntie, she hisses and fusses more'n givin' the facts." Gram's willowy chestnut fingers tapped lightly on the rocker arms.

Renee studied the old woman. Since Gramps' death two years before she'd been more than a little concerned about the elder's health. She had hesitated to ask Gram's younger sister, Lydia, to move in. Gram had always been the calm in the center of her sister's storm; without her, Lydia was battered by the wind, often taking more energy than she gave. Gram was the caretaker, and Lydia, armed with her '54 Chevy and beaded dab-a-dot bingo marker, the Queen of the Rez at eighty-three. The two were polar opposites. But Gram needed someone, so after a while they settled in alongside each other. The only thing Gram insisted on before the move was that Lydia either spread Eldon Poussaint's ashes somewhere, or bury them. Auntie's half-breed companion had died a year before, and Lydia had been hauling his ashes around in a Converse shoe box. A week after moving in she buried Eldon on the hill behind the old tobacco racks, in the Coon family cemetery.

"Facts are, Gram," Renee began, "somebody broke into the high school over at Elko, or more likely, was hidin' inside. After the janitor left, they smashed the lock on the display case and made off with the whole exhibit. Everything, Hobey told me. Pipe, cradleboard, eagle bone whistle, flute, rattle. Everything loaned to that history teacher, Richards." Bringing her gaze back in from the old oak tree next to the cabin, Renee tried to catch the elder's reaction, something she often relied on. Gram was Renee's role model. The elder's willingness to be called to doctor bruises, pneumonia, or problems brought on by decades of stoop labor, as well as her carefully tended spiritual life, served as an example that Renee tried but consistently failed to measure up to.

Something was always changing the younger woman's direction, it seemed. The world could distract her easier than the old one.

With Gram's silence, her granddaughter continued. "It'll probably be impossible to identify fingerprints on the case even though the janitor'd jus' cleaned it. No other clues 'cept a piece of striped tape stuck to the top of the case. No witnesses yet, either. But anybody walkin' round that parkin' lot got a hell—oops, sorry Gram—got a heck of a lot of red clay on their boots. That stuff sure is sticky. No wonder it's so good for chinking log cabins, eh?"

"Oh, Renny, you're here," Lydia croaked sleepily, raised from her nap by the talk. Her sparrow limbs balanced her five-by-five frame silhouetted now in the bedroom door. Lydia loved her sleep. "Practicin' for eternity," she called it.

"Came by to tell you I checked on the robbery," Renee said. "Gotta go now though, Auntie. Sam and Jenny are waitin' on us, eh *ahnimoosh?*" She gave Mukwa a pat.

"Go ahead, my girl," Gram offered. "Lydia and me, we got all night to talk. You give that *anikobidjigan* a kiss from her great-granny. Say hi to Samantha too, eh?"

Gram had treated Samantha as part of the family from the jump, but it hadn't surprised Renee. Gram was the one she went to at sixteen bursting with her secret. "I've been waiting for you," Gram began quietly, after listening to Renee. She wiped the teen's tears then with her long apron. "You were named Wabanang Ikkwe for a reason. Morning Star stands between—not night or day, but guiding each. You live in the space between women and men. We are Great Spirit's pure thoughts, *nojishe,* all of us. Here to love, so do not be ashamed of who that is. Creator made you and we don't question the work of our Creator." Gram's attitude about her being a lesbian wrapped Renee with the love she needed. "Two-Spirits have always been part of our community, *nojishe.* It's good you're ready to accept it."

It was good, Renee thought, kissing the two elders as she turned to leave. Still is.

Pulling out the drive, Ren broke into a broad grin as she looked back at the elders' house. It felt good to be home after ten years of not coming home at all and ten more years of hopping back and forth between the rez and the city. She never had fit in at college. Classmates took her on as an exotic hobby: get to know an Indian. It was the '60s after all, and the wannabe tribe was growing by leaps and bounds. "Seems like a lifetime ago," Renee said aloud. She was happy to be home for many reasons, not having to pay for the land she lived on being one of them. Her part-time teaching job at the reservation school and what she made selling her beadwork and baskets was enough to keep their bellies full and the fire burning. "Yahoo, Mukwa, this is the life, eh?"

Mukwa raised an eyelid, then returned to her dream of chasing that bothersome *waboose* invading her space. *Darn rabbits, jus' don't know their place,* she growled, already back deep into her dream.

Renee hit the last turn a little too fast, and the fishtail took her twenty yards down the drive. "Damn! Pay attention, LaRoche." She whistled a breath through her teeth. Mukwa gave a loud agreeing bark as Renee coasted to the wood pile and killed the motor. "OK, girl." She leaned back as she opened the door, but the dog's leap caught her on the inhale. "Ugh. God, Mukie, you little *maka kossag.* You gotta lose some weight!" Bursting through the door moments later, they were met with an icy stare.

"I got your message, Renee LaRoche. Why are you getting involved in this robbery business? Just because your Aunt Lydia hinted at it? What kind of reason is that? You're not the police, you know." Samantha stopped to take a breath, the anger vein bulging on her forehead.

"It's traditional for younger ones to protect the tribe's honor, Sammy." Jenny giggled. "Though sayin' *younger* for Ma's kind of a stretch." Her round Ojibwa face hung over the cabin's loft railing like a full moon. Hidden at first, her smile was all the more infectious as it burst across her face. Great-granddaddy Coon's for sure, everyone would comment the first time they saw the girl. Sometimes the glimpse Renee caught of Jenny sent her back a century. Jenny on a horse, leading the tribal hunting party through the woods. Or at the fire, her turn on the camp meal.

"Ah...*megwetch, abinodji.* You just wait though, you're not always gonna be fourteen." What Renee didn't say was that tonight she felt about as ancient as her daughter thought her to be. And the last thing she wanted was to fight with anyone.

"Well, tradition's one thing," Samantha continued, glaring at her partner, "foolishness something else."

Leaning against the cupboard, Renee glanced up through

hooded eyes. "What'd you say, Sammy?"

"I said tradition's one thing, stupidity a whole other matter."

"Tradition...tradition. Mm, I wonder." Checking her watch and groaning silently, Renee pushed herself up. "Listen, gotta run into the Malt Shop. Shouldn't be long, though. And don't worry."

She gave Sam a quick kiss and was out the door, Mukwa at her heels, before Samantha yelled, "I'm losing my grip here, LaRoche. When you get back, we talk!"

Renee sipped the Coke she'd grabbed off the cupboard. Her thoughts drifted between the robbery and her relationship with Samantha as she drove the fifteen miles to Elko. Lydia had just come from selling eggs at the farmers' co-op earlier in the morning when Renee ran into her.

"You know white folks, Renny," Lydia began, "they talk 'bout us like we're not there. Lampposts. So I jus' listen, an' best spot's always been the co-op." Renee felt a twinge whenever her Aunt Lydia described people's treatment of her, but she knew the tree stand around the elder's heart was penetrable only by those who knew the way. "The sheriff's jawin' with these other two sayin' us damn Indians are always causin' him trouble. He says the liberal teacher at the high school was showin' stuff from Red Earth and the whole bunch gets stolen last night. Thieves left a note sayin' *Boo! Happy Halloween!* Then he says, 'Now I gotta go talk to those idiots over at tribal police. 'Course, maybe I'll run into that cute little new girl they hired!' And they all laugh it up."

Lydia paused, her face crinkled and flushed like it got when she was into telling her story. "It's a sour tongue in that man, Renny. Seems those Christians got just enough religion to learn to hate, but not enough to love. And how 'bout them robbers? After our stuff, eh? Somebody might wanna check on this."

It was Lydia's last comment that was now causing Renee so much grief with Samantha. She knew she had to make Samantha understand, but most white folks just didn't get the bond Ojibwa have with their elders. Renee worried her lip, stopping when she tasted blood. "They're too busy throwin' their old folks away, eh Mukwa?" She patted her friend.

Samantha was a love like she never dreamed she'd find. Especially after moving back to the reservation four years ago. A relationship full up with wishes and plans. An intimacy so intense from the jump it was like they had the same spider web filament connecting their hearts. It hardly seemed a year had passed since they met at Red Earth's fall pow wow. She smiled as she remembered the first time they made love outside on a bed of pine needles that warm fall day. Laughing until their stomachs hurt at the curious pair of eyes peering at them through the bushes. And how, at the sound of their muffled laughter, the timid red fox scurried off, scolding them loudly. *Who'd believe a chimook just up from the city—a professor no less—would be sharing my bed!*

But she knew sharing her bed was not the problem. Sharing her culture was. And this wasn't their first go around. Times like these, Renee wondered if Samantha was comparing her to past lovers. Was it too much of a hassle to be involved with an Indian? Way up here? Samantha had only intended to remain up north for nine months. Three semesters as guest lecturer in the boonies teaching women about women. Did she really stay because of her? "God, Mukie, why do I torture myself like this?" She had to believe they'd work things out. They loved each other, didn't they? Lydia would say it was all known ahead of time anyway. Fate. "All depends on if you're born on the hill or in the valley."

Renee pulled into the Malt Shop parking lot twenty minutes later, then walked in the side door. Her eyes narrowed at the sudden overhead glare. A few Generation X types sat on stools spotted at intervals along the counter, faces forward as though waiting to take a test. Surveying the rest of the crowd, thinner now than right after school, she spied Mindy Johanson in her usual booth. "Thank the Creator for creatures of habit," Renee sighed. Talking to Mindy was a long shot, but they'd been friendly since the American Indian Traditions class Renee taught last summer. The young townie slurped the last of her Coke.

"Yep, we drove by there, musta been 11:30 or so 'cause I've gotta be home by midnight, and we were headin' back. Only one we saw was Lou Blank. You know, the death police? Sunny sees him around the hospital so he beeped. Blank was busy talkin' to some guys in a car. Barely looked up."

"Did you see who was in the car?"

"Blond guy, older...'bout thirty, I mean." Mindy giggled, peeking at her friends. "Indian guy drivin'."

"Car?"

"Old. White, I think. Like in class—what you called a rez car. Want me to ask Danny more 'bout it?"

"Might help. Give me a call then?"

"Cool. I feel real bad about this, Miss LaRoche. I helped organize that exhibit."

Renee nodded, leaving Mindy with her phone number. Driving back she reflected on what she'd heard. She didn't know Lou Blank very well but couldn't imagine his being friendly with an Indian. She did know he was a bigot, an anger-dweller on the knife's point, honing his rage on Indian lives. During high school, Blank and the other jack-booted thugs liquored up, piled into trucks, and raided pow wows to bash heads. Since working for the county coroner, he limited himself to verbal assaults. *So what in hell was he doing in the Elko High School parking lot that time of night talking to an Indian?* The traveling neon above Sparky's warned it was the last chance to tip one before entering the reservation. The parking lot was full, as usual. An uneven mix of rez cars and ones made in this decade. But she hardly noticed the place she used to white-knuckle it by in her early years of sobriety. She turned onto County Road 3 past the *You Are Now Entering Red Earth Reservation* sign. A better description of the white car would help. The blond could be anybody from the Scandinavian-filled border towns. *But it's a start.* She yawned.

"Making connections is complicated." Renee could hear her grandmother. "When the woolly caterpillar crawls, it affects the cardinal's song. Cardinal changes the firefly's direction. The flash of the firefly lights the eye of the Kagagi Clan people. All this affects us and the ant in the hill over there." She turned to Mukwa. "Those guys are involved. Or they saw somethin', Mukie. I can feel it."

Before Renee installed the larger wood-burning stove last winter, the cabin often captured the cold night air and refused to give it up. But tonight the *ish ko day* was spreading warmth generously.

"OK to come in?" She peeked her head in the cabin door.

"Get in here, LaRoche. Jenny and I talked before she left. She told me about your propensity to wear the savior's mantle."

"Left?" It felt good, she thought, having help parenting. She knew Sam tried hard to respect Jenny, be a friend but not a mom, and she appreciated it. Especially on nights like tonight.

"Gone to Jody's to spend the night."

Ren sank into the couch, releasing a huge sigh, the coffee air inviting.

"Did you get what you went for?" Samantha's petulant look raised a smile on Ren's full lips.

"Mm. Maybe."

"The chief called."

"Hobey?"

"Said he had a tip. Wants you to call."

Renee leaned back and closed her eyes, remembering just two short days ago when the only unusual thing in their lives was next weekend's trip to Minneapolis for the pow wow and Samantha's job interviews. This is that wrinkle in time, she thought, the interruption in your journey that forever changes you. For good or bad, depending on your take on it. Either way, their peace was fading fast. Groaning, she stood and walked to the phone.

"*Boozho,* Tribal Police."

"Hobey? Renee here."

"Renee, listen. Thought you might be interested. Irene Bird called. Works at the hospital. Says she thinks Billy Walking Bear might know somethin' about the robbery. Know him?"

"Know the family a little. His sister plays basketball with J.J. Mrs. Walking Bear works at the day-care center. Far's I know, Billy works at the hospital. Not sure about Dad."

"Irene said he hasn't been to work in four days. She saw him today, flashin' a lot of cash. Gossip at the hospital is he was at the school the other night. Is he livin' at home?"

"Was, but his girlfriend just had a baby. They're livin' together now. Rice Lake I think."

"Baby, eh. Reason to steal and try and sell the tribe's stuff?"

"Possible." Renee relayed what she'd learned in Elko. "White car Billy's maybe?"

"Reason to steal" stuck in Renee's mind. Billy had more than just the baby for a reason. He had Janice. Janice was a "tweener," someone caught between two realities, the elders explained, with a soul in such a hurry to come back to this world it hadn't disengaged from the spirit world. Janice made do with family help, especially Billy's, but Renee knew she had two speeds: zombie and hysterical. If Billy or another relative wasn't close by when the hysterics came, the sixteen-year-old usually ended up in the tribal jail until one of them came and got her out. Ojibwa madness didn't mean throwing people away, and it wasn't defined by gender like in the white world where, as Samantha's last magazine article charged, a female's craziness is explained to her by the father, husband, doctor, minister, priest, or other male in her life. Ojibwa madness was bad medicine, spiritual wandering, or a family thing, depending on the generation talking about it. A rumor of bad medicine swirled around Janice at the Elder Center, the most recent talk being that she left the footprint of coyote in the dust. *Some folks use the label* crazy *nowadays as an excuse because they can't handle difference,* Renee sighed to herself. *Name calling, insecurity's dead end.* Billy and Janice struggled continually with poverty, boosting to supplement Billy's meager salary. And now the baby. That worried Renee. Mind-bending poverty drove people to do many things.

"Bedtime?" Renee queried after a few hours of listening to Samantha's sighs and grumbles over her current piece for the *Lusty Ladies!* feminist monthly. Watching her, Renee remembered how cautiously she'd responded to this woman and her typical *chimook* questions last year at the fall pow wow. It wasn't long, though, before the white woman's charm won Renee's heart. Sam's open, expressive face set Renee at ease, contradicting what she imagined East Coast bluebloods to be like. The contours of Samantha's face certainly fit the stereotype, though—wide-set blue-green eyes, cleft chin, and broad mouth. "A classic beauty," according to Renee.

"OK, I'm coming," Samantha sighed. One final save and the computer whir faded into the night's silence. Renee reached for her lover's hand, pulling her up. Sam's hair stuck up from the twisting and tugging it endured as she worked. Smoothing the auburn mop and hooking it behind Sam's ears, Renee brought her hands softly to Samantha's cheeks, drawing her face close. Their lips met tentatively, then Renee leaned into the kiss, feeling the sudden surge of passion that always accompanied their initial touch. A familiar hotness exploded in her chest.

"My love. My beautiful *saiagi iwed.*"

"Uh-huh. You conniving woman," Sam whispered. "You're more obvious than the big *E* on an eye chart, LaRoche!" Sam tightened the squeeze around her waist.

"Whatever do you mean, my darling? Surely you're not accusing me of using sex to settle an argument?" Ren flashed her quick smile, a smile that caught Samantha's breath in her throat. Kissing her lover again, waves of desire washed over Renee and, pulling Samantha down on the bed, she reached up to dim the lamp on the log wall to a soft glow. She unbuttoned Samantha's shirt, sliding it off her shoulders. Renee kissed her ear, then moved slowly down her neck, across her chest, circling her lover's breast with her tongue, chestnut face ornamenting Sam's vanilla skin. "Now, come into my wigwam, dear," she whispered, as if the murmur put even her voice tight next to Samantha. "Let me show you why they say we Indians are so good with our hands."

Mukwa, sleeping by the bed, cocked an ear to the window, her lips curled back from her teeth. Her nose caught the acrid odor of fear, and a growl started deep in the *ahnimosh's* throat. She was more than a little protective of her very own personal two-legged. Glancing back at her constant companion of the last five years, she could see she'd get no help there. Renee's attention was taken up with the woman next to her. The cocker laid down at the door, nose to the air currents drifting in.

The wind had calmed at sundown. Smoke meandered out the fieldstone chimney on the north wall, merging with the night sky. Crispness in the air told of an early fall. A few yellow aspen leaves held lonely vigils on once-full branches, but the strikingly colorful part of fall was over. Snow blowing in Mother Earth's northern doorway was making its first appearance as the birch trees began their soft *si si gwad*. Grandmother Neeba geesis had disappeared early behind moisture-heavy clouds, and the stars soon followed. Darkness clung to an outside world where only four-leggeds moved surely on nights like tonight.

Watching the first snowflakes patchwork his jacket, the intruder debated what to do. A light flicked illuminating a watch face: 10:27 P.M. It looked as if they were going to bed. He was cold and tired, irritated it'd taken the guy so long to show up with his new car. As the lonely figure leaned tentatively against the woodpile, a sound from the back of the cabin split the stillness.

"Mukwa, sometimes I think you interrupt us on purpose," came a scolding from the dimly lighted doorway. The stranger stepped back into the woods. "You stay around now, it's starting to snow," Renee yelled before closing the cabin door against the night chill. But Mukwa tore off toward the southeast corner of the clearing, her fluorescent fuchsia neck scarf all that was visible in the swallowing darkness. She hit the clearing's edge and drew up. With the wind shift under the tree canopy, even Mukwa's woods dog nose was bombarded with more scents than it could decipher, the unique odor she'd been chasing lost to the wind. Running her nose back and forth along the ground, she picked up the scent, only to lose it again in the next gust. Several false starts later she gave it up. *So you're clever. You got away this time, but I'll be watching,* she scolded the darkness. Raising her long, shaggy ears and tilting her black nose to the sky, the *ahnimoosh* howled to the hidden Nokomis Moon.

"*Be in digain,* Mukwa. Come in. You'll wake the Spirits with that howling!" Renee called from the cabin door.

Little did she know that that was exactly what Mukwa intended.

2

The sun rose slowly, escaping through the trees and bushes to glint off the small mounds of new snow. Around the LaRoche cabin, the forest spread like a giant mitten. North and east, large stands of aspen, northern hardwoods, and oak ran to Eagle Butte Ridge, merging with the sugarbush. Looping west, a soft thumb of birch and evergreens hid the cabin from the rolling meadow beyond. Flicker's familiar *cheer up, cheer up* echoed through the trees, greeting the cardinal family in their favorite Norway pine. Morning rounds were under way in the west grove where Woodpecker and Chickadee pecked at Birch tree, freeing it from the itchy grubs and beetles. In turn Birch rewarded them with a thirst-quenching sap—a long-standing agreement.

Mukwa jumped on the bed and nuzzled Ren's face. "Hey, you old rez dog, hold your horses. I'm coming." Renee rolled over, stretched, and kissed Sam lightly on the cheek. "We're going for a run, *saiagi iwed*. Be back."

"Mm," Samantha murmured, barely noticing the kiss and increased activity. Turning, she burrowed deeper into the warmth.

Renee had slept fitfully, waking twice from the cold with no covers. She'd been drawn down into the shadow world to retrieve a message, the dream becoming reality, the dreamer the link:

She was on the thieves' trail. They tried losing her at the north end of the rez on the abandoned logging road, but she knew the area well and managed to keep them in sight. She didn't recognize the old white car, and the thieves were too far ahead to get a good look at them, but she couldn't shake the feeling of familiarity. Maybe it was how they took the remote trails. Suddenly, she lost them. They just disappeared. A great gray owl sat high up in the Douglas fir at the bend where they'd been, malevolent eyes barely visible behind the ring of feathers. Tragedy was in the air. The owl...

Picking up her medicine bag, Renee stepped into the warming early morning air. She remembered trying to collect fog on mornings like this. Swinging the jar through the air, then snapping the cover tight and running into the house to proudly announce her capture. To this day she couldn't figure out why foggy air outside wasn't foggy air in. "*Boozho, Gitchie Manitou*, this is Wabanang Ikkwe. I offer the *ah say ma....*" She burned a pinch of tobacco with a special prayer for the safety of the tribe's sacred pipe. At the east side of the clearing, she sprinkled the rest on remnants of the summer garden, grabbed an armload of wood, and returned to the log cabin she'd built herself—with a child's measure of help from J.J. The cabin's white cedar logs, harvested from this spot, had been machine-hewed at the tribal mill after-hours by an old classmate. Renee was grateful for how much money it had saved her. She loved being close enough to Gram and Auntie to hear their rooster's morning crow.

Living on ancestors' land intensified life's dimensions, eased the emptiness she sometimes felt being the last LaRoche. Besides Jenny. Ojibwa died young, and the LaRoche side of her family was no exception. *Cause of death: G.I. hemorrhage due to final-stage alcoholism,* was her father's death announcement. Alcoholism in one form or another, or poverty, killed most of the LaRoche family. Her last brother dead with his hands full of grass and his face in the mud. Another LaRoche ending as tragic as the rest. Renee thanked Creator every morning for turning her around in time. Before life in the city under the bridges near the Ave. took hold. Before the hand-to-mouth-beyond-the-law existence swallowed her up, too, and spit her out all twisted and hollow.

She slipped into her running shoes, making the careful double knot she'd used since tripping and spraining an ankle. "OK, *niji*, let's go. I know you're tired a waitin' on me." She grabbed her anorak and a pair of light gloves, and they quietly left the cabin.

Mukwa headed straight to the woodpile, barking excitedly.

Come here. Niji here. Whoever had been there had been careful, the *ahnimoosh* noted. Nothing was disturbed. An Indian, or savvy *chimook*.

Ren looked around curiously. The red plastic casino bucket used now for hauling bird feed was tipped over, but nothing jumped out. "Come on, girl. I really need this run," she whispered, scratching absently behind Mukwa's long ears and wishing for the old days when everyone spoke a common language. Before the forest uprising where Skunk was pissed at two-leggeds for being so bossy, and Deer said two-leggeds were killing others for food without respect for their spirits. Everyone was mad. *Until you can respect us as equals,* Bear announced to the two-leggeds angrily, *we will stop speaking so you can understand us.* And that was that.

The language barrier frustrated Mukwa, too, but there it was, she had to make the best of it. Turning back now, Mukwa looked peevishly at the spot by the woodpile. *You two-leggeds,* she growled, *two seconds and you lose interest. And your sense of smell...* She shook her head and ran to catch up with Renee.

Ren's shoes hit the trail with familiarity. She'd run this way so often she could do it with her eyes closed. The kind of routine athletes strive for. Something to put them in the zone. Adjusting her stride to a comfortable level, this morning she wanted to rid her mind, however briefly, of the nagging questions about the robbery. She knew her motives for getting involved in the investigation were mixed. Renee believed deeply in her traditions, in respecting elders, but in the privacy of her own heart she had to admit another reason. It made her blood surge. The endorphin hit from this was as addicting as the one she got from running. For now, however, she let it all go.

A truck pulled away at the river's edge, spinning its wheels up the rutted, nearly hidden tracks to Old Bridge Road, the graded route that split the reservation east to west. Turning from the bridge, the driver skidded and spun down the road, while on the sand, a dark form was beginning a different journey. Renee first slowed, unaware of the activity below, then collapsed on the large rock just off the trail. The engine sound tugged at her momentarily. Then it was gone.

The two always stopped here at Ren's spirit rock before heading down to Old Bridge and cutting back around on another of the dozen trails that forked and twisted throughout the five miles of woods and prairies on the west side of the river. The rock sat on the edge of a cliff that fell 150 feet to the Baba ma dizi win River. Beyond here, the trail made its way through the sugarbush until it caught up with both the road and the Journey River below, winding gently through the valley of the *mis skwa ah ki*. White farmers' fields spread east through the valley as far as the eye could see. John Deere's clan, Renee had thought as a kid.

Gazing at the river, Renee found her mind lingering on a memory at once so painful and so meaningful that words spilled uncontrollably through her mind. "Couple hundred years ago that river bank was thick with red and white cedar, cottonwood, and willow," she had allowed in a quiet voice, standing on this spot a year ago. "The river was like a silver thread woven through red earth my people walked for hundreds of years. Then Europeans came..." She'd had a twinge of guilt telling Samantha the ugly history of this area's *chimooks*. She didn't want pity for the past, and she knew it was sometimes hard for whites when confronted with the reality to get beyond the past. At first, anyway. But this wasn't a sound bite, it was her life. So she had continued.

"The Peterson farm bordering the rez plowed up bones along with trees, crushing 'em under their machines." Then, after a long pause, Renee had said, "And this generation's no different, Sammy. They laugh at how fertile the bones made their land. We duked it out in court in the mid '80s. 'What's past is past,' one said. 'Why don't you people get on with your lives? This ain't your land anymore.' They carried on like that. We won in the end, but it didn't mean much. The wind is steadier than any damn government promise. The new law imposed fines on anyone desecrating burial sites, but it took a long time before farmers started to change their ways. Some still grumble about it down at the local Eat & Meet Cafe."

Renee recalled the stricken look on her lover's face when, as she was finishing, she'd said, "It reminds me of Martin Luther King's comment: 'The law can't make them love us, but it can make them treat us right until they do.'" Samantha's joke about life not evolving much beyond when giant sloths, mastodons, and saber-toothed tigers roamed the area eased the tension, but they walked back to the cabin in silence that day.

This spot was important to Renee. It was where she first became aware of time, of time on the move. Time passing in her child's life, ever more slowly in her rock, seasonally in the river's water, so much faster in her alcoholic father.

As she looked over the cliff, Renee's thoughts drifted to the bluffs below where caves, undiscovered until Jenny and her friends stumbled on them while rock climbing last spring, held their ancient vigil over the valley of the red earth. Here, time stood still. Experts called in to examine the caves thought they were as much as three thousand years old, possibly older. Native archeologists were contacted, elders consulted. Technically the caves were on Coon land, making Gram, Auntie, and then Renee the official decision-makers, along with the tribal council, about what to do. The landslide of reporters, collectors, archeologists, state, federal, and BIA officials nearly buried the family. After several months, Gram and Lydia dug in their heels. Everything drew to a screeching halt, the caves were declared off-limits, and the search into them was put on hold until an organized investigation could be planned by the tribal council.

"All of those goings-on, now the robbery, this whole thing could end up like Browns Valley Man," Renee mused aloud, calling up the discovery seventy-five miles west of Red Earth three years before. It raised a big fuss because it was believed to be the oldest human skeleton found in the western hemisphere. And, if she remembered right, its notoriety attracted grave robbers who escaped, after killing the security guard, with articles recovered with the skeleton. They were never caught. Those in the know figured the stolen goods were moved quickly overseas and sold to rich private collectors. "Could this robbery have any connection to that one? Whoa now, don't get ahead of yourself here, LaRoche," she scolded herself. "It *is* something to check on, though."

Renee started off, stretching her legs, then slowly lengthening her stride to shake the kinks out after sitting in the chilly air. Below, a great gray owl lifted off the abandoned osprey nest it had laid squatter's rights to. Swooping from atop the dead giant pine, she glided up river past the dark form on the sand. The owl circled, just clearing the old wooden bridge, and landed on the bridge's sagging railing. Renee gulped in the morning air, running comfortably now. In the distance a deep *koo* echoed through the valley, then another. The owl calling someone's name. It was fleeting, almost unnoticed by the Native runner until, after the final *koo*, something stirred within and a shiver escaped down her back.

3

" **F** ather M. called," Samantha yelled, as Renee and Mukwa fell through the door. "More mystery?"

"Oh, he's jus' checkin' on a rumor Jenny heard at school. Found somethin', maybe," the runner panted. Shucking her sweats, damp from the run, she flashed her deer eyes. "Come here, my love. Puhleese, give me a proper good morning." Ren tossed her old running shoes into the corner just as Samantha dove onto the bed on top of her, planting a big kiss on her cold cheek.

"Were you impressed with my creativity before sleep, Ms. Salisbury?"

"Mm, yes I was. Good morning, my sweet. You're awfully sexy all sweaty like this." They kissed a lingering kiss, lying comfortably in each other's arms, the tension from before supper last night forgotten.

"Remember our first time?" Renee whispered. "We both knew it was going to happen after the movie but still were surprised when it did."

"Think we should thank Thelma and Louise for getting us together?" Samantha responded languidly.

"Oh, oh, and in the movie. You, slick, with your hand on your knee tryin' to sooo casually slide it onto mine! Too, too cool. A city move, no doubt?" Ren leaned over with another kiss.

"Renee, my dear, we don't make anything as vulgar as a move in New England. Subtlety is our way. Especially in our two-thousand-dollar-a-month apartments overlooking the harbor."

"Jeez, Sammy, for two thousand dollars here you could get a small farm and a little farmer. Vulgar move thrown in for free." Samantha laughed, enveloping Renee in her arms and squeezing her tight. They both closed their eyes. After almost falling asleep Renee whispered, "I'd love to stay and make you happier even than you were last night, but I gotta take a shower and—"

Reluctantly, her partner rolled over and got up, blowing Renee a kiss as she returned to her writing spread out on the kitchen table.

Renee stepped into the shower minutes later and was soon singing her favorite pow wow song at top volume.

"Oh God, Mukie, you hear that? She's in there singing the bark off the trees!" The cocker looked up from her food and gave a playful woof. "It's something to behold, isn't it?" Samantha laughed.

Sure is, Mukwa responded. *Ain't she somethin'? And she's all mine!*

Ren toweled her short raven hair, then slipped a favorite sweatshirt over her runner's body. *Celebration of Sobriety: Red Nation School, New Year 1986,* the faded red shield on the front advertised. Sam watched lovingly as Renee pulled her ragged Levis on, moved to the table, and sat down, all in one motion. She wore all clothes the same, unaware she had any on.

"J.J. call?"

"She'll be home about five after basketball, though she was very angry when I told her she had to come home. She wanted to go back to Jody's."

"That girl's busier than a robin at a worm farm, but it channels some of that teenage energy, eh? Helps her attitude a little...maybe." Renee glanced at Sam and burst into laughter. "Funny, ya know, when Jen was ten we were at the Jordans' for a feast when Angie Jordan had a screaming fit about somethin'. Jenny was so shocked. Swore to me later that when she got to be a teenager she'd never act that way."

"So much for delayed promises!" Samantha chuckled.

"Especially in competition with raging hormones. Anyway, you two seem to be doing pretty good these days, eh?"

"Not bad. I wonder sometimes if I was going to fall in love with a mom, why I didn't fall in love with one that had a toddler, or a child in grade school, or maybe even one married and gone," she laughed. "But a teenager!"

"They're a challenge all right. I appreciate how hard you try."

"I do that all right," Samantha smiled weakly.

"God, I slept terrible last night," Renee said, changing the subject.

"I noticed. Thought I was going to have to hog tie you."

"Ooh. I like the sound of that!" Ren reached over, tweaking her lover's cheek before wrapping her hands around the thick blue mug of hot chocolate Sam set in front of her.

Renee's call to Father Murphy at Holy Rosary was short. He was on his way to an accident on Old Bridge Road and promised to stop by later.

"*Boozho,* Tribal Police," came through the cracking gum on Renee's next call. "Oh hi, Renny. Hobey? Hold on, looks like he's on the other line." The minutes stretched.

"Mm, the wonderful smell of Clorox." Renee grinned over at Samantha. "Red Earth's a hell of a lot cleaner since I captured the white tornado!"

"And to think you don't even appreciate it."

"Oh, but I—"

"Renny? He's headed out to the Walking Bear place. Sorry. Thought it was him on the phone. Anna's here on a student intern program. She was talkin' to her boyfriend. Oops, gotta go. That's the nine-eleven."

"*Megwetch,* Bobbi. See ya."

Ren set the phone back in its cradle. Bobbi had been a friend of the LaRoche family for years. She'd been dating Renee's brother Ben when he was arrested and beaten by Elko police. "Trumped-up possession of heroin charge," Ben said, and Renee believed her older brother. The white prosecutor didn't. The all-white jury rendered a guilty verdict and sent Ben off to prison for five years. Bobbi babysat Renee and her younger brother Joe until Conway Twitty McMillan, a Choctaw draft resister, came through on his way to Canada. They returned to the rez five years later, married with two kids.

She knew how different tribal police departments could be from one another. Some were as corrupt as the U.S. government—harassing people, using public funds for private enjoyment, aligning themselves with the Feds against their own. Others were ineffective, made up of drunks and losers and deputies who understood little or nothing about keeping the peace. But there were some that were central to the life of the tribe, where keeping the peace was viewed in the traditional way of providing safety, honor, and respect. Renee realized it hadn't always been that way on her reservation. It was Hobey's doing that had restored the old ways to the Red Earth tribal police. She noticed the difference soon after she, Jenny, and Mukwa moved home, so when she was asked to sit on a police-community task force called to find better ways of working with youth, she agreed. That started a renewal of her friendship with the chief, a relationship dating back to when Renee had played in the mud with his daughter Sharon—now living in France. Ren smiled at how often in the last three years she'd been involved in one thing or another at the tribal police station. Gram said it was because the family was Bear Clan, peacekeepers of the tribe. Ren figured it was part that and part her thinking she could fix everything.

"RENEELAROCHE youarethemoststubbornwomanIknow!" Samantha yelled as the door slammed behind Renee and Mukwa a half hour later. "Are you trying to get yourself killed? That security guard in Bemidji was murdered, you know. Don't you realize how dangerous this could be?"

"Only one thing I know for sure, Sammy. I *luv* you. Catch ya later!" Renee yelled.

The silver streak in Ren's hair was a match for the woman's silver tongue. Sam knew that, knew that she wasn't embarrassed to use that tongue either, to talk Samantha into late-night lovemaking on the bluff, or into putting money down on a one-runner sleigh to go along with the still-empty horse barn. Normally, Sammy didn't mind. It was one of the things she loved about Renee. But not today. "Am I nuts?" Samantha screamed to the air. She slid the curtain shut, shaking her head, then turned and strode across the room. She placed her hands flat on the desk. Side by side. Neat, symmetrical. Applying enough pressure to feel the wood from wrist to fingertips. Focusing. Noting how they appeared. She shifted the left to better match the right. This felt good. Manageable. Sam was tempted to leave them there for the rest of the day.

"Why doesn't she stay home and clean her side of this damn desk if she wants to do something helpful?" she muttered to herself, brushing aside Renee's notes cluttering their shared space. Samantha's irritation at their differences was easy for her to focus on here, confronted with Renee's blizzard style of neatness. Her files were everywhere, and Post-its stuck to the lampshade and computer were her idea of organizing her thoughts. Opposite of how Samantha believed things should be: files prioritized, everything stacked along the back, labeled clearly, neatly. Shaking her head, Sam slipped a diskette into the disk drive. She punched the mouse button with her short, round forefinger, then waited impatiently until she gratefully escaped to another realm.

To Ren's surprise, the *Minneapolis Star-Tribune* article was in the periodicals section of the Granite Rock library.

> Minnesota's Browns Valley Man, the ancient skeleton lost for decades in an amateur archaeologist's fruit cellar, has been radiocarbon-dated to about 9,000 years ago, making it one of the oldest and most complete skeletal remains of a human ever found in the Western Hemisphere.

Renee shook her head. *How the fuck can you forget a whole skeleton for decades, for Chrissake.*

> The preliminary dating tests, conducted on a small fragment of bone from the upper part of the skeleton's right leg, put the age of Browns Valley Man at 8,790 years, plus or minus 110 years... The final test, on a purified sample of one of the 20 amino acids in human bone, is expected to pinpoint the age even closer....

The article continued:

> Browns Valley Man was a "paleo-Indian" and a close descendant of the Asian population that migrated across the Bering Sea land bridge. Archaeologists have long believed that migration took place about 12,500 years ago, at the end of the last Ice Age, but that theory is now being challenged. Humans may have migrated to North America in waves beginning as long as 30,000 years ago, according to newer theories.

"Newer theories," Renee chuckled, imagining Gram's answer to how life began in North America. "Everyone knows Anishanabe came from Gitchie Manitou breathing life into the *megis* shell," Gram would say. "White people have forgotten their instructions, *nojishe*. You have to be careful they don't try and trick you into giving up yours."

Renee closed the huge book holding the original article. "I won't forget, Gram, I promise," she whispered. Renee felt the seriousness of the moment straighten her back and stiffen her thigh muscles as she sat at the large oak library table.

She recalled that experts investigating Red Earth remains last spring explained that radiocarbon dating came into use in the early 1950s, revolutionizing the science. Initial examination of the bones in the caves put them at three thousand years old. Renee figured they were relatives of Browns Valley Man from the middle of the Terminal Woodland Period.

The next newspaper article she found when she reopened the reference book reported the robbery and murder. Flint knives and spears, throwing spear shafts, reassembled pots, animal skin remnants probably used for clothing—all disappeared from a Bemidji State College Indigenous Peoples Exhibit early the morning of October 7. This article ended:

> Authorities suspect it may be someone familiar with the area and the type of security around the exhibit. Giving few details of the theft and withholding identification of the murdered security guard until notification of next of kin, they promise more within a few days.

During the joint news conference held later by the Minnesota Indian Affairs Council and the state archaeologist's office, a five-thousand-dollar reward was offered to anyone who came forward with information. At the time Renee thought this was a good enticement. Now she realized it was a drop in the bucket compared to the millions to be made from the illegal sale of Native artifacts.

The library was nearly empty. Three preteen Red Earth girls giggled over a book in the corner. An elderly white woman was immersed in old 78 rpm's stacked around her in the lounge. A young Ojibwa mother stood at the counter, checking out several books for the two-year-old she had in tow. No wonder we're the smarter sex, Renee thought. She smiled, then leaned back, stretching her legs. *Wonder if this poor Browns Valley guy ever made it to the spirit world with the* chimooks *interfering like that.*

Returning the reference book and microfilms, Renee asked for copies of the articles. The librarian slid a large ledger in front of her. "Mind signing? Helps at funding time."

"Everything's about quantity nowadays, eh?" Renee said, picking up the pen. Turning away from the retreating librarian, she traced her finger up through previous signatures and the reasons for their signers' visits. *Our Bodies, Ourselves* caught her eye, and she smiled at the girls who were now huddled on the floor. Four pages back and sixteen lines up she found three books on Native artifacts signed out. Two weeks ago. Tribal Chairman Jed Morriseau's name was next to all three. Renee slammed her hand palm down on the counter. Jed's notation, written no doubt in haste and without a thought, surprised her. *Damn, Jed. What in hell you up to now?*

Renee walked into the cabin just as the phone rang. *"Boozho."*

"Renee?" a male voice said.

"Yeah, who's—hello? Hello? Damn." She dropped the phone back in the cradle and, hearing a car pull up, stepped out the back door.

"What a morning," Father Murphy declared, unfolding his huge frame from the old Ford station wagon. "That accident was bad. White guy. Skidded his truck down the bank when he missed the curve over by Goodbears'. Must have taken it too fast. They had a devil of a time prying him out of the wreck, he was so big. No one recognized him, and he didn't have an ID. They're checking the license plate, sending prints out."

Renee stared at the priest. "Who wound you up?" she teased. The two friends hugged. "Didn't see any books about selling Native artifacts did ya?"

"Huh?"

"Nothin'...wishful thinking. Accident sounds bad. Hope they find his family. But enough, let's go in. I'm starvin'."

Father M. tossed his suit jacket on the couch. "Samantha, how're you today, honey?" accompanied a big bear hug before he perched on the high phone stool. The frayed cuffs of his priestly pants came into view on his crossed legs, witness to the purer form of vowed poverty Father Murphy practiced than his predecessor at Holy Rosary, Father Ambrose. Father Ambrose, the infamous spreader of Indian women's legs, was part of the 1933 "Gang of Six" caught selling stolen tribal goods back East to a very wealthy man named George Haynes who used the money he made in oil to open a museum in New York City. It housed all the Indian artifacts he could obtain from around the country—stolen or not—and whatever he could acquire by descending on remote Indian communities in his chauffeur-driven limousine and buying up everything within reach. Father Ambrose's secret cache of money was discovered by church officials assigned to investigate. Stealing Native people's things was not a new thing.

"Father, can you convince Agatha Christie over there that we have a police department on Red Earth," Samantha begged the priest.

"Tonto," Renee interjected playfully. "Mukie here's the Lone Ranger!"

"Whatever, Renee!" Samantha's voice was as unforgiving as a January Alberta clipper. "This isn't funny. Twice today someone called and hung up when I answered. And, I hate to even tell you this, but Betty Atori called."

"Jed's sister? I haven't heard from her in years." Renee looked puzzled.

"She knew about the theft and wanted to talk to you. Asked how Jed was, too, which seemed strange given what you've told me. Said she would call back. I almost suggested she call the police and not *you* but—" Samantha threw her pencil at Renee, who fell onto the bed clutching her eye.

"Ooh, she got me, Father! You're my witness."

Father Murphy's portly frame shook with laughter. Shrugging his shoulders he looked at Samantha. "Saints preserve us, Sammy, I've known this woman for almost forty years. Since she was just a little bit of a thing. She's Gram and Aunt Lydia all rolled into one. 'Itchy mind,' Lydia calls it. You know the difference between you two? You deal with fear by making a detailed plan of action, anticipating the worst. You like your corners squared. Renny runs headlong into it. I'm not sure if she's trying to face it or scare it to death!" The three friends laughed easily. Having grown up in the shadow of the Catholic Church, Renee knew the "grave sin against nature and God's law" that she and Samantha were supposedly committing. But if Father Murphy had a problem with their relationship, he never mentioned it. They just didn't talk about it.

"Renny," Father Murphy began, "I came by to tell you I checked on that rumor Jenny heard at school about somebody with a Holy Rosary bumper sticker hanging around the river bluffs. We only had those bumper stickers for a month last summer, during our festival. Sold about two hundred of them. We checked the parking lot during all three masses. Found thirty-three cars with the sticker still on. Four matched the description the kids gave—new Dodge, Chevy, or Ford sedan, metallic blue or gray. I'll be checking with those four soon. Why do you want to know?"

Renee combed her black hair back from her face with the fingers of both hands and leaned back, linking her arms behind her head. "Well, with this robbery in Elko, it got me thinkin'. I remembered the kids talkin' about the bumper sticker thing after Halloween. Then I thought about the Browns Valley Man, so I went over to the library."

Samantha moved to the kitchen, listening but not wanting to. Trying to blot out what Renee had told her about the murder of the security guard at the Browns Valley exhibit. She didn't want to overreact but she knew she was heading full speed for the edge.

"Do you think there could be any connection between our esteemed tribal chairman taking out those books and—"

"Wait!" Samantha yelled with a voice as swollen as the lip she'd been biting. "Please, no more!" A sickness was starting deep, in that place she reserved for things she tried to bury.

A beam of light streamed down from the skylight in the loft, tucked into the south side of the roof's pitch. The new silence echoed off the walls.

4

"Boss, got a nine-eleven. Somebody says there's a body down at the river flats just south of Old Bridge."

"I'll head over. Not far from there. Who called, Bobbi?"

"Wouldn't say. Sounded like one of us though."

Chief Hobert Bulieau set the microphone back in its holster on the dashboard and, traversing The Narrows between Portage Lake and the river on Low Crossing, turned onto Old Bridge Road heading west, accelerating rapidly.

He felt, rather than saw, the motion. Felt the gentle softness of a breeze puff, the air move a millisecond before something whistled by his left ear. Then silence. Chief Bulieau dove behind the patrol car, laying there for what seemed like an eternity, clutching his .38. *What the hell happened?* As the downed tree by the water's edge, the old bridge beyond, and the lifeless form he'd come to investigate began returning to focus, he marveled at the terror and deadliness of something so fleeting.

The radio crackled. "Chief? Chief Bulieau come in. Hobey, you all right? Are you at the river? Want me to send someone?"

He slid into the car and grabbed the microphone. His words came haltingly as he glanced cautiously over the edge of the dashboard. "I'm OK. I'm at the flats. There sure is a body here, and somebody just took a shot at me. Though, if they'd really wanted to hit me, I probably wouldn't be talkin' to you. Anyway, get Jesse down here. Tell her to bring the kit."

"She's at an accident. Not far from you, actually, but might've gone to the hospital by now."

"Call Harvey or Josh and send one of 'em to relieve her. I need Jesse here." The Red Earth Tribal Police included eight sworn officers, any two of whom would be on duty together. Jesse Johnson was a specially trained crime scene investigator, and the chief had come to rely on her. "You better call the coroner and get him over here. It's near ten, and it'll take 'em a while. Call the Feds, too, and let 'em know we got a body. You know how they get if we don't call right away. Oh, and send both cameras with Jesse."

"You got it, Chief. Sure you're OK?"

"Tell Jesse to circle around on Eagle Butte before she comes down. Just to be sure. And tell her to be careful for Chrissake. We don't need any more dead bodies."

"Will do. You be careful too, eh? Oh, Renny called lookin' for you."

"Gotta go, Bobbi, ten..." The chief's sentence trailed off. His arms felt weak, like he wanted to hold tight to something big enough to stop the dizzying whirl of events. Walks In Winter, Hobey's uncle, taught him as a boy that life was full of challenges and experiences that, if taken humbly, teach a person how to live. The chief prayed that his sixty-six years had been teacher enough for him to cope with these latest events. Taking a deep breath, Hobey surveyed the murder site. Suddenly he had a longing—much to his embarrassment—for the yellow *Police: Official Business. Do Not Cross* tape city cops used to cordon off a crime scene. The tape implied there were crowds of people watching and that this was important, very, and since he could go beyond the tape, that made him important, too. The chief peaked around him sheepishly, as though his grandiose thoughts had been broadcast throughout the valley. "Not a very humble start," he muttered.

As Hobey moved toward the lifeless form, he first noticed a dark spot in the sand. A fine film already drifting over its outer edge put the death about three hours back. His eyes moved up. "Right between the shoulders," he noted of the single gunshot. The victim, as if holding what life was left, had curled into a fetal position facing the river. Two sets of footprints came to the body. One left. There were minimal signs of a struggle, but Hobey reasoned that the footprints, together with the blood in the sand and the bullet's exit spray of blood about three feet west of the body, placed the murder here.

The victim's head was covered with a small maroon blanket, but the right hand was now visible. Indian male. The boots, fancy lizard-skin type with hand-tooled feathers up the shaft, looked familiar. The man's belt had been wrapped around his wrists. The chief could see the initials *J.M.* beaded into the buckle. Having a similar buckle, he recognized Renee LaRoche's skilled artwork and knew this one belonged to Jed Morriseau, Tribal Chairman of the Red Earth Ojibwa Nation. "Jesus, Mary, and Joseph," he muttered. "What in hell have you gotten yourself into *now*, Jed!" Lifting the blanket, Hobey looked into Jed's contorted face. "Hard a time dyin' as ya did livin'," he sighed, squatting alongside the body. Drawing a deep breath and releasing it slowly, the Ojibwa chief continued his examination. After checking for a pulse in the neck and finding none, he moved down the body. No other gunshot wounds. He found debris under Jed's manicured fingernails. "Finicky Jed wouldn't leave the house like that," he mumbled, slipping a plastic bag over Jed's right hand and securing it to the tribal chairman's wrist. No evidence of a robbery. His wallet, still in his back pocket, had three hundred dollars in it. The watch on his left wrist and turquoise silver ring on the same hand were visible. Hobey cursed, grunting as he pushed himself up. He remembered the crouches and twirls and leaps he'd been known for as a grass dancer. The sneak-up warrior unable to sneak up. "Hard to admit," he murmured to the wind.

The chief backed away using his same tracks. Like most kids growing up on the reservation, Hobey learned tracking, and the first and most important lesson was: disturb nothing, observe everything. Out of the corner of his eye, he saw the sun reflecting off something on the ridge. He stopped, still as a jacklighted deer, and slowly looked up. Officer Johnson flashed the Bronco's spotlight, then continued along the path high up on Eagle Butte and disappeared back into the woods. The chief's hands rested on a belly beginning to severely test the buttons on his uniform shirt. Cocking his head, he let his breath out slowly, thoughts drifting to the officer on the ridge. Some weren't happy he'd hired a woman, especially the tribal chairman, but Hobey thought it was time Red Earth joined the modern world. Besides, he felt lucky to have lured Jesse home after four years at Arizona State University. Folks began to change their view of his decision when, three weeks after her hiring, Jesse broke the marijuana ring on the reservation. Growing it in Chippewa National Forest to avoid land seizure if they were caught, the dope dealers had over fifteen hundred plants, worth about two thousand dollars apiece. The bonfire was seen for miles when the DEA came in and burned them out. After she cracked the case, Bobbi's father—a tribal judge—nicknamed the new officer Jesse James, and it stuck. Now people thought it was a given name.

"Get some pictures of Jed. Let's get all that outta the way before Peterson gets here," Hobey said to Jesse as she stepped out of the Bronco. "Then all we have to do is bag and tag him. I've done a prelim on the body, but we need pictures and a check on the side by the river. Where the footprints are."

Jesse swallowed her questions, waiting for Hobey to finish, but traditional Ojibwa respect wasn't so easy this time. "Chief—did you say JED! Jed Morriseau?" she burst out on the heels of Hobey's last syllable. "What the heck! Bobbi didn't tell me who it was."

"Bobbi didn't know. Me either till I got here. I know nobody liked the guy, but Jesus Christ, Jess!"

The chief was a serious fellow, with a soft voice you strained to hear in the wind. Much of that composure was missing today. A frown split his forehead as he looked back at his deputy.

Hobey and Jesse had an uncomplicated relationship. His deputy respected him not only because he was her boss, but because he was a tribal elder. After he called her at college and offered her a job, the next thing she knew he showed up at her dormitory one morning a week later.

"I like to do things face to face," he'd told the surprised young woman. "Besides, I told your mom I'd bring you back home to work." Jesse was completely charmed by this man old enough to be her grandfather and, after lunching on Mexican food and visiting the famous Heard Museum, the elder again offered her a job as his deputy. It was an easy decision for Jesse to say yes. If the visit was an indication of their work environment, Jesse thanked the Great Spirit for her good fortune.

Now she stared at the lifeless form of her tribal chairman. Someone she'd always called *Sir*. Flat-out dead in the sand. Swallowing hard, she turned her professional acumen to the work at hand. She took pictures of the area and Jed's body from every angle with the 35mm. About thirty feet from the body, next to the footprints, two dark spots jumped out. "Looks like blood here," Jesse called, snapping several pictures before Hobey came and scooped them into evidence bags. "Shooter hurt, eh?"

The chief nodded. "And look at these footprints," he said. Describing the person as over three hundred pounds, with size twelve feet wearing work boots, he added, "Looks left-handed. See the detail of the left heel is more pronounced than the right. He favors that side. And Jed came in first, his prints are under Man With The Work Boots.'"

"Guess you can't learn *everything* in school, eh Chief?" Jesse smiled respectfully. Nearer the bridge she found a Camel filter cigarette butt. "Looks new," she muttered to herself, retrieving it as another piece of potential evidence.

By the time the coroner arrived from Thunder Lake, the county seat some fifty miles away, the two Ojibwas' investigation was complete. Polaroids accompanied bagged evidence. Hobey grunted acknowledgment to Dr. Gerald Peterson. "Sure as hell took ya long enough. Did ya go by way of Canada?"

Dr. Peterson turned to his assistant. "Well, well. Look, now they're killing their leaders," he said, nodding at the dead tribal chairman. "Probably had a bottle somebody wanted and wouldn't give it up." His familiar half-snarl smile appeared and Lou Blank joined his boss's laughter.

Gerald Peterson, MD, County Medical Examiner, was built like a wide-receiver who'd lost his training manual. Small, delicate shoulders and hips gone to seed with a rotund middle. "The kinda person your dog'd bite," Lydia said once. The ME's job was providing an impartial, scientific view of investigations, but Peterson couldn't be trusted to do that when Indian people were involved. Hobey knew from experience Peterson's reaction to Indians. The hatred, the anger—sometimes fleeting but always there—then the pause before deciding whether to just be nasty or out-and-out cruel. A so-called sport fisherman, rumor was he hung a sign in his office during last year's state legislature debate on Native spear fishing rights: *Save a Walleye—Spear an Indian.* "Hatred of us has always been his ugliness of choice," Hobey warned Jesse before her first encounter with the doctor.

"Just do your job, Peterson," the chief responded to the doctor's sarcasm, making a silent scrawl of irritation in the air. "If you mess up one thing in this investigation, I'll have your damn license. Some day we're gonna be able to do this ourselves. Until then we gotta put up with you. Finish up and get the hell outta here. And you, Blank, what're you laughin' at? I wanna talk to you. You come by my office tomorrow mornin'. Early."

Blank drew up, his face draining a pasty white. "What do you want to talk to me about?"

The desperate sharpness of his look almost softened Hobey. Almost. "Not now, Blank. Just show up tomorrow morning."

"Tomorrow? That's my busiest morning."

The police chief's glare answered the question.

Blank snuck a quick look at Peterson who, it seemed to Hobey, was deliberately avoiding his assistant's gaze. He watched as Blank's hands shook visibly. Lou Blank was a garden-variety lackey, and in the presence of his boss, he had the glassy look of a team player who always rode the bench. He loaded the body on the stretcher and wheeled it to the waiting station wagon, avoiding Hobey's stare.

Peterson silently handed the chief his clipboard. Hobey signed the attached form and just as silently handed it back. "Any idea who did it?" Peterson asked suddenly. Pressing a fist against his burning abdomen, the doctor remembered he hadn't eaten today.

Surprised by the question, the chief replied, "Well, how 'bout you? You'd be a good suspect. You hate all of us. 'Prairie Niggers,' isn't it?" The doctor's face turned the color of new brick, and for the first time that Hobey could remember, Peterson was speechless. It was a delicious moment, but he let it go. Lowering his voice to its most official register, Hobey asked, "Any idea about the time of death?"

"Around nine this morning. He's halfway through rigors," Peterson responded curtly, poise recovered. Turning, he retraced his steps to the wagon. Hobey watched the retreating figure and debated what he'd just heard. The body was too cold for Jed to have died less than an hour before his arrival on the scene, plus the sand film he found on the blood was at least a few hours old. He made a mental note to follow up on his suspicions.

"When'll the autopsy be done?"

"I'll call you."

"Yeah," the chief said, turning away.

"That was weird, eh?" Jesse said, staring after Peterson.

"Sure got a rise outta him. Did you see his face?"

The chief and his deputy made a final sweep of the area, one behind the other in decreasing circles. Finding nothing more, Hobey checked his watch. "Jesse, you'll get the bloody evidence and the cigarette butt to the hospital? Tell 'em to put a rush on the blood type and a DNA on the cigarette. We're lucky to have a lab in Minneapolis accredited to do that fancy DNA testing. I'll be in to help catalogue the rest. Oh yeah, call over to the sheriff's office and see if they got any leads on who shot at me. Bobbi called it in." Heading to his patrol car, Chief Bulieau looked across the river at the fields. A bald eagle was circling. "*Megwetch*, Migizi, for stopping by."

"You say something, Chief?" Jesse called from the Bronco.

Hobey nodded to Eagle, who was just beginning a dive. Starting far off she came quickly, flying into the sun ahead of her shadow. She flew like a shot, wings tucked, her white head an arrow tip, speeding toward what only she could see. The prairie dog looked up too late. With fur flying, Eagle quickly released the animal's spirit and rose up into the heavens with its earthly remains. The tribal police officers turned inward to their own thoughts. "The natural cycle continues," Hobey reflected. Watching the eagle, he thought about definitions. Migizi identified by her eyes, the impenetrable pupils. The deer's sinew strapped tightly to the marrow in its legs to make for a higher leap. The wolf's stretch at full run. And on and on. So what about us, he pondered. Is this our identifying trait, that we kill each other for who knows what ridiculous reason?

Jesse swung left onto the down slope of Chippewa County 3 toward the hospital, knowing they didn't have long before everyone knew about Jed's murder. From house to house, faster than a phone call. Down the back roads and into lone cabins in the woods, the moccasin telegraph was surer than Western Union, more personal than police scanners, if not always as accurate.

Hobey stayed on Old Bridge Road until Gi sina Nibi Lake, then headed south to catch the short cut to tribal headquarters. The moon on the horizon hung in the cold, clear sky like a giant globe in the dusk of coming night. Approaching the curve at Goodbears', he could see where the accident left the road and smashed into the wall of the ravine. He switched on the radio. Fatigue drained down his shoulders and spread through his body like a seeping oil slick. The tribal station's mix of pow wow music and country usually distracted him, but not tonight.

Unresolved questions swirled in his head. He wondered where it would all end. The robbery, he figured, had a local connection. Someone knew the exhibit was there. Someone knew when the janitor left and when the first sheriff's check was. Billy Walking Bear? Lou Blank? Then, according to Jesse, a stranger with no ID runs off the road on an 803-square-mile reservation and dies in an accident within a half mile of Jed's murder site. Coincidence? And what about Jed? Was his murder a coincidence so soon after the robbery? Even he wouldn't steal the tribe's stuff—would he? Everybody knew Jed Morriseau was a mean and vicious man. Proud of his have status in the have-not world of the reservation, he was the guy who, in the midst of starving people, would complain about having indigestion. Without intending to, Chief Bulieau found himself praying for Jed's journey on the Path of Souls. Ojibwa knew that the difficulty of the journey depended on how you lived your earthly life. Jed's trip would be an arduous one.

"God, I could use a sweat," the chief cried out to Neeba geesis as he made his final turn on to Anishanabe Circle.

5

Walter Leaper's clearing stretched out before Renee. The only cars visible in the early morning fog were Walter's three dead ones. She'd made it in time. As she and Mukwa jumped from the jeep, the old man's skinny, stooped frame emerged from the one-room house. A Twins baseball cap kept the long silver-black hair off his leathered, whiskerless face. Morning Star—last of the Night People—tipped the Douglas fir behind him while chickadees whistled their first-of-the-day proclamation. Mother Earth was a morning person, and Renee loved it.

Laying against the front of the house was the bottom third of a two-hundred-year-old spruce tree trunk. A cello-maker in Granite Rock, hearing about the downed spruce felled by lightning in a summer storm, notified the elder he wanted to buy the part of the tree he could use. Old spruce is the best wood for making cellos, giving the instrument the velvety sound that's so admired in the classical music world, but a good piece is a rare find. Rumor had it the cello-maker camped out on Walter's doorstep until the old man agreed to sell the tree. Leaper's fifty-five-gallon shower barrel peeked above the curtain on its twelve-foot stand just left of the house. Hidden back behind it in the woods, Renee could see the eastern side of Leaper's sweat lodge, the door flap open awaiting its next visitors. Next to the shower a shed leaned precariously against a nearby Jackpine, its only apparent means of support. Walter had spread a deerskin atop the shed's roof, and from the smell at the fire pit, Renee knew he was cooking brains for massaging into the hide in the last stage of tanning. Off to the side of the clearing was the Leaper outhouse. Paths worn between the buildings told visitors the family had lived here a long time.

The littered look of the place was deceiving. Instead of junk, reservation yards held items not yet needed, items that someday would be, could be. Tires, oil drums, fenders, transmissions, horseshoes, sled runners, board ends. Renee smiled, thinking, City folks don't know beans about recycling.

"*Boozho,*" she called after the old man's back.

Leaper squinted momentarily in the younger woman's direction as he walked to the fire. Adjusting the skinning knife on his hip, he tossed a log on the fire and slowly straightened. "Emma Coon's *nosijhe,* eh?" the elder replied without looking back. No matter how old Renee got, matriarchy bid the elders on Red Earth call her Emma Coon's grandchild.

The chief had phoned Renee at 5:00 A.M. and asked her to head over to Walter Leaper's house. It seemed the old man had found a gun on Old Bridge Road the morning of Jed's murder that could be the one used to kill the tribal chairman. As usual, the FBI insisted on butting its nose into the investigation. They were going to interview Leaper, futile as it was, about the find, and Hobey wanted someone there. Feds were not a welcome species on the rez, especially with the elders. They were just another invader's face: starting with the missionaries, evolving into the cavalry, becoming the pioneers, who turned into immigrants to railroad barons to the FBI. In the light of day or the dark of night they came, leaving only the dot of the i to the Anishanabe. The elders had grown weary of it. Renee, herself, was no stranger to FBI agents, confronting them many times during her years in the Movement, so Hobey knew she'd be a good buffer. And, Ren figured, it'd be fun watching the elder run circles around the nosy ef-bee-eye!

Walter squatted near the woodpile, motioning to Renee with his lips, Ojibwa-style, toward the tall grass. A bullfrog's *barrumpff* sounded as Ren kneeled next to the old man. The jump-out-at-you smell of sage mixed with the oily odor of cedar wreathed Walter in "elder's perfume," as Jenny called it. Hunkered down, the frog was holding his ground and glared at the two Ojibwa, obviously not happy with this intrusion into his preparations for winter. Walter whispered,

"Look, the grass stem." A tiny red spider stretched out on the blade of grass, chin on her front feet, studying the job of creating a web in the canyon she saw between blades of neighboring grass. After a while Walter offered, "Patient little thing," and returned to the pot, leaving Emma's *nosijhe* to draw her own lessons. As Spider finished her second leap, Renee left her to her work and set about making herself useful. She hauled wood to the fire and pulled the deerskin off the roof. "Mr. Leaper," she said finally, "Chief Hobey sent me over. The FBI's gonna pay you a visit."

There'd been another freeze overnight, and their breath steamed the air as they worked this morning. Time passed easily until Walter commented, "Crickets've stopped." Someone was coming. Mukwa took a position at the overgrown tracks along with Leaper's two *ahnimoosh*. Soon the hum of an engine lifted Ren's gaze away from the fire, and a brown, late-model Chevy crawled into the clearing. Two men emerged from the plain two-door sedan. As they approached, Renee chuckled at the short one tugging irritably at his suit jacket. She'd seen it before. A new guy, not used to anything but a police uniform, and now he found himself in a job requiring suits. Exiled to watch the Indians because he'd messed up somewhere else, maybe. She smiled. He'd be fun to confuse.

"Good morning...ah...Ms. LaRoche, isn't it? Special Agent Lawton," the tall one said. "This is Agent Tommy Lancaster." Renee didn't react to the familiarity of the greeting, much to Lawton's disappointment. Instead she watched in amusement Lawton's attempt to locate the smell irritating his nose. "Mr. Leaper?" Agent Lawton turned to the old man, who continued stirring the brains. "Mr. Leaper," he repeated, yelling this time, "I'm Special Agent Lawton and this is Agent Lancaster from the FBI. We need to ask you a few questions." Their practiced pushiness wasn't working on the old man, who stopped stirring finally and looked up at Renee. Eyes snapping, he moved his lips in the agent's direction.

"*Anishwin wegonen wendji biwide?*"

"*Winawa aiawa gagwedwewin gega pashkisigan,*" Renee responded. "They have questions about the gun," Renee repeated for the agents' benefit.

Walter understood English well enough, even used it, but he wasn't going to let the Feds know.

Game time! Ren smiled at Walter, then added, "*Gowengish*

kimagams, eh!" Strange fellows indeed!

The old man grinned widely, looking at the agents for the first time before turning his back to spread the skin on the grass.

The door to Walter's cabin squeaked open just then, and a man emerged. Like a wounded soldier refusing to lay down for fear he'd die, Melvin moved through the group. His glassy eyes still held last night's excess, and his gaze was fixed on the other side of reality as he disappeared into the woods, on a trail visible only after he turned onto it. Ren snuck a glance at Walter. An imperceptible tightening of the face drew his pain to the surface. He never looked up at his youngest son.

Melvin's story was no less tragic for its familiarity. A rowdy, angry kid, he'd joined the military to "straighten up." Back from Vietnam after a two-year tour, he was no longer rowdy. No longer angry. He came home to his father, but most conversations nowadays were with himself. He roamed the rez, taking drinks where he could get them, huffing down at the dam with others in almost as bad shape. He would show up places suddenly out of nowhere. Watching him, swallowed up by the beech and aspen, Renee could almost hear the trees whisper, *Rest your soul under us, we'll wrap our arms around your spirit.*

For the next hour, the FeeBees tried swimming upstream, following the aged river otter. Walter finally lost them after one of his dives. *Walter, Walter*, Renee smiled. *Don't they know that as long as you don't want to be trapped you won't be? Besides, it's such stupid make-do work.*

Walter had already told the whole story to Hobey. How he'd been out on his morning turtle hunt in the sloughs along Old Bridge Road. How, after rounding Willow Bend, he'd noticed what at first he thought was a turtle's head in the water. How, when he saw that it wasn't, he walked on by. But it had called him back. "Drew him over," he told Hobey. "The power of it." When he picked the gun up, the old man said he could feel it had just been used. Renee knew the FeeBees would never buy that, but she did, and so had the chief. When Leaper's son Ben came by with supper and heard his father's story, he brought Walter and the gun in to the tribal police. They were sitting at the station waiting for the chief when he got back from the murder site.

The Feds finally gave up on Walter, recording once again the "total lack of cooperation" they received on the reservation, unable to see any reason for the rude treatment they were met with. They retreated down the narrow trail, leaving Renee and Walter behind, with a weak plea for the elder to contact them if he remembered anything.

"When bears don't hibernate," Walter muttered, and the two Red Earthers had a good laugh.

"Hobey? Say, I like this car phone, or cell phone, or whatever this is you gave me," Renee said, pulling on to Loon Road a short time later.

"They do come in handy, eh?"

"Well, we all came out alive at Walter's. He gave it to 'em, though. Pretty entertaining. I'm free now. Blank come in yet?"

"Haven't seen him."

"Want me to track him down?"

"Jesse's handlin' it. He's starting to piss me off royally. Pardon my French."

"OK, I'll be there soon. Give you a full report. This case is startin' to feel like we're opening a milk pod in the wind," Renee scoffed. "I'll see you in a bit." She counted four law-enforcement agencies now interested in the robbery and murder, five if you included the BIA "law and order department" who usually watched from a distance but never met a camera they didn't like. Ren understood why Hobey hated to involve the Feds. The Chippewa County sheriff and his shoot-from-the-lip attitude, along with the Elko police, were more than enough *chimooks* to deal with. But federal law required that the FBI be notified of any felony on a reservation. Special Agent Lawton would have to dance a little though before the chief gave him much. FeeBees were stingy about sharing evidence, and bad publicity was to the Feds what mortal sin was to the Catholic Church. They were a pain in the butt to work with, and it all irritated tribal police. Ren smiled at the image of BIA Indians and narrow-tied Feebees fighting over the press ink in the case. "Let 'em go at it," she smirked.

Red Earth was a mix of conifer and broadleaf forests, prairies and wetlands. County Road 3, on the drive in from Walter's, had prairie to the west and forest east to the river. This time of year, with an Arctic storm poised in Canada ready to begin its great winter sag on to the reservation, changes were palpable. Blue jays darted from oak to nest retrieving acorns, no time left for teasing. The last butter-flies staked out warm spots in the sun, waiting to begin their transition to the Spirit World. Even the tiny box mites busily filled up on dead leaves in preparation for the Long Snows Moon.

Hibernation was on the mind of everyone from chipmunks to black bears. The little four-leggeds would foray into the wintry world every week or so, needing to warm their small bodies, but bears would be in for the season, birthing in the first month, then snuggling down for the duration with their newborn cub or cubs. Rarely using the same den, the bears' wanderings were more intentional now as they sought safety for the big sleep. Even the wood duck would have chosen its nesting hole high in a tree trunk and prepared it for winter occupancy. Come spring, mother duck would leave the nest with her newly hatched right behind, tumbling over each other as they floated down to the soft composted earth. Hibernation's a great solution to winter, Renee thought. No goin' south, only need a little food. Too bad we're not smart enough to do it.

Renee was reminded of the chief's admonition to watch for patterns as she drove. "A cop's best friend is patterns, Renny, meaningful patterns. Chains of events that are, or turn into, a picture." She knew it took trained eyes. She was getting better.

"*Boozho*, my Anishanabe *nijis*. This is O Gitchi Da Gi ghi kiwa ansi, Tony Coon." Ren smiled, hearing her cousin Talk Dance Brother's voice over the air waves, one more success story in the wreckage of reservation life. "Before the news, let's hear from one of our CW brothers." The twang of an electric guitar blared from the dashboard, followed by words of pining love and betrayal.

"My God, Tony, that song's so bad, how'd it ever stick to the tape?" Renee yelled at the radio, turning the volume down to a murmur.

"No more news on Tribal Chairman Jed Morriseau's murder at the river flats yesterday," Tony began after the song, and Renee turned the volume up. "Cause of death appears to be a gunshot to the back. The tribal chairman's body was taken to the county coroner's office over at Thunder Lake. No funeral notice yet, and Chief Bulieau has asked KAIO's listeners for help contacting Jed's sister and brother. If anyone knows how to reach them, call the station. We'll pass anything new on to you as soon as it becomes available."

Renee's breath caught in her throat hearing the news broadcast. The reality, the finality, of death was startling. Pulling onto the shoulder of County Road 3 she took a big breath and picked up the cell phone, hands shaking.

"Hello?"

"Sammy?" Renee whispered tentatively, remembering her partner's anger about where she was headed this morning, but desperately needing to talk.

"So I'm told," Samantha responded icily.

The pause was long. Finally Renee said, "Please, Sam. I'm sorry we fought this morning. I know you don't get any of this, but I really need to talk."

There was another long pause, then, "I can't right now, Renee. I'm not ready, and besides I'm on the other line with Mollie. I have to go. I'll talk with you later," Samantha said with heavy finality. Renee sat there for a long time, looking at the dead phone and wishing she was the one talking to her old friend Mollie.

Samantha hung up the phone a short time later. "Willa Cather said there's only five or six human stories that keep repeating themselves," she mused. "Wonder which one she'd put Renee and me in?"

White, not exactly debutante class but barely a step below, Samantha hadn't been prepared by New England society for life on the reservation. Coming from one of the Seven Sisters colleges, she'd signed civil rights petitions and attended a few anti-Vietnam war demonstrations. She read about Chicago in '68 and Woodstock in '69. That was about it, except for feminism, her consciousness-raising support groups, and her coming out in '78. There'd been one Japanese and one upper-class Mexican girl in her dorm. A few African-Americans lived across the quad. Not much of a cross-cultural experience. She'd never met a Native American, that she knew of, until she moved up to these north woods. And, she was finding, they definitely were a different lot.

The miracle to Sam was how deeply she felt for Renee, and how hard she was working to understand her. It wasn't one of those "I think I was an Indian in another life" things, but she now knew what Renee meant when the Ojibwa woman told her that the soundless, pulse beat of the wilderness—Indian Country—would fill her up if she let it. She knew she'd been overreacting to Renee's involvement in investigating the robbery at least in part because she didn't feel so self-assured here.

Renee's commitment was born of the same consuming passion

she brought to their bed—and who could quarrel with that? Renee wove her life's web so elaborately it was hard to keep up with her. A Monarch butterfly flapped its wings in the forests of Mexico and Renee felt it. Samantha knew she'd never be an insider, completely, on the rez, or even in Renee's heart. But Renee had opened the gate to her culture, invited her in, and she hadn't refused. Besides, in the area of love they spoke the same language. Samantha wiped tears from her eyes and, on impulse, she grabbed Renee's leather work gloves, heading for the stack of cordwood and the unsplit rounds. It was usually Renee's job, but who said it had to always be that way? It had helped to talk with Mollie. She'd call Renee at police headquarters later.

Renee couldn't always keep up with what she was doing wrong in Samantha's eyes—dirty dishes, discarded clothing, messy desk, lack of sensitivity—but she could usually tell with one glance at Sam's face that she wasn't happy. She imagined her partner's frown right now was pretty deep.

Tony's voice broke in. "Continuing news from around Indian Country." Renee drew herself away from her funk and slid the volume on the radio back up.

—"Northern Wyoming: The Park Service is planning to commercialize the great medicine wheel, a sacred site for over thirteen Plains tribes.

—"A world-class telescope is being built at Mount Graham in Arizona, endangering both the red squirrel and the most sacred mountain of our Apache brothers and sisters.

—"Grave robbers are at it again. Remote burial sites of the Navajo, Zuni, and Lakota people have been found desecrated and empty. FBI and U.S. Park Service spokespeople state they are investigating.

—"And speaking of burial sites, the U.S. Forest Service is looking for Indians to sign up for their Passport In Time project. Working with the U. of M.-Duluth Archeology Department, they're opening some new digs in the Arrowhead region. Come on all you Injuns, call the station and sign up so we can keep an eye on these folks.

"That's it for now. How about a song from the Sacred Directions Women Singers, an all-women's drum group from Minneapolis with their first album. Help all you folks still tryin' to get outta bed to start your week. Aha. Aha."

"All of a sudden this grave robber stuff is everywhere," Renee said, reaching for the phone. "Think I'll give Tony a—" She snapped her mouth shut, swallowing loudly. "Oh my God, Mukwa!" Glancing sidelong at the *ahnimoosh*, she pressed her back against the seat, elbow-locking her arms, and took a deep breath. Renee pulled back off the road. The grave robber news was a memory jog, and the dream she had last night came flooding back.

She was flying over Gi sina Nibi Lake with a pair of eagles, trying to talk to them. Samantha flew up and distracted her because she was not such a good flyer, being so new at it. But Ren had to talk with the eagles about the pipe, get their help. She could see the stem and bowl still separated in their red flannel wrap, the way to keep its power suspended until the keeper began the ceremony. Renee started screaming at the faceless Europeans who were handling the pipe way down below, warning them that if they looked at it without understanding its sacredness, it could hurt them badly. Then she realized nothing was coming out. They couldn't hear her. Her lungs hurt, she was screaming so loud, but all was silent. Just as the tallest man took the bowl out of its beaded bag the stocky bearded man said something and both laughed uproariously. The Living Pipe called to Renee. It had witnessed the birth of babies. It had called out their names to the Great Mystery. It had whispered the way in Healing Ceremonies and promised the People's word during the peace signings. Its power was limitless. The Living Pipe called again, and Ren tried again to warn the men. Just as Tall Man With No Hair picked up the pipestone bowl and feathered stem, Renee woke up. With tears streaming down her face, she turned quickly to be sure of Samantha's safety, then rolled into her lover's arms.

"Listen to the Shadow World, *nosijhe*," Renee could hear her grandmother. "Your gift is also your responsibility." The words swirled before her. She'd been given another message from the Spirit World, and she felt the responsibility, deeply. She needed to talk through this dream with Gram. Maybe she'd go by after her meeting with Hobey, or after teaching her class. Or tonight. "Creator, I need a patch of blue here. Help!" she yelled out the window.

6

"*Boozho*, Esther, awful about Jed, eh?" Renee greeted the elder on the steps of the tribal police station.

"To tell you the truth, Renny, I'm surprised it took this long. He's been a *Windigo* since he's a little boy." Esther shook her head sadly and leaned against the step railing. "I said to him just the other day, 'Jed, one of these times you're gonna step over the edge with someone who's already over it.'" She slit her throat with her finger.

"What'd he say?"

"He laughed, but took on a very funny look."

"Who'll lead the Council now?"

"We're meetin' in a half hour."

"Open meeting?" Ren queried.

Esther nodded, then walked down the steps, the bounce in her walk belying her age. "You say hi to your gramma and auntie, eh?"

Esther was Lydia's buddy, and the two of them could be found on almost any Wednesday or Friday night at the Elder Center, green accountant's visors shading their eyes, one dab-a-dot bingo marker in each hand. On Wednesday they played seven cards, on Friday, fourteen. Seven being an important number to Ojibwa, they figured doubling it would be extra lucky. Six years before, at age seventy-seven, Aunt Lydia had talked Esther into going back to high school with her, and they both had earned their high school diplomas from the newly organized Red Earth traditional school on the reservation. No one quite knew why Lydia did it: she was often heard mumbling, "I can tell more from the swayin' trees, how they spread their branches and lean into the wind, than from anything I get from books." Much to the school's horror she had told the graduation audience, "I get more from where the moss grows and the height of the flowers than any book learnin'. My best teachers are in the forest." But every year after they graduated, Lydia and Esther could be found at the school as elder volunteers. Esther said Lydia was prouder of her diploma than she was willing to admit in public. Maybe that's why it hung on the wall in her bedroom.

Inside tribal police headquarters, Chief Bulieau was having trouble concentrating. His uncle had taught him to clear his mind and visualize what he was trying to focus on. But today it wasn't working. *Is it just the murder, or is it the murder and something else, the robbery maybe? And what about the truck accident, could that be connected? The gun was found along there.* Mulling it over, Hobey didn't know if they made more sense separate or together. *Maybe they're all part of something bigger. But what?* It had given him a headache.

"You're a happy sight, Renee. Damn, where is that stuff?" the chief mumbled, rummaging in his drawer. Since learning how to dig the dogbane root, cut off the elbow, and pound it into powder, he'd given up commercial aspirin. *Dewi kwewin mus keeki* had no preservatives, and with the plant's spirit added, well, he just believed it worked better.

"Anything new?" Ren asked, watching Hobey curiously.

"Just this damn headache. Tryin' to find my medicine," he muttered, slamming the drawer. "Start of the week frustrations, I guess. When I got back to the office last night Walter and Ben were waitin' for me with the gun. Me and Jesse worked late, then I left for a sweat over at George's. Didn't get home till three this mornin'. Called you at five, and here I am. Nine forty-five," he said, glancing at his watch. "Life goes on."

"Funny," Renee added, "you'd think the world'd stop when somebody's murdered. But I got up this mornin' same as always, had my run, drank my juice, got dressed. Even had time for a fight with Sammy."

Bobbi stuck her head in. "Jesse called. She talked to Blank and he swears he was just out for a jog the night of the robbery. The two in the car stopped to ask him directions. He couldn't explain an Indian needin' directions, though, and she said he was very cranky."

Headed to Rice Lake now to look for Billy Walking Bear again. And two suits, *chimooks*," she whispered, "here to see you. Say it's official business."

"Show 'em in, Bobbi. Just what I need this mornin'—*chimooks* in suits!"

"Chief Bulieau?" The first man through the door held out his hand. "Special Agent Lawton. This is Agent Lancaster. We talked on the phone." Noticing Renee, he added, "Nice to see you again, Ms. LaRoche."

Renee nodded, unsmiling.

"What can we do for you now?" Hobey's slow, deliberate look at the agents stated clearly who was in charge.

"We want to talk to you about the murder and the theft of tribal artifacts."

"They were sacred ceremonial items." The chief hated when *chimooks* said "artifacts."

Despite his outward appearance of calm, Hobey's voice was changing. "Why does that concern you?" He fixed the agents with an icy stare.

The FBI men glanced at each other. "Well," Lawton said over tented fingers, "I'm not at liberty to go into details, but I assure you it's serious. If it becomes necessary for you to know, we will certainly bring you into the loop."

Chief Bulieau stood, looking from Lawton to Lancaster. "And I can assure you, gentlemen, if we need your help we'll be sure to open our loop to you. Now, if you'll excuse us, we're due at a meeting." Chief stared down the two agents. Stared down five hundred years of disrespect and lies, of arrogance and murder. Stared them down for all the times as a little boy, clutching his BIA ID card, he would line up for commodities for the family, load them into his rickety wagon, and before he'd be allowed to leave with the month's food allotment, have to "dance like an Indian" for the Federals. And the agents of the U.S. government looked away.

Walking out, Renee turned to Lawton. "Know anything about grave robbers out west? Heard it on the radio."

"It's being investigated," he replied. The coldness of a FeeBee's stare didn't phase Renee anymore, and Agent Lawton wasn't capable of warming his up. "Ma'am," he tipped his hat, and turned into the parking lot.

As they made their way to the council meeting, Renee held out her hand. "Gimme five, Chief. That was some standoff. Skins One— Long Knives Zero!"

The chief laughed, slapping Renee's outstretched hand. "Pushed me too far. That guy acted like their Jesus hisself. Don't like them ef-bee-eyes."

Hobey's last few words were whispered as they entered the circular chamber of the tribal council. A new building, it was constructed with local materials—pink granite, cedar, basswood—with the circular council chamber in the middle. The ancestors' spirits were everywhere: old ricing baskets, an *aneak akween* for harvesting wild rice, and bows and arrows hung on the walls next to the ricing pole. A *wigwass* canoe was strung from the ceiling. Renee brought her art class here when they were on the section about traditional uses of birch bark. The table from Red Earth's first council lodge sat in the center of the room where people stood to address the council. Along the wall behind the seated semi-circle of council members, photographs of Minnesota Anishanabe at various times in history were hung. Chief Bug O Nay Ge Shig (Hole In The Day)—named that because he was born during an eclipse—was the last chief recognized by the people. His picture held the place of honor behind the council chairman. There were pictures of children standing at attention in front of the windmill at Holy Rosary boarding school in 1905. Another of a later class riding down Learner's Hill bunched into the school hog cart in 1913. A picture of the tribe's first newspaper office—the *Bow and Arrow*—about 1910. And, of course, the popularized portraits of women, men, children, and families in traditional dress, in front of wigwams and trading posts. Or stuffed into European-style suits and dresses.

The 1934 Indian Reorganization Act forced Red Earth and all reservations to elect a tribal council and chairman. Though many on the rez had come to accept and even respect tribal government, Jed Morriseau was not a respected chairman. Renee's brother Benny used to say of his classmate, "Yeah, Sticks To His Fingers has trouble remembering what's his and what ain't." Jed Morriseau's scams were legendary, from selling powdered maple leaves to white folks as herbal medicine, to ripping off tribal elders by taking half their allotment checks for "a retirement community." Some stories about him were true, some were the imaginings of a people terrorized by his larger-than-life image.

The story that enraged Renee most, though, was from his sister. When Betty first came to class with black eyes or split lips—once with a broken arm—everybody believed her stories about falling out of a tree or getting poked in the eye with a ricing pole. The worst Renee remembered was the day Betty arrived at school barely walking. As she undressed for gym, she tried but couldn't hide a bruise, about the size of the volleyball they were batting around, on her right inner thigh. Jokes made were soon replaced with whispers of concern. "Renny, it was so sad. Jed was doin' it, and she told us he was forcin' her to have sex with him," a friend told Renee later. After finding out about Betty's late-night revelations to her friends, Jed suddenly left the reservation. No one saw him for ten years.

Traditional *ahos* rose up around the room following Esther Little Wolf's opening prayer. Smudging smoke drifted above the council members, and the sweet smell lay as a calming blanket on the people.

"*Megwetch*, Esther," Don LaFleur nodded. "This is a sad day for Red Earth," the deputy tribal chairman began. "No matter what anybody thought of Jed, he didn't deserve this."

"Wanna bet?" The muffled comment came from the community section behind Renee.

Shifting her eyes, she caught Hobey's slight nod, indicating he'd heard it too. But wanting to be neither impolite nor obvious, she filed it away. Male voice, young, about two rows back.

"Today we have to plan the transition, the election of a new tribal chair." Don droned on, and Renee turned her thoughts back to Betty and Jed.

After high school, Betty went off to college, married a Mohawk, and stayed East. The reports were that she was happy living in upstate New York with her husband and five kids. Until about six months ago, when rumors started that there were problems. "Flashbacks," Bobbi said, "about the abuse." No one knew for sure what was going on. Some said Betty was drinking, trying to blot out the memories; others that she was near a nervous breakdown. Gossip was it was affecting her marriage so bad, people thought she might move back to Red Earth. But not as long as Jed was around.

Jed's life had gone a different way. The rumor on him was that when he left the rez, he was up to his neck in gambling debts. Then ten years ago, he suddenly moved back. Showed up one day with his truck packed full of his worldly possessions. "Got homesick," he said. Of course, no one believed Jed cared enough about anyone else to get homesick. "He squawks like the blue jay," was the comment from the Elder Center. He bought the next tribal election, or so people on Red Earth believed. And he'd been holding court ever since with puppets on the council. Then two years ago, elders were elected a majority on the council for the first time in fifty years and a return to traditional ways began. This all made Jed very irritable.

Chief Bulieau stood to address the council. "*Boozho*. First off, I want you all to know I got ahold of Jed's brother. Wants Jed buried in the reservation cemetary. Can't get down from Canada. No one's talked to Betty yet, she doesn't have a phone, but Bobbi's workin' on it. Don, what kinda things were goin' on here at council the past few weeks? Anything might have put Jed's life in danger?"

"Routine stuff," the deputy chairman began. "Road repair, plans for an elder feast, money for the basketball teams. There was that aide at the hospital caught stealing—strange things, like formaldehyde, big sterile plastic bags, operating room packs. And elementary kids wanted to take a field trip to the caves."

"Why wasn't I contacted about the hospital incident?"

"Jed said he took care of that, Chief." Don looked to the other council members, who all nodded.

"Never heard a word, but...I'll talk to you later about it. *Megwetch*."

When Hobey finished, Renee stood. "*Boozho*. Do you know when the kids went to the caves?" Don informed Renee the students were denied permission for their field trip. "By Jed?" Renee asked. With a nod from Don, Renee returned to her seat.

Hobey nodded toward the door. On the way out, Renee scanned the rows as she passed them: two middle-aged women and their children, an elder man, and a young man in his late teens who was slouched low in his seat. They made their way to the front steps, then Renee stopped abruptly. "Billy Walking Bear! Hobey—that guy, the one who made the 'wanna bet' comment, I think it was Billy Walking Bear." They turned and ran back into the council chambers.

"He's gone!" Renee hissed. "Damn. He musta gone out the side door."

They canvassed the building and parking lot. No sign of the white car or Billy. "We gotta talk, compare notes." Renee tugged

Hobey's arm and nodded to the restaurant.

"I'll be over after I put out a call to pick Billy up." The chief strode off in agitation toward the station, his cowboy boots clicking on the sidewalk circling the cul de sac of tribal buildings on the outskirts of Rice Lake. Renee crossed the road and, entering the cultural center, glanced back at the tribal offices. A new black Pontiac Grand Am caught her eye as it pulled out from the side of the building. It was a standout amidst the dozens of rez cars and trucks, and she watched the fancy car squeal off Anishanabe Circle onto Chippewa County 3 with Billy Walking Bear at the wheel.

7

"Call ya later," Renee said to the thirtyish woman sitting in the back of the cafe. She caught up with Hobey as he walked to their table. "Guess who burned outta the Circle in a brand spankin' new Pontiac Grand Am right after we left the meeting?" she began. "Our own Mr. Billy Walking Bear! Now where'd he get money for a fancy new car, and where in hell is his old one?"

The air split with his frown as the chief put down the menu and picked up his cellular phone. "Bobbi, change the all-points on Walking Bear to look for him in a new Pontiac Grand Am—hold on a sec."

The chief looked at Renee. "Color?"

"Black."

"Bobbi? It's black. A black Pontiac Grand Am."

When he clicked off the phone, Renee said, "You know Sally? Woman I was talkin' to?"

"Teacher at Heart of the Nation?"

"She's the one that wanted the trip to the caves. Told me Jed didn't give her any reason for refusing. Just said the tribal council's answer was no. When she told him maybe she'd check with me or Gram, Jed got pissed. Said he was chairman and she shouldn't be botherin' us. Played on her bein' an outsider, so she backed off."

Hobey took another sip of coffee, shaking his head, "'Course he probably didn't ask the council, just told 'em."

"No doubt. It's one more strange thing around the caves,

though." Her laugh was short and unamused.

The chief nodded. He looked tired, stress from the past week showing in his eyes and the lines around his mouth.

"Ever try that Indian violet tonic?" Renee shrugged, not wanting to be pushy.

"Long time ago, but that's a good idea, LaRoche. I'll ask Donna to bring some. She'll be in later with the grandkids for supper. I could use a little pick-me-up." The chief leaned back, stretching his arms out wide. "Anyway, Renny, let me add to the pot of confusion." Hobey rifled through his papers. "Now wait, it's here somewhere, last thing Bobbi handed me when I walked out the door. Here it is. OK, after the accident on Old Bridge—you know the unidentified *chimook?* I sent the license plate number through the computer. That and fingerprints. Here's the report." He handed a sheet to Renee and sat back. Hobey noticed the way Renee's eyebrows bunched, then twisted, as she began reading the report. Cute, he thought. She looks just like that cocker spaniel of hers.

Renee read as she munched on her lettuce salad:

> MN plate #RFM 635 is registered to John Anderson, 3720 Pleasant Ave. S, Mpls. The 1992 Ford Ranger was reported stolen the morning of Nov. 1, from the owner's residence. Sighted once in Mpls after the theft, driven by a large Caucasian male, 45-50 years of age, wearing a denim jean jacket. The owner has been informed of the accident and agreed to come to your location for positive ID of the vehicle.

The faxed message came from the Minnesota Department of Motor Vehicles and the Minneapolis Police Department.

"Jeez, this doesn't help much. That description fit the victim?" Hobey shrugged. "Far as it goes, I guess."

"How 'bout this John Anderson. We know anything about him?"

"Nope. Not yet, but that stolen part doesn't quite—" Hobey grew quiet. After a long silence he said, "I was thinkin' about the story my mother used to tell, 'bout the cedar tree?"

Renee waited.

"It's about when plants and animals were created. Everybody wanted to be on a hill because it looked like the nicest spot, all sunny and bright. Nanabush suggested some live in the valley, but everyone said, 'No, no. Too wet. Too dull.' Only Cedar tree saw the winding valley stream and said, 'I'd like to live there.' Nanabush answered, 'You'll see, all is not as it first seems.' 'Course, Trout found the stream, bugs and insects lived in the trees, birds came, and Waboose thought it a great place to raise her bunnies. Winter came and Cedar tree broke the cold wind for everyone. The maples and birches were shivering and bare way up on the hill where they'd argued to be." Hobey stopped. "I was thinkin', things not bein' as they first seem."

The two friends sat quietly until Renee asked, "You wondering 'bout John Anderson?"

"Just a feelin'," the chief replied. "Fax says he reported the truck stolen yesterday morning. The accident was yesterday morning." He picked up his phone, "Bobbi? We're still at the Center. You comin' for lunch?"

"You got it, boss. Leavin' now," came the hurried reply.

"Do one thing before ya come, eh? Call Minneapolis and get the exact time that truck was reported stolen."

"OK, be right over."

Renee set her Coke down. "What're you wonderin'?"

"Mm, not sure yet." Hobey smiled absently.

When Ren glanced up to see Bobbi standing at the table, she realized how long they'd been sitting there lost in their own thoughts.

"Ah yes, super trackers hard at it, eh? Gettin' ready for the latest clues in Red Earth's grand mystery!" Bobbi teased. "Anyways, here's what you wanted. The stolen vehicle report came in at 8:20 A.M."

The chief took the sheet. "OK, given that it takes four hours from the city if you drive straight here, and the accident was reported at 8:15, the truck had to have been stolen at least by 3:00 A.M., probably earlier. So we have a few unanswered questions: Did Mr. Anderson not discover his truck stolen until 8:15? If he knew it earlier, why didn't he report it? Answers to these two'd be good for starters. Oh, one more thing, the accident arrived at the hospital at 8:10."

"Could be we'll get some answers sooner'n we thought." Ren nodded to the door. "*Chimook* at the counter with *Anderson & Sons* on the back of his jacket." The words on the black rayon jacket surrounded a flaking orange stencil of a bulldozer.

"Gotta go eat, Boss. Catch ya later." Bobbi turned to the table occupied by Jean, the school nurse who had been her best friend since high school. She threw a "good luck" back over her shoulder.

"OK, Bobbi. *Megwetch.* See ya." Hobey's voice trailed off, his attention turning to the new customer seated now at a table near the windows. Renee and Hobey sat in silence observing the visitor, who didn't have a clue his every move was being monitored. He brushed wispy, corn-colored hair off a high forehead, his pale blue eyes darting about.

Suppose he's handsome enough, Renee thought, looking him over. For a white boy. She knew her images of white men were broadly drawn, maybe to the point of being prejudiced, but she didn't spend much time feeling guilty about it. From a visual point of view, her taste in men had always been men of color.

Hobey stood. "Wanna see if Mr. Anderson can clear some things up?"

"Look how nervous he is, Chief, checkin' out everyone comin' in, almost like he's lookin' for somebody, or afraid he might see somebody."

"Think we can add to that nervousness?" Hobey winked.

The soon-to-be-identified John Anderson, a son in Anderson & Sons, looked up, startled, as the two Ojibwa approached.

"Mr. Anderson?" Chief Bulieau said in his official voice.

"Yes?" Anderson replied, obviously surprised at hearing his name.

"Back of your jacket," Hobey smiled. "Guess we have something of yours, eh?"

"I don't know." John Anderson hesitated, glancing down at Hobey's revolver.

"Didn't you report a truck stolen in Minneapolis yesterday?"

"Oh, right." A giggle betrayed his nervousness.

"What time was it you called the theft in?"

Anderson stared at the chief.

"What time did you report your truck stolen?" Hobey tried again.

"Morning...early morning. I...I noticed it was gone and called the police."

"Do you remember the time?" the chief persisted.

"Exactly?" Anderson, who was looking out the window, turned back to Hobey and snapped, "I don't know—seven, seven-thirty, I guess. That's when I leave for work." John Anderson began to fidget, his demeanor becoming hostile.

"Which was it? Seven or seven-thirty?"

"I don't know, what the hell difference—" Hobey's solemn stare stopped the man. "Seven. I called at seven."

"OK, just so we understand each other now," the chief began. "You went to your truck at seven yesterday morning to go to work. It wasn't there so you immediately called the police?" Hobey and Renee were watching Anderson carefully.

"That's what I said, didn't I?" he responded angrily.

The ensuing pause was long enough for Renee to notice sweat beads forming on Anderson's upper lip. "Mm," Hobey nodded unsmiling. "Well, why don't we go take a look at the truck. By the way, this is Renee LaRoche, I'm Chief Bulieau, Tribal Police."

The weather outside was getting colder. The chill in the air ran through Renee, setting off a shiver. Zipping her jacket a little higher, she followed the two men to the the tribal police car. "Still not drivin' the jeep or the Bronco, eh?" Ren teased the chief.

"I'm too old to be bouncin' around in those things," he growled. "Hop in, Mr. Anderson, we might as well all go together. You gotta come back here to get to the highway, anyway." Hobey opened the back door.

Renee got in the front, smiling to herself. Any other visitor would've been given the front seat out of courtesy, but Hobey apparently was trying to work on the guy. "Worry his last nerve," Lydia would say. Anderson got in the back without comment.

They rode in silence past Red Earth Indian Health Service Hospital and Odeima Anishanabe Kikinoamading. Passing the large grassy field behind Heart of the Nation School that held the pow wow grounds, softball field, and playground, Ren thought back to when all it was was the local dung heap. Full of broken beer and wine bottles, rusted cans, garbage, old couch springs stretching prayerfully through torn cushions to the God of the Throwaway.

Ojibwa knew every meadow held a mood reflecting its spiritual state. Destroying any of it changed that mood. The spirit of this meadow began to die as the grass succumbed to pollution from the trash. Soul-spirits of the sumac and berry bushes collapsed under the weight of refuse blown in on winds to this orphanage for junk, and it became the stereotypical poverty war zone seen on nightly news clips. Soon people started walking around it to avoid injuries as well as the depressing feelings it evoked.

Shortly after Renee and Jenny moved back to Red Earth, Renee noticed a change in the meadow. Drunks, inspired by the "return to traditions" campaign of the tribal council, started sobering up. As their eyes cleared they saw the results of their spiritless lifestyle. Interviewed on the then-new reservation radio station KAIO, Rob, a Wigiwam of Nin gige client said, "When I sobered up I felt so bad I'd helped make this mess. Thought we should clean it up." Renee remembered driving by in the evening and seeing Lodge of Healing clients hauling truckloads of trash out. The woodland meadow returned. Lady-slippers, bluebells, roses, and Indian paintbrush jumped out. Free at last! Elders told the story of Odaemin—turned away from the Land of Souls because he was in turmoil and sent back to live as a heart-shaped strawberry—as bushes bloomed and berries returned. The people held a Pipe Ceremony honoring plants and their gift of life to others. *Red Earthers are kickin' butt!* Renee cheered quietly to herself. *This latest stuff, the robbery and murder, isn't really us.*

She realized that Jenny and her friends would be out at lunch soon. Even in cold weather, students from Heart of the People often ate in the meadow. Renee liked to bring her youngest students—first-graders—to the meadow with Lydia, who'd tell them stories about this flower or that bush and what they could be used for. Then they'd all stand in the parking lot to watch Lydia leave. That was the kid's favorite part: trying to guess which tree she'd hit or bush she'd back over this time as she drove away.

Renee was jolted by a bump in the road. Looking through the cage between the seats she said to the stranger, "Weird eh, somebody steals your truck and ends up dead here in the north woods. Wonder what brought the guy way up here?"

Anderson shrugged, not taking his eyes off the passing landscape.

"Any chance you might know him?" she continued, eyeing him carefully.

"What do you mean by that? How would I know somebody that stole my truck?" the man in the backseat responded curtly.

"Yeah, right. Guess I was thinkin' of around here. Everybody knows everybody."

The patrol car's passing raised raucous chatter from the flock of blackbirds lining the wires. That, and the whine of tires—the only sounds now as the three rode along Deer Lodge Trail. The landscape today was crushed under an incoming bank of rain, or snow, clouds. The day grew dark and gray as they approached, and splots of wet snow began hitting the windshield. The air had turned cold and raw. Renee daydreamed about skimming the cross-country ski trails the tribe groomed to entice winter vacationers to the area. Tribal members used the trails free, and last year it had been a favorite pastime for her and Samantha.

Soon the world outside faded. Drawing upon her lesson from Walter Leaper's red spider, and Hobey's story about the cedar tree, she began to sketch an outline of Mr. Anderson. Defensive. Definitely defensive. Almost sullen, impatient. Why? There was no doubt he was hiding something about his truck and when it was stolen, if it had been. Why? If it wasn't stolen, what was his relationship to the driver and why is he hiding it? Maybe the driver was on his way to some drug deal or something. If he knew the driver, was the time of his call to the police connected in any way to the accident, or the time they showed up at the hospital? Did someone tip him off about the accident? Was he looking for someone he knew in the restaurant? Who? Renee didn't like John Anderson. Something about the way he moved. He didn't look you in the eye, either. If he was Indian, okay. But his name and appearance was Scandinavian—she knew *chimooks* were supposed to look people in the eye. Things not being as they seem, for sure, she thought, that's right on with this dude.

They passed the Red Earth saw mill turnoff, and half a mile down drove by the *Jed's Reclamation Next Right* sign. Hobey slowed and the whine quieted. It was always hard to find the turn, overgrown as it was with meadow grasses and an eastern burning bush leaning lazily across Jed's sign. The chief pulled off down the rocky dip and parked next to the fence. A visitor to the rez might wonder who this guy was who had his name on so many businesses around here—the Indian taco stand at the pow wow grounds, the novelty shop in Rice Lake that sold *Authentic Indian Gifts* made in Taiwan, this place. But the people knew it was their tribal chairman. Their tribal ex-chairman.

Like the one in town, this sign, too, was misleading. Jed's was short on reclamation and long on junk. Behind the fence, and stretching for seventy or eighty yards, was a graveyard of the most bombed-out junkers Anderson had seen. "This it?" he asked, looking around.

"These really *are* junkers."

"Actually," Hobey winked at Renee as he turned the motor off, "this don't look much different than any parking lot on the rez."

Anderson stared blankly at the chief, obviously missing the inside joke. Hobey unlocked the gate, and the three went into the yard. The junkers reminded Ren of the old car they'd used as a playhouse as kids. It sat in their front yard for as long as she could remember, the kids sharing occupancy with a couple of wild turkeys. Her dad only worked on it after downing a six-pack, so it never did get fixed.

"That it?" the chief said, pointing to a truck halfway down the first row.

"Jesus, he really wrecked it," Renee heard Anderson mutter, seeming to have forgotten all about his two companions. As he reached for the truck's twisted door, Ren noticed that his hand was shaking.

"Doubt you'll get that open," she said. But after several angry yanks, the door came off entirely, falling at their feet. Anderson looked up, startled.

"You really wanted that open, eh?"

"I just wanna get my stuff," came the frustrated reply.

"I guess!" Renee smiled. "Well, go to it then," she said, sweeping her arm toward the truck's cab.

After collecting ownership papers and maps from the glove box they pried open the tool box in the truck bed, retrieved the tools inside, and then piled silently back in the patrol car for the return trip. As they passed the hospital, Hobey suddenly pulled into the emergency entrance, parking in a *Reserved for Emergency Vehicles* spot. He turned the motor off and glanced back at Anderson. "Let's go in and take a look at John Doe. Just in case."

"Waste of time," Anderson replied, folding his arms across his chest like a defiant child.

"Yeah, probably, but humor me, eh?"

"Oh for Christ sake, let's get it over with then," the *chimook* grumbled. "I...I don't like dead bodies." He stepped angrily out of the car.

Reaching the morgue, Hobey knocked on the door. A minute later he picked up the wall phone and the hospital operator said she'd send someone. It wasn't long before the shift supervisor came down the long, dimly lit corridor and, after introductions, opened the morgue door. Hesitating, Anderson had to be guided into the room by Renee. Mrs. Effie opened the door behind the John Doe label, sliding the steel drawer out. With the sudden release of cold from inside the wall, and the eerie squeaking of the rollers, Ren half expected music from "Murder She Wrote."

Mr. Anderson, however, was having no such thoughts. In fact, he was barely holding himself together, standing with his eyes averted until the chief asked if he knew the man. Glancing at the body with unfocused eyes, Anderson said, "I...I...no. HE'SNOBODYIKNOW."

"Look a little closer, eh." Hobey stared into Anderson's eyes. "Here, how about this tattoo on his arm?" He turned the man's huge left arm over, revealing the faded image of a naked woman, legs wrapped around the U.S. Marine sword.

A slight expression change flashed across Anderson's face, so quickly that Renee almost missed it. Like the shadow of the eagle passing in front of the sun. "I don't know," Anderson responded, but it was too late. The eagle had flown with the truth before Anderson spoke his lie. So, Renee thought, he does know something. But what? Struggling to get words out of a mouth as dry as a Tucson sidewalk Anderson said, "I gotta get out of here. I don't know him and that's—" He turned and ran out the door.

Renee and the chief looked at each other, then at Mrs. Effie, who was smiling after the retreating Anderson. "A lot of folks have trouble seeing dead bodies," she offered sympathetically.

"Thanks for coming down, Mrs. Effie. Please don't let this body leave without notifying me."

"It's your call, Chief," the shift supervisor said as they walked out of the room.

"Would you happen to know who was working the other morning when he was brought in?" Ren inquired. After twenty years on the staff, the woman from Elko knew everyone.

"In the ER?"

Ren nodded.

"No, but it wouldn't take much to check."

"When you track it down, will you call Bobbi at my office?" Hobey asked.

"Say," Renee drew up at the bottom of the stairs, "do you keep a record of when the county coroner's here?"

"There's a logbook in the morgue, and if he comes in after visiting hours he'd have to sign in up at the front desk," the nurse explained.

"Could we see the logbook?"

The three returned to the morgue, where Effie retrieved a black book with a red spine from the desk in the corner of the room. *Sign-In Log* was the adhesive-taped message on the front.

"Looking for anything in particular?" she wanted to know.

"A sign-in for Dr. Peterson or Lou Blank on Halloween," Renee told her, glancing at the chief.

Checking through the logbook, Renee discovered that Dr. Peterson had signed in on the twenty-fifth, but not again after that. Mrs. Effie, turning away from the phone, announced there was no sign-in at the front desk by Dr. Peterson for the last fourteen days.

"Any reason other than morgue work that Dr. Peterson would be here?" Renee asked.

"Staff meeting maybe, but he usually doesn't come to those. He's not around here any more than he has to be," she answered, a hint of sarcasm edging her words.

"Staff meeting's during the day, eh?" Hobey said.

"In the morning, and far as I know, our last staff meeting was at least two weeks ago."

Ren and Hobey looked at each other. *"Megwetch,"* Renee nodded to the woman, and they retraced their steps up to the emergency room.

"Told you it was a waste of time," Anderson said, shoving the ER door a little too hard and slamming it against the wall.

"Mm," the chief replied, walking silently to the car. The rest of the ride back was even quieter than the ride out.

Hobey turned into the Center parking lot, pulling up next to the car John Anderson pointed out as his. Reaching up, the chief took a card from behind his visor and handed it to the stranger. "'Preciate a call if you think of anything that might help. What do you wanna do with the wreck?"

Anderson took the card, picked up the bag of personal items he'd recovered, and moved quickly to his vehicle. "It's not worth hauling down to the city, so do what you want with it."

"Will do. You take care, eh." The chief nodded to the man who was so anxious to leave he didn't bother to shake Hobey's outstretched hand or say good-bye to Renee.

"Wonder why he bothered comin' up here? He's got somethin' on his mind, that boy, somethin'." Hobey shook his head. "Just don't know what...yet. Didn't even ask for verification of the accident for his insurance company."

Renee wrote down the fleeing man's license plate, noticing as she did the sticker on the back bumper: *Anderson & Sons Excavation —We Dig Your Desires!* She turned to her jeep and opened the door. "Come on girl. Out ya go." Renee walked slowly, Mukwa trotting beside her. Just ahead, Hobey shifted the brown gun holster at his side. The stoop to his shoulders was new, and for the first time Renee became aware of the sixteen long years the chief had already lived as an elder. His vulnerability scared her a little.

"Did you notice the cut on John Doe's left thumb? And the bruises and scratch on his face and neck?" Hobey remarked. "Probably not from the accident, but I wonder where they're from. Definitely new injuries."

"Is the guy left-handed?"

"I noticed a watchband tan-line on his right arm, and the middle finger on his left has that bump you get from writing, so I'd say it's a good bet." The chief shrugged his shoulders, grinning broadly.

"Do you think it coulda been him at the flats with Jed?"

"That guy was left-handed, too," Hobey answered. "But if it was, who the hell is he and why would he want to kill Jed? We've gotta identify him. Maybe we'll get lucky and his fingerprints'll turn up in a file somewhere."

"Did he have any personal effects?"

"A few things, I guess. Bobbi and Josh signed it all in. Was wearin' a beaded watchband. Carried some change. That was about it." Hobey opened the door to the station.

"This is gettin' pretty whacked," Ren muttered, then noticing the puzzled look on the chief's face, she added, "Whacked means weird, lousy. One of Jenny's words. I can't believe I just said that." The two Ojibwas had a good laugh.

"Come on, girl," Renee called to Mukwa. The dog perked her ears at the sound of screeching tires in the distance.

As Renee and Hobey made their way across the Circle, Mr. John Anderson peeled out from the stop sign at the intersection of County Road 3 and Highway 7. "Goddamn it," he cursed, "Fuckin' Indians." He slammed his fist against the steering wheel, roaring off down the highway.

Renee sat for a long time at her desk after teaching her three o'clock class. Her mind jumped from one thought to another. She couldn't help but wonder if what was happening with the robbery and murder was a consequence of the slash-and-burn attitude many on the reservation had about their traditions. While the tribal council's "return to traditions" campaign had stirred many people's souls, there were still some who were bored by it. She took a notepad from her briefcase and began to write:

> It's like the forest, same thing. Ojibwa traditions are the forest, and just like the forest, our traditions are dying because of greed and our losing sight of what's important. Assimilation into the dominant culture for us is as deadly as clear cutting the trees was for the forest. It's not that I want to go back two hundred years. I know that's not possible, and really, I don't want to go back. Some changes have been for the better. But some things we have to hold on to. We're adrift in no man's land without our traditions. How can we give our kids moral direction without our traditions? And that's what I have to get Samantha to see—that's all I'm trying to do.

Oh God—Samantha, she thought, setting her pen down. Well, suck it in, LaRoche. It's time to go home.

8

"Bobbi, anything on John Doe's prints this morning?" Hobey glanced at the mail on Bobbi's desk. He wasn't hopeful about the prints, but his prints would be on file if the man had ever been arrested.

"Check the computer fax for Doe, Chief. NIS's usually pretty quick," Bobbi called from the back room, where it smelled like she was making the morning coffee.

"I can't work that damn thing."

"Got it, Bobbi," Renee called, coming into the station chased by a gust of cold wind.

The computer hook-up was a department purchase after the drug bust and rash of rapes on the reservation the year before. "Our borders are expanding," Chief Bulieau had told the tribal council. "We need more sophisticated equipment to track people coming onto the reservation and committing crimes." Everyone expected Jed to protest an expenditure that wasn't a project of his, but this time he was especially hostile. The chief figured it was because he liked isolating his little kingdom, the better to control it. The system was installed over Jed's objections nonetheless, and within two months tribal police had arrested two *chimooks* in Granite Rock for the rapes. The computer had provided the key data.

Renee handed the fax to Hobey as Bobbi came into the front office.

"Mrs. Effie called with the names of who was working the other morning," Bobbi announced. She also said she had to talk to you soon, Chief, something about gossip going around the hospital."

"I'll call her in a bit." The chief looked down at the National Information Service report in his hand. "Well, well! Mr. Doe does have famous fingerprints."

Leaning over, Renee read:

> Peter John Thompson, DOB: 5/3/42. AKA: P.T. Thomas, T.P. Peterson. Last known address: 1824 Water St., Syracuse, New York. Arrests: B & E, 3/10/72, convicted, served 3 months with 1 year probation; Aggravated Assault, illegal possession of firearm, possession of cocaine, 11/15/88, pled guilty to count 1 and 2 with count 3 dropped, served 5 years, 8 months—released on parole 6/15/94 from Attica State Prison, NY.

"Nice fella, eh?" Ren looked up.

"Mm, he's a dandy. I'll call Attica, see if we can get any more on him, a next of kin maybe, somebody who might know why he's out here." Hobey went into his office.

"Oh yeah, Betty Atori also called," Bobbie added. "Said she tried to get you, Renny. Anyways, she wants to donate all Jed's stuff to the elder and daycare centers. Was very chatty. Sounded happy as a lark. Scared me a little. It's so different from what we've been hearing. When she was hangin' up she mumbled what I think was, 'I expect to be hearin' from Renny soon anyway.' Know what it might mean?"

"Nope, not a clue."

"Oh well, I probably didn't hear her right."

"I'll try and give a call before I go down to the pow wow," Renee shrugged. "I got the number of one of her neighbors. Betty called my place the morning Jed was murdered," she added, "before we knew about Jed. Could be takin' the news harder than she, or we, thought. Family, eh. No matter what they do to us it's still not easy to turn your back."

"You know, I been thinkin', Renny, you should make Hobey deputize you. You've got a real knack for this. You Bear Clanners, it's in your blood."

"Oh, it's not much different than how I do my art, really. You know, ya take a mental picture and turn it into something real. Hobey talked to me once about patterns. Made a lotta sense 'cause in bead-work and basketmaking, setting up your pattern is the most impor-tant thing you do."

"Well, you should get some money for all this work you're doin'!"

"Thank you, you're too kind. 'Course, you've always been in my corner! Even when Benny tried to get the best of me. Remember the time you dislocated his little finger when he was ticklin' me? Did he howl!" Renee threw her arm around the older woman's shoulder.

"I thought of him the other day, Renny, after the pipe was sto-len. He'd a been blisterin' mad about that. Can't hardly believe it's been almost ten years." Renee leaned heavily on her hand, then sat down hard.

Ben had been his little sister's teacher and protector. He taught her how to set snare lines and hit a baseball, but they had the most fun tracking. Her older brother helped her identify different marks—the deep cleft of the moose hoof, the shallower, narrower one of the deer. Large, sticklike impressions out from a center ball were wild turkey tracks, and, of course, there were the easy ones like bear and wolf. He also showed Renny how to set natural traps for land birds by digging a hole, camouflaging it, and laying out a trail of Indian corn. His most important job, though, had been covering her body with his own when their father, in his drunken tantrums, beat them with a switch, or took off his belt and started swinging wildly. Ben would turn his back, enveloping Renee in his arms as he headed out the door and ran for Gram and Gramps' place to hide until morn-ing. Though almost nine years apart, Renee and her brother were emotional twins. Lydia said Benny only claimed part of his spirit at birth, saving a piece for his little sister.

With difficulty, Renee forced herself to return to the present to write a report on yesterday's visit from John Anderson, turning on her "last cow in a line headin' for the barn" mode. It helped quiet the pain of memories.

Bobbi squeezed Renee's hand as she walked by. "I'm with ya, sweetie. I miss him too."

The phone rang. Bobbie was already down the hall and Renee lifted the receiver. "Tribal Police. *Boozho.*"

"Ah...booz what? Who is this?" a confused baritone on the other end queried.

"Means *hello.* Ojibwa for a greeting. This is Renee LaRoche.

Who's this?"

"Minneapolis Police. Ran into a little more information on that truck theft and wanted to pass on what we found. Mike Swenson here."

"Go ahead, Mike. 'Preciate it."

"OK. Was over there last night answerin' a nuisance call."

"Nuisance?"

"Noise. One neighbor was complainin' about a racket on the block. Anyway, got to talkin' with some of Anderson's neighbors so I asked a few questions 'bout the truck. Thought they mighta seen somethin'. Two of 'em said they hadn't seen the truck since before Halloween. In fact, one thought he had sold it."

"You don't think maybe they just didn't notice?" Renee felt her excitement growing but reigned it in. Remember the red spider, girl, she said to herself.

"I wondered, but they all have their own parking spots behind the townhouses. Anderson paid for an extra one for the truck. Neighbors said his car's been there, but no truck."

"*Megwe*—thanks, Mike. Thanks again. We'll be in touch." Renee hung up, tapping the desk with her pencil and contemplating what she'd just heard.

Officer Johnson came in the door. "*Boozho*, Renny. I've got to go over and check Jed's office and house. Interested?"

"Let me try and get Jenny." She dialed the school and asked for her daughter. "Hm, that's funny, she's not there. Oh, wait a second. Let's see, it's Wednesday. What the heck's her schedule on Wednesday? Wait—she helps out at Children of the Circle for God's sake. The mind goes first, I guess!" The two women bent over laughing. Renee's high school yearbook had described her well: "Her Auntie Lydia says she'd forget her head if it wasn't attached." And she never failed to live up to it.

She dialed again.

"Children of Red Earth."

"*Boozho.* Lookin' for Jenny LaRoche. She's there today, eh?"

"Hold on," the teen who answered said. "Yo, J.J., stop dissin' him and take this call."

There was a loud noise and then a breathless, "*Boozho.*"

"J., it's Mom. Sounds like a stampede over there. What're you guys doin'?"

"It's cool, Ma. Wass' up?"

"What time're you done? I have some things to do this afternoon. Could be a while. I'm at the police station and wondered when I should be home?"

"Now, Ma. NOW! You're gonna get hurt...or killed. I told Sam—oh, forget it."

"You told Sam what?"

"Forget it, Ma. We're just worryin' about you. I'll be home 'bout 6:00 or 6:30."

"I'll be there too, J., and don't worry. I'm a big girl. I gotta do this. You know—"

"I know, Ma. I still worry. Gotta go. Bye."

"Bye J., I love you!"

"Back at ya, Ma."

Renee hung up and turned to Jesse. "Teenagers! What was Creator thinking!" After relaying Mike's call to the chief, the women left. Jesse walked the short distance to the tribal chairman's office, set a little south of the tribal council offices, while Renee ran back to her jeep with Mukwa.

"Sorry, Mukie. You can get out and run when we get to Jed's." Mukwa slouched in the driver's seat, chin on the window Renee left open, ears hanging down. She looked after her own personal two-legged with eyes that said, *How can you leave me here all alone?* "Oh Mukie, puhleese. You are so dramatic. Guess this is where the saying about 'having a hang dog look' comes from," Renee called over her shoulder as she crossed the street. The *ahnimoosh* maintained the vigil until her *niji* was out of sight and the last hope of changing her mind went with her.

Oh well, I tried, she thought. Turning round and round, Mukwa made her nest in the seat and fell asleep.

Jed's secretary offered a slight nod in response to Renee's greeting. "She's in there. Told me you'd be coming," she mumbled, turning back to her work.

"*Megwetch,* Sharon. 'Preciate it." Their usual banter, it seemed, wasn't in the cards today.

"Jess?"

"In here, Renny."

Officer Johnson was sitting in one of the overstuffed chairs against the wall, drapes pulled and lights off. Renee slid onto the new leather couch next to her. Silence fell dramatically.

"Ever been here before," Renee whispered.

"Once, right after I was hired."

"This is his second redecoration since takin' over in '84. Fancy, eh, all this leather? That artwork on the walls and those soapstone sculptures aren't cheap either. There's a Martinez bowl over there that musta cost five or six hundred bucks. She's that elder potter from Santa Clara Pueblo, the one who started the rage for black pottery in the late '70s. Fired pots in the backyard in a homemade kiln using cow pies covered over top with old license plates. She discovered that if you take the pots out at a certain point in the firing they turned black. Some oxidizing thing. Family and pueblo members are carrying on now."

The two sat quietly. Jesse had come to respect Renee like an older sister. She knew Ren's life had been much different than hers, much harder. Jesse told her mom that her respect had to do with the way Renee had turned her life around, the strength of her spirituality and how seriously she took her role as a tribal dreamer.

Ren's commitment to the people of Red Earth impressed Jesse, and challenged her. Jesse didn't quite understand the two-spirit side of her new friend. While she'd known a few lesbians at Arizona State, she didn't know there were any Indian ones. A common myth, Renee had told her, but the admission still embarrassed Jesse. When she talked to her mother or her grandmother about their beliefs, Jesse got very different responses. Granny acted like it was just another way of living, while her mom recited bible verses against it. Looking at Renee now, Jesse had to admit she didn't seem any different than anyone else, which made her tend to side with her granny's point of view. Renee's voice broke through Jesse's reflections.

"Look at this place. Looks like the goddamn president of Honeywell's bring-and-brag office. You know, the kind that scarf up our art, thinking they can buy into some kind of spiritual life without committing themselves to it? Spirituality by osmosis, eh?"

"Maybe that's why it feels so strange in here. You walk inside and it's like another world from out there." Jesse looked very sad.

"Partly the energy, I think. Close your eyes for a second, Jess, feel how unsettled it is. Everything's in turmoil. Some of that could be because he was murdered and his spirit's confused, but that's not all of it. Somethin's been goin' on in here, Jess. I can feel it."

A shadeless floor lamp tilted precariously in the corner, curiously out of place and leaning, as if seeking light itself, toward the window. Flipping the wall switch, Renee walked to the shelves on the south wall. Books on Ojibwa culture and treaties, tribal law, and a few odds and ends titles took up the top two shelves. The bottom four held the pottery and sculpture Renee had commented on earlier, plus Ojibwa and Zuni baskets, Hopi Kachinas, and an Ojibwa pipe. "These were just things to you, weren't they Jed...the pipe, everything. They didn't mean a damn thing to you. Just trinkets." Anger caught in her throat.

Jesse interrupted Renee's perusal, holding out a checkbook. "Every month a five-hundred-dollar deposit—like clockwork. Five hundred in cash still here, with a note that says, 'Per our phone call.'" Renee and Jesse looked at each other.

"I'll ask Sharon."

Ren took the note and checkbook out to the front desk. "Ever see this?" she handed the checkbook to the secretary. "Jesse found it in Jed's locked drawer."

"I've seen it," Sharon replied coolly.

"Can you tell me anything about it?"

"Not much. Jed told me it was his special account. Like a savings account, 'cept it was easier to get to," Sharon answered, not looking up.

"Know anything about the deposits? Or this money and note. Who it's from, maybe?"

"I made the deposits," she shrugged.

"These monthly ones of five hundred dollars?"

"Uh-huh. Said he got the money gambling. Always gave it to me after a trip. I don't ask questions. I mean, I didn't."

"No, 'course not. I understand. How 'bout this five hundred dollars?"

"He musta just got it in the last couple of days or he'd of given it to me."

"*Megwetch*, Sharon." Noting a slight warming, Renee gently touched the other woman's shoulder. "This must be hard, eh?"

The secretary's pause was pregnant. Swinging her gaze up, she said, "It's not easy, Renee. Not easy. I'm pretty much in shock. You know, I don't know if I have a job or what's going on. Jed was always good to me. Gave me extra time off for Jeffy's surgery, even an extra Christmas bonus last year to help with the bills. He was always good to me," her voice trailed off.

Renee nodded, giving her former classmate a quick hug. She returned to the inner office.

"Sharon thinks it's gamblin' money," Renee said quietly. "Too consistent for luck though, doncha think? Somethin' else was goin' on. Same time of month, same amount every month. Seems more like a sure bet than a gamble."

Jesse nodded, handing Ren a piece of paper.

"Invoice?"

"Looks like it to me. I leaned across the desk and the blotter slid. That was under it."

"He was hiding it?" Ren looked more closely at what she held, a generic, carbonless invoice with no company logo. The only word in the section for name and address was "Jed." In the description column Renee read: "Per phone call 10/28. Two (2) caribeeners, petons, ropes, belays, harnesses." The signature was unreadable. "Whadya make of this?"

"Do you recognize those things?"

"You know, it's rock climbing equipment, isn't it? Jenny and I had a huge fight over her wantin' money for stuff like that."

Jesse nodded. "Trying to get to the caves?" She smiled at Renee, shrugging her shoulders. "Think we're onto something?"

"Maybe. Damn. One more piece of the puzzle, anyway. Or one more piece of one of the puzzles!"

An examination of the rest of the office turned up nothing, so Jesse asked Sharon for the last six months' phone bills and, with the invoice, checkbook, and note, the women left to begin the second leg of their investigation. "I'll drop this stuff off and meet you at Jed's place, Renny." Jesse turned and hurried back up the road to the station.

Renee pulled off at the river flats on the way to Jed's. She looked around, standing where Jed breathed his last. The quiet, interrupted a day ago by the crack of gunfire, today had the place to itself. *Guess it was your name Brother Owl was calling, eh Jed? Your death the one in my dream. Did you hear the call? Know your time was up? Was Esther right?* Thoughts drifted through her head. *Were you invaded by a* Windigo *that never left, something evil and devious you couldn't shake? Suppose we'll never know now.* The old bridge's darkened wood, home after all these years to carved messages of love and anger, scrapes and dents from off-course traffic, stood out from the surrounding scenery. "Probably one of the last things he saw," she heard herself say out loud. Looking out at the river, Renee mused, "If I could understand your song, what would it be today? After all you've seen."

Settled back in the jeep, Renee and Mukwa turned across the bridge, following the gravel road along the river's edge to the turnoff to Jed's place. The state highway department, previously unwilling to smooth-scrape Red Earth's roads, changed its policy in the '70s when reservation activists exposed the state's neglect. Now most roads, like Old Bridge, were in pretty decent shape.

Three miles up river, the Morriseau land was a beautiful spot, deep in a heavily forested part of the reservation. The drive in from the road was far from beautiful, though. Jed's driveway was rutted, overgrown, unattended, and obviously easily flooded, judging from all the mud. To the left, Mosquito Creek wound its way to the river from its origin somewhere far north of the reservation. True to its name, the creek spawned millions of the pesky insects. Bumping along next to the creek Renee pictured Ba pee wug O day Ikkwe, the old medicine woman who'd sit in a swarm of mosquitoes and never get a bite. "Make yourself one with the mosquitoes," she advised. "They never bite their own."

"Now that's a spiritual power I wouldn't mind havin'!" Renee chuckled.

Renee and Mukwa pulled up next to Jed's Lincoln Town car and Ford Ranger. "Musta left here with someone else, his murderer no doubt," Ren said, stepping out of the jeep and noticing the same strangeness she'd felt in Morriseau's office.

Mukwa felt it too and crowded Renee's leg. *These smells could drive a bear's nose crazy.* The *ahnimoosh* sniffed the air.

The Morriseau house was typical of reservation dwellings built three generations before. Rain and snow had scoured off any paint once protecting the plywood and clapboard walls, leaving an eerie look of bone in the woods' lonely stand against the elements. Tangled, barren vines covered the west side. The old peony bush was spare and flowerless in the new chilly air, but Renee remembered its beautiful pink blooms from past visits.

Making her way around the land with Renee, Mukwa stopped at the old shed, scratching and whining at the door.

"Somethin' in there girl?" Ren tried the door. Locked.

The smells, niji. *In here.* Mukwa jumped excitedly on the wider than average door. The one window was covered from the inside and locked up tight. Running back around the front, the cocker was getting more and more insistent. Respecting her friend's nose, Renee took the tire iron from the back of her jeep and inserted it between the door and jamb, just below the knob. The lock popped. As the door sprung open, Mukwa ran inside, nose to the ground. She recognized the smell in the shed. The smell of death.

"What is it girl? Hold up a second." Renee squatted, wrapping an arm around the *ahnimoosh*. "Wish I knew what you're so excited about *niji*." Renee stared into the darkened recesses of the shed, her sense of dread growing.

Along the creek's edge, downwind, the speckled alder and red dogwood parted slightly. A cowboy boot stepped into the remains of a family of thistle and vervain. One of the season's last pine beauty moths escaped off its spot as a hand spread the brush where it had rested.

The overcast sky and the coming night threw a blanket over the inside of the shed. Renee turned back to the jeep. She took a deep breath and closed her eyes, trying to calm her rising anxiety. After pulling the jeep up facing into the shed she hit the lights. It was moments before her eyes adjusted, but what she saw then was as confusing as the darkness itself.

The walls were lined with shelves holding more than a dozen large bundles. A three-legged table—the fourth a tree stump—sat in the middle of the floor stacked with a cradleboard, pots, baskets, several pictures, and a wrapped bundle. The bundle wrap was a pale-green heavy cotton. Opening it, Renee noticed *RE IHS HOSPITAL OR* stamped in the corner. Under the last fold, resting in its original deerskin bag, was the tribe's ceremonial pipe. Next to it lay the eagle bone whistle, the rattle made from a badger bladder, cattail seeds, and willow stem—the last of its kind, Renee had been taught—and the carved willow flute. Everything stolen from the school in town seemed to be on the table.

"Oh God, Mukwa look at all this!" Renee felt light-headed and more than a little sick to her stomach. "Goddamn it, Jed. Soon as I saw your name at the library, I wondered, you low livin'..."

Ren circled the table, staring. She had never before handled the band's ceremonial pipe. Its first official ceremony with the new Europeans was in 1825, but it was used for generations before that for tribal and intertribal ceremonies. Brought out again in 1837 and 1854, it sealed treaties that outlined the band's fishing, hunting, and wild rice gathering rights. The pipe was smoked by all Anishanabe bands in 1867 when they were forced to merge onto one reservation, and at every tribal ceremony until the 1930s, when it was put away. The bowl, made from pipestone, was carved in the shape of a turtle, its crudeness dating the pipe to the early 1700s when there were few tools for carving fine lines or intricate details. Male and female eagle feathers hung from the sumac stem, their contrasting light and dark bodies striking in the jeep's headlights.

As she moved toward the shelves Renee noticed the sameness of the packages. Gingerly lifting one off the shelf, she cleared a space on the table. "Weird wrap," she paused, clearing her throat. The outer cover was a heavy plastic with tape fasteners attached. Opening the plastic she found the same green cotton with the hospital stamp. Next was a white cotton wrap closed with a piece of striped tape. A light went on in Renee's head. *That's where the tape at the robbery came from.* She hesitated. *It's how they tell when equipment's sterilized in the operating room.* She shook her head at the brilliance in hindsight, remembering the tape now from her days as a nursing assistant in high school. Opening the last wrap, Renee reeled back. "Whew! Mukwa. What's that smell? I've smelled—" Her pause was only momentary before, "Holy shit, the morgue. That's it—it's formaldehyde!"

After her eyes stopped watering from the fumes, Renee saw the contents of the package: bones. Long bones. Several of them were laid side by side in formaldehyde-soaked cloths, along with a human skull. She sank to the shed's floor, bursting into tears. Mukwa, off searching the far corner, came and stared into her eyes, resting her head on Renee's shoulder. They were still like that minutes later.

"Renny?" Both looked up and saw Jesse standing at their side. "Oh Jeez, Jess, I didn't hear you come up."

"I know, I called but you didn't even look up. You OK?"

"No, not really," she said weakly, taking Jesse's outstretched hand.

"What is all this?" Jesse was looking a little stunned herself.

"God, I'm so glad you're here. Look at this. The pipe, the rest of our stuff from the school, and those..." Renee moved her lips toward the bones, unable to speak the word.

"Renee? What the heck—bones?" Shaking off the momentary

shock, Jess said, "Hold on, I'm going to call the chief."

Renee felt frozen in time. The realization washed over her that they probably were the bones of her ancestors from the caves. A possibility so horrible she wanted to throw up, and the more it pushed through her consciousness, the faster tears streamed down her dirt-streaked face.

She repackaged the bones carefully, wishing she knew for sure what to do. Shaky hands refolded the wraps, then rested lightly on the package as she offered a prayer.

Jesse returned and sat next to her two friends. "Hobey's on his way, Renny," she said in a hushed tone, putting an arm around Renee. "He's bringing Esther and your gram with him."

"It was like a cold fist closed around my heart," Renee began. "Finding all of this—how could this happen, Jess? How could one of us do this? If these are bones from the Old Ones, how'll we recover?" The two women sat in the doorway of the shed in the fading light, crying for their people, for the Old Ones, and for the miserable mess made by their tribal chairman.

In the near darkness, only the wood ants and mosquitoes saw the figure downwind step back into the creek, hurriedly wade through the freezing water to the other side, and, with trained silence, disappear into the night.

9

The squad car pulled in behind Jesse's Bronco. Had the women sitting in the shed been looking, they would have seen the elders approach up the long, rutted drive, but Renee and Jesse had drawn their worlds in to the edges of the shed. Hobey left the lights on and stepped out of the car. "Jess, Renee?" His call into the shadowy darkness was tentative and, after saying something to the elders, he started slowly toward the shed, hand resting on the service revolver he'd just finished cleaning before the call.

Renee and Jesse stood at the sound of his voice. "Over here, Chief. We're over here," Ren waved.

"Everything OK?"

"Well...no, but we're alone, if that's what you mean," Jesse replied.

The chief lifted his hand off the gun, resnapping its safety strap.

Renee walked to the passenger side of Hobey's car, opening the doors for Gram and Esther. Several minutes passed. "You know, my girl," the ninety-two-year-old began, "I am part of the last generation of the old way and the first generation of the new. I've believed it was our role to adjust to the modern things while still passing on traditions. When I see something like this, something coming from the greed of this new world, I weep for the old days, the old ways. Once we spoke the language of the animals, now we speak word winds of deceit. It pains me to think that one of our own was so taken in by what he thought money could get he would sell the spirits of his ancestors. And now he's dead. I wonder about the job we've done preparing generations after us to adjust to the changes of our people."

Everyone stood, eyes downcast, listening. "Many of us from generations after you had ears closed to your voices for a long time," the chief offered. "I was given a second chance and took it. Not everyone did."

They stood in silent reflection until Renee finally said, "I was thinkin' of checkin' in the house a little. Don't think I can be around here anymore."

"Go ahead, Renny. We'll let you know if we need you." Hobey stepped aside. Gram nodded, kissing Renee's cheek.

The younger woman made her way up the path, rubbing her hands over shivering arms. She couldn't remember the chill being so deep this early. Mukwa, matted and dirty, trotted along behind.

Jed lived in the house he'd grown up in, a makeshift structure with two rooms inside and a double-hole outhouse fifty yards down slope. Simple—not alternative-lifestyle simple—poverty simple. Renee passed the old water pump, or what was left of it after years of use, misuse, and no use. The forest east of the clearing was almost impenetrable, choked with white spruce, birch, the pine family, and willow thickets. It was a beautiful stand despite the fact that one hundred years ago, railroad and lumber barons had infested the area, buying up the land they couldn't steal for as little as fifty cents an acre and then clear cutting it. Second-growth timber was not the same regardless of what anybody from the outside said. According to Lydia, though, no matter how small or changed each Red Earther's plot of Mother Earth was on the surface, they were still all four thousand miles deep. And, she would add, "We are grateful for every inch."

In later years Jed added plumbing and electricity to the Morriseau site, and replaced the tar paper and cedar bark roof with shingles. There was ongoing speculation on why, with all his money, he never did more work on the house. The elders said it was just a stopping-off spot for Jed, not a home, and he treated it that way.

Stepping onto the back porch, Renee felt the cold seeping through her jeans, assaulting her thighs and calves. It was different being outside and not exercising. The cold steel cramped her hand as she turned the ancient door knob. The unlocked door squeaked open on dry hinges, and Renee entered. Flipping the switch just inside, she was startled by the brightness of the bare ceiling bulb. "Keeps his shed locked up tight and his house is wide open," she scoffed. Renee was sure that now any worry about stealing Jed's possessions came from non-Indians or unbelievers, the only ones who would rob the dead. Ojibwa knew that stealing from those who'd crossed over meant being haunted and hunted by their spirit. Fear took away any interest in what the dead might have.

Standing inside the Morriseau house for the first time since Betty moved away, Renee felt her pulse quicken as the memory of what had gone on here flooded over her. She remembered the story Gram told her and her friends about Nanabozho marrying a daughter. Worrying about what people were saying, he went from village to village asking, "What's the news?" Each time people answered in disgust, "Nanabozho marries his daughter." Finally he climbed to the highest tree, hoping to have the gossip blown away by the wind. But even at the top of the trees he heard the news of his disgrace. "Europeans. Taught us to ignore Nanabozho's disgrace, and to believe that Two-Spirits are sinners. Now *there's* a moral code I'd be proud to hold." Renee shook her head.

On the west wall of Jed's living room hung a beautiful Navajo weaving Ren thought was a Two Gray Hills design. Below the weaving sat an old wooden rocker. She easily imagined Grandpa Morriseau in the chair. Back and forth, back and forth he'd rock, day in and day out, observing everything, saying little, the rocker creaking under his weight. You could always tell when he was listening extra hard because the creaking stopped. He went to the spirit world in silence. Whatever had been in his thoughts all those years went with him. "Wonder what he'd have to say about his grandson now, the bottom feeder of the Red Earth food chain," Renee sneered.

A determined rebellion was starting in her stomach, but she resisted it and continued her perusal of the house, wanting to finish before giving in to her growing hunger. The walls held remnants of the days when light came from kerosene lamps. On one wall the whole lamp was still in place; on another only the base remained. "The old ways and the modern," she reflected, thinking back to what Gram had said out by the shed.

The wind was picking up outside, sounds of night shrieking in the growing darkness. A 1950s green couch stood sentinel along the south wall. It blocked the front door from intruders but not from the wind that whistled and whined around the frame. Moving to the worn table in the kitchen alcove, Renee sat on one of the plastic-covered chairs. *This baby-poop green sure was popular in the '50s.* Ren smiled, running a hand across the green Formica tabletop that matched the chairs. An ashtray with a filtered cigarette butt sat next to an empty coffee cup on the table. She knew that Jed didn't smoke. "May belong to the murderer," she mumbled, her pulse quickening as she sat staring at it. "Camel filter, smoked 'bout half way down. Smoked here from the looks of the ashes in the tray." There was no match in the ashtray and, she noted, no lipstick on the cigarette. Retrieving the butt, she placed it in one of the plastic bags Jesse had given her, and included a note on where it had been. A mug, almost empty, sat next to the ashtray. *Looks like one of 'em was doing most of the talkin' here. Musta been a* chimook. Again she labeled the evidence, listing details as she deposited them into separate bags.

Ren opened Jed's under-sink cabinet with a pencil. "I'd never hear the end of it if Josh found my prints here, eh, Mukie?" A dozen cleaning supplies stood in a neat row, the nozzles all pointing forward. His plastic-lined trash can contained just an envelope and letter. Taking the letter out at its corners, she noticed the week-old date and the fact that there was no postmark on the envelope. "How the fuck did this get here?" she muttered. "Hand delivered?"

Renee was shocked to find that the letter was from Jed's sister Betty. She started by telling him she'd gotten counseling. "You'll never know how much you've messed up my life, Jeddy. I think the worst time was that night at the river with your so-called friends." Renee was amazed that Betty could still call him Jeddy after everything he'd done to her. Closing the letter Betty said, "I hope you will admit what you did to me, how much pain and suffering you've caused me. I don't know if I can ever forgive you, and maybe soon you'll understand just how deep my pain is." Renee set the letter down on the table and leaned back in her chair. "Where in hell did this come from?" Renee looked around the room as if somewhere, out there, she'd see the answer.

There was little else of interest. Rewinding Jed's message tape, Renee shook her head sadly. "All the sound left now of our esteemed tribal chairman is the message on this stupid tape machine." The tape had one hang-up on it, no messages, and she figured the hang-up must have come from off the reservation. Anyone on the rez would have heard by moccasin telegraph within a short time after it happened that there'd be no use calling Jed anymore. His bedroom added little to what Renee already knew. The bed was made—either from neatness or because he hadn't slept in it the night before his death. With the clock alarm set for 5:30 A.M., Renee would have put money on the former. Neatly stacked on Jed's nightstand were the three books on tribal artifacts. "You stupid jerk, Jed." Renee picked up one of the books and threw it on the bed. "A lot of goddamn good these did ya, eh?"

Renee gathered up the evidence and aroused Mukwa, dozing by the door. She could feel generations in the loosely rattling shank of the white porcelain knob as she turned it. Renee was about to flip off the light when she noticed the doorstop: streaks from a recent washing darkened the floor, and bits of red clay stuck to the stop itself. "Mukie, look at this, will ya. Clay, red clay. Well, well, well. Did the Great Spirit bring rain that night just to help us out, girl?" Closing the door behind them, they returned to the group outside.

"It's almost 7:00," Hobey was saying. "What say we finish up for the night. Everything's loaded into the Bronco, we'll take it in. Josh'll be out to dust for prints."

"Seven? Goddamn...oops. Sorry, Gram. I told Jenny and Sammy I'd be home by now. Gotta run." Renee handed the evidence she'd collected to Hobey. "They all have notes in 'em. I'll call later. Especially wanna talk about the letter from Betty." She waved an evidence bag. Ren kissed Gram and piled into the jeep with Mukwa, the thought of going home brightening her exhausted mood.

Mosquito Creek and Journey River's confluence sharply curved Old Bridge Road a mile down from Jed's turn-off. Gusts of snow momentarily obscured Renee's vision at the curve and she nearly missed it, jerking the wheel at the last minute to avoid a very chilly accident. Slowing to a more sensible speed, she settled into a review of the day, beginning with the bones of the Old Ones. Their medicine burned over clean ground, mourners would have gone to the river, calling the names of the dead to the other side so relatives could begin preparations to meet the new soul. The body would be wrapped and set to rest. After a year of mourning the bundle of things left behind would be opened for a giveaway, the saved lock of hair burned, and a feast in the deceased's honor held. *Just like Gramps and Benny.* Renee's brows furrowed at the memory.

Making the last turn, she pulled up next to her cabin. The headlights brightened the clearing just as a doe and her fawn made their way along the back edge onto Ren's running trail. "On your way home *wa wa shkesh she?*" She leaned back to enjoy the moment. "OK, Mukie, here we are." She turned the ignition off and stepped out into the snowy evening. *Sisi gwad* in full chorus, the oak and birch limbs whipped about as northern doorway's wind rose and fell in schizophrenic frenzy. "Restless world tonight, Mukwa, a *Windigo* maybe, out stirring up trouble?" At the door, Renee brushed aside the last of the autumn moths hovering around the outside light Samantha had left on, and went into the cabin.

10

"This wouldn't of happened if we hadn't found the caves." Jenny threw the forks she was drying angrily into the sink.

Renee looked up from the paper. "We don't know if that's where the bones are from. They could be cow bones for all—"

"Oh, right, Ma. Whatever!"

"OK, OK. But we can't be blaming ourselves. We've gotta find out who murdered Jed and what their connection is to the robbery. Gram said we're gonna have to set aside being pissed at Jed, send some positive energy out to the universe. Creator'll tend to his soul." Renee frowned. "Can't say I'm up to that, though. Not yet, anyway."

Jenny hung the towel by the sink and moved to the phone.

"Ran into your old friend Harriet today at the college," Samantha said when the two were settled on the couch. "Up for a conference. Said to say hi to you." Samantha combed her fingers through Renee's hair. "I'm no match for that babe," she pouted.

"Sammy, you're totally different from Harriet. She's the head radical lesbian commando and you, well you..." Renee ran a thumb seductively across Sam's shoulders. "First off, on our second date you didn't come over driving a fully loaded U-Haul. I liked that."

"You're not interested, Renny? Come on, even a little? I don't believe that. The look on Harriet's face said you two used to have a lot of fun." Sam's martyred sigh came out long and slow.

"Not interested. She's got a vegetarian snobbishness now that irritates me. Doesn't even eat fish 'cause she says it's killing another life. Hah! Wonder if she hears her broccoli scream as she whacks its head off?" Renee took a breath. "Life's life, far as I was taught. We're always eating souls. That's what Gram says. Only thing to do is be grateful. And not greedy."

"OK, I believe you. She's not your type. Thank God," Samantha sighed.

As Renee's lips touched Sam's, she offered, "You're my type, sweet woman. I've waited a long time for you."

Renee turned away from the kiss and returned to the *People's Circle,* a weekly newspaper "from a Native American perspective" published in Minneapolis. She flipped the pages to the events section where the weekend pow wow was listed. "What time ya leavin' for the Cities, Sam?"

"Early. I want to get settled at Mollie and Alice's before my first interview at 1:30. You're still coming in Friday, right?"

"You bet. It'll be so good to get away." Turning the pages, Renee let out a hoot. "Holy shit, listen to this, Sammy:

> The Zuni tribe of New Mexico reported the return of six Zuni war-god carvings this week after they were recovered in an FBI sting of identified grave robbers. The carvings were stolen, along with other items and the skeletal remains of Zuni ancestors, three months ago from a remote grave site on the reservation. Tribal leaders were stunned at the theft because they believed these sites were known only to tribal members. Early investigations led to dead ends until the FBI joined in the hunt.
>
> The wooden figures, called Ahayuda, are guardians of the Zuni, protecting the people and their land, bringing rain and prosperity to Zuni and their neighbors. Zuni spiritual leaders are grateful the powerful figures from the Spirit World have been found. The only item not recovered was a kachina mask of the trickster, believed to date back to the 1500s.
>
> Upon their return, the bow priest of the tribe performed a purification rite for the figures, announcing they will be reburied in an all-tribal ceremony

> sometime in the next few weeks. Tribal Chairman Daniel Rides Alone stated, 'We have been in a mourning period since the robbery. Now we will celebrate and give thanks for our great fortune.'
>
> FBI Special Agent James Lawton stated the trio was arrested and charged under the Archeological Resources Protection Act of 1979 enacted specifically for these kinds of crimes. "We are still looking for the kachina mask and would appreciate any help we can get in locating it."
>
> Robbery of Native American graves has increased dramatically in the past five years. According to Navajo archeologist Dr. Laura Begay, buyers of the ancient 'artifacts' are usually wealthy Americans, Germans or Japanese.

"Can you believe that!" Clenching and unclenching her jaw, Renee turned an angry face to her partner. "'Germans or Japanese.' Do you think they know they're buyin' stolen property? This is too much." Picking up the article again, she said, "And our good friend Lawton's in on this, too. I asked him about grave robbers the other day. Goddamn."

"Ma! Renee!" The reproaches from her daughter and her lover were simultaneous.

"OK. OK. Sorry," she whispered sheepishly. "Jeez, you guys are gettin' as bad as Gram. Come on, Jen. I need the phone."

"Two minutes." Jenny held up two fingers.

Renee began to pace. This could be significant. If Lawton was working on the Zuni case, he might really be able to help with what was going on here, maybe with suspects. Lawton didn't know about what they found at Jed's yet. Her mind was racing, trying to put all the broken pieces together. The faster her thoughts raced the faster she paced.

Samantha came up behind her, encircling her waist. "Honey, calm down. Your mind's going to spin right out your ears." Renee leaned back into Sam, closing her eyes.

"Mm, you feel so good. What would I do without you?"

"Can't imagine." Samantha tweaked Renee's nose. "By the way, you were late tonight. For our family time."

"I know. I'm sorry, really. I got involved in all that at Jed's and lost track of time."

"I think I'll put that on your tombstone. *She lost track of time.* Samantha pushed down her disappointment. Now was not a good time to get into anything. Again. Instead she said, "We see any less of you and you'll qualify as a rumor!"

Renee noticed the pain flick across Samantha's soft blue eyes. Embracing her, she sighed, "I love you, *saiagi iwed.* I know this isn't easy for you."

"Ma, Ma! YO—I'm off." J.J.'s voice interrupted their intimate moment.

Renee dialed the station. "Hobey? Glad I caught you. Got a minute?"

"You sound excited."

"Have you seen this week's *Circle?*"

"Not yet."

"Got a copy?"

"Hold on." She heard Hobey set the phone down. Moments later he returned. "Renny? Got it."

"OK, page two. Top. About the grave robbers?"

Minutes passed. Then, "So, Lawton's been a busy boy, eh?"

"I'd say so. I asked him about other stuff like this goin' on around the country, but he jus' locked up those lips of his."

"The Federal Bureau of Irritation."

"You gonna call him?"

"I guess. He doesn't know about our find at Jed's. We need information from him more'n we need to keep the suit from snooping around. I'll call him in the morning. Good job Renny. Bobbi's right, you're worth big bucks."

"Naw. A medium buck and a small buffalo'll be enough." Renee laughed. It felt good to hear Hobey's respect after the day they'd had.

"Comin' by tomorrow?"

"Couldn't keep me away."

"Good girl—oh. Sorry, Ren. Hard to teach an old dog new tricks, eh? By the way, I was wonderin', you found red mud inside Jed's?"

"Just a little. His place was really clean. The guy was a damn fanatic."

"Wonder if Jed, or his friendly murderer, were actually the ones at the school?"

"Don't think it'd be Jed. I heard him bein' interviewed on KAIO that night. You know, he's been talkin' to that Golden Nickel Gaming Company from Minneapolis about opening a casino on the rez. Turning us into Bingo Indians."

"Yeah, OK. I was just wondering, hoping we could clear up one piece of what's goin' on."

Renee usually rubbed her daughter's back before she went to bed. It gave them time to talk.

"I don' know 'bout all this, Ma."

"You worried?"

"No, jus' want things back to normal around here. Want you to be a teacher and a mom. You never have time for me anymore."

"I don't think it'll be much longer. And don't forget, we'll have the weekend." Renee gave her daughter a big hug. She hoped she sounded more confident than she felt.

"I'll believe that when it happens. You'll spend it all with Sam and Mollie and them." Jenny stuck her lip out like she'd been doing for fourteen years.

"You're gonna step on that," Renee teased. She had to smile at how well Jenny had perfected the hangdog look over the years. She figured Mukwa must have learned it from her older sister. "I'll do my best, OK? You'll be with Jody, anyway, so I'll probably never see you. Go to sleep now, honey. I know you're tired."

"Ya, I am. Been havin' some hard practices. Night, Ma." J.J.'s usual crooked smile barely crossed her young chestnut face. Her mother watched her climb up the loft ladder and disappear behind her privacy curtain.

Renee stoked the fire before hauling Mukwa into the shower. "I know grunge is a style, Mukie, but it's not becoming on you." She soaked the *ahnimoosh*. "Besides, Alice and Mollie would not be happy campers if you showed up packin' half of Red Earth."

Samantha turned on the TV to try and catch the news. A Pepto Bismol bottle was two-stepping across the screen. "Don't you look happy," she mumbled. As the news dissolved into another commercial, she collapsed onto the couch.

A damp Renee returned and lay her head in Samantha's lap. "Felt a little frost on your name when the Bean said good night."

"We had an argument before you got home. She came home

late, threw her basketball stuff down, and went up to the loft without even a hello. It went downhill from there because the less she talked the more I pushed, and on and on like that until I finally gave up. No winning power struggles with teenagers. I should know that by now," Samantha moaned.

"Parenting's some trip, eh?"

"Mm, sure is. Do you ever worry about Joe showing up wanting to be involved in his daughter's life?"

"Doubt it. Long as he's underground, runnin' from the law."

"I can't imagine being on the run like that. God, I've led a sheltered life."

"I could've done with a little shelter. Things were intense in the '70s and early '80s in Indian Country, you know. We'd finally begun to feel some pride and our power in numbers." Renee sighed deeply, remembering those years of little sleep, eating on the go, driving back and forth across the country from a sit-in at Alcatraz to a march on BIA headquarters in D.C.

"When was the last time you heard from Joe?" Samantha had a superstition about things like this. If you talked about it, it would happen, so she didn't often bring up the subject of Renee's ex-lover. But sometimes you just had to know.

"Before we moved here. Probably six, seven years ago. At that time he was in Canada, living on one of the reserves. Athabaskan tribe, I think. Sometimes I wish he'd come back and take his chances with the courts. He didn't beat up that FBI agent, but after what's happened to Leonard Peltier, I can see why he stays underground. I'm not interested in the guy, but Jenny might want to get to know him."

"It must be scary to take a chance and come back, risking spending the rest of your life in prison." Sam's last comment brought a long silence.

Finally Renee said, "How're you doin' as a parent?" She kissed Samantha, brushing a wisp of hair from her eyes.

Sam set her book down. "Just when I think we're making progress I press one of Jenny's buttons." A note of discouragement edged Samantha's voice. "I never thought much about kids till I met you. Besides, my mother told me I could either be a lesbian or a mother, not both." The two women giggled. "Guess the four million gay and lesbian parents raising their ten million kids haven't heard from Mom yet!" They folded themselves in each other's arms and laughed quietly.

Renee got up to let Mukwa out and returned, lying back in Sam's lap, brushing her fingers across her lover's face. "How're ya doing adjusting to my current passion?" She dropped her words gingerly into the silence. Ren desperately wanted Sam to accept, if not understand, it. But, after their fight the other day, she'd been afraid to bring it up.

Samantha stared for a long time into Renee's eyes. "Have you heard, 'Night is when the shadow of death is darkest'? Dickens wrote it. Fits me, because I know I don't feel so hysterical about this stuff in the light of day. It's not just your involvement in the murder and robbery, it's everything. Things are different here. A lot of time I feel like a fish out of water. After I spoke with Mollie today she put Alice on. It helped to talk with another white woman involved with a Native American. And since she's been at it longer, she's better at it. We're going to form a support group."

"We're not from Mars, you know."

"No, I know, Renny, but it *is* different. It's just different. Anyway, save your question for now, OK?" The crackle and hiss of the fire embraced the quiet as exotic shadow images danced and leapt across the wall. A nighthawk let loose its *wee* from somewhere in the darkness. Samantha lay her head on the back of the couch.

Half an hour later she started awake. "Let's go to bed. I'll give you a nice long back rub, Tonto," Sam murmured in Renee's ear. Ren stirred, warmed by her lover's attempt at lightness. Turning off the lights, the women were hit full force by the shimmering northern sky. The three of them—two- and four-leggeds—headed for the door. Mukwa leapt in the air, making a half ballet turn at the top. Outside, brilliant northern lights in white, green, and pink on a black canvas streaked across the night sky. "Creator's modern art," Samantha marveled, squeezing Renee. They stood for a long time arm in arm on the cabin porch before they went back inside.

They didn't stir the next morning until Jenny came out of the shower, dozing off again until she was getting ready to head out the door. "Ma, I heard you upstairs last night talkin' in your sleep." She sat on the bed rubbing Mukwa's ears.

"I kinda knew I was restless but I don't remember my dream," Renee said, sitting up. "How 'bout you, sleep OK?"

"Good enough. Gotta go now, though."

"Hope you have the day of your dreams today, my girl."

"That all my teachers'll die and school'll close? I don't think so, Ma. So, better get to it. Don't wanna miss my bus. See you tonight, eh?"

"Get all your homework today, J.J. We leave tomorrow. And gimme some of that brown sugar before you go." Jenny leaned over and kissed Renee, then as an afterthought bent down and gave Samantha a peck on the cheek. "See ya in a couple days, Sam. Have a good trip, eh?" she mumbled on her way out the door.

"Great to have a kid old enough to start a fire for us," Renee said after Jenny left. "It's nice and cozy in here." She lay back, resting her chin on the heel of her hand and smiling her I-know-you-luv-me-'cause-I'm-soo-cute smile. Eyelids lazily shading dark eyes, she pulled Sam's face close. "I love it when you purse your lips like that." She rubbed her finger along Sam's jaw.

"How about giving these pursed lips something to do?" Samantha's smile was easy and inviting. These were the moments that kept her going.

"Do you have all your stuff ready? Did you take your articles?" Renee asked, following through on the kiss invitation.

"I do. Just hope they like them."

"You're an incredible writer, Sammy. Jeez, you make a living at it. Thank God I don't have to. I couldn't write home for a bus ticket!"

"Lots of writers out there, Renny. Billions, trillions of words written. Do you know the history of the world is stored under a park in New York City? Bryant, I think. There's everything under there, from George Washington's beer recipe to Melville's old trunk. And probably most of New York doesn't even know."

"Mother Earth's bookshelves, eh? I like that."

"Me, too." Samantha smiled at the image.

"Mm, but back to the moment, my pet. It's good that we're both morning persons, eh?" Renee whispered, rolling on top of Samantha.

"Whoa, hold on there, Sharon Stone. I've got to get going. My first appointment's at 1:30." She wriggled free before Renee could sneak another kiss and headed for the shower.

"Okee dookee, Mukwa, let's get goin' too, eh? We can take a rebuff gracefully. We're runnin' behind now, too, 'cause your auntie wouldn't let me out of bed." She raised her voice.

"I can't hear you!" Sam yelled from the shower.

Renee used her grandfather's tobacco, grown behind the Coon family cemetery, for morning prayers. Harvesting the plants each fall, drying them on wooden stands, Gramps recited the same prayers Anishanabe had been saying since the beginning of time. Once dried, each leaf's nicotine veins were stripped, the leaves crushed, packaged, and given to family and friends at ceremony. After she finished her prayers, Renee distributed the pile of raked leaves out over the pine needle layer already on the garden. Gramps had taught her soil acid replacement had to be done to have good crops the next year. She hauled the sack of Indian corn leaning against the woodpile to the back porch. Mid-winter they'd shell the corn, soak it in warm water, and set the sack by the wood-burning stove until the corn sprouted. Come spring, the sprouts would go back in the ground and the circle would continue.

The *nijis* headed into Rice Lake, coming around the back way. Renee remembered taking this road as a kid, everyone bouncing around in the back of the truck like popcorn. The old part of Rice Lake crouched together at the west end of town as though defending itself against the rest of the world. The 1950s BIA-built brick houses came first—cold and forbidding, family after family of Anishanabe still crammed into the four-room rectangles. Following them was the double line of tar-paper shacks standing like rows of decaying teeth. Once home to single lumberjacks who'd migrated to the area to make a quick buck, or any buck, depending on the state of the economy, they now housed solitary drunks. Gathering outside around a communal fire and communal bottle by night, they slept it off in their own private eight-by-eight caskets by day. The prefabricated section of town came next, hauled in from some far-off birthing place on giant railroad flatbeds right into the middle of town. Several pre-fabs stood empty, the darkened windows peering out at the street as though looking for their people. Renee imagined the factory workers who'd built the prefabs, home at night, shirts saturated with their work, bandaging torn and cut hands from the sharpness of the day's labor. She turned up the alley just before Hole In The Day Avenue. The telephone pole next to the turn advertised a garage sale at Josie Barrett's, a prayer meeting at Holy Rosary every Wednesday evening, the AA/Al-Anon tandem at the Cultural Center on Saturday morn-ing, and a flyer offering a reward from the Anishanabe Traditionals and Holy Rosary for information leading to the arrest of the person or persons who stole the tribe's "sacred, historical items." Billy Walking Bear and Janice were supposed to be living in the apartment above the drugstore on the corner. Neither his old white Ford or the new Pontiac Grand Am she'd seen him in were in the space between the end of the building and the dumpster. "Oh well, was worth a try," she grumbled.

Hobey and Jesse were already sipping coffee when Renee walked in. Hobey's small gray desk, a stark contrast to Jed's seven-foot mahogany one, looked like the desk he'd had in junior high school. The chief sat, fingertips pressed together, lips pursed. Finally he spoke. "How 'bout we try and make some order out of this, after that we'll call Lawton, fill him in and find out what he knows. The sheriff and Elko fuzz've been keepin' a low profile. I don't know what's up with them. Think they'd just as soon stay out of it. We're gettin' some help now from Detective Swenson in Minneapolis. Renny?" The chief looked over to his friend.

Renee nodded. "OK, let's start with Jed and see if the rest will fall in place, since that's where we found everything and I doubt they were storing it there without his knowledge. I'd say he's been involved from the jump. He took those books out of the library two weeks ago." Ren was watching the chief carefully. "You OK, Chief?"

"Little frustrated. Just got off the phone with Peterson before you came." Hobey said the name as if the speaking of it left a bad taste in his mouth. "He's been draggin' his feet on the autopsy report. Gave me a headache. But he finally faxed it over. BCA called too. They're all backed up and can't send anyone. Wish they'd get some more help down there. So we're on our own on this one. Thank God you guys are here. I'd be hidin' in the woods if you weren't." Jesse and Renee smiled at each other.

Peterson's autopsy report was formal and cold. Renee began reading. "Let's see. Jed's name. Weight: 210 lbs., height: 5'10". Then it says: 'The victim's body is clothed in blue shirt, Wrangler blue jeans, boxer underwear, tee shirt, cowboy boots, and socks. Body temperature is cold and rigor mortis is present throughout. External examination of the body reveals one entrance gunshot wound between the scapulas, to the left of thoracic vertebra #4, splitting the rhomboideus major muscle. The victim died instantly. Negative otherwise.' Then he describes the damage done to the left lower lobe of the lung, says the bullet nicked the aorta and liver, and exited the body just above the waist on the right. Quote: 'The deadly path of the bullet extended downward in a left to right direction causing massive hemorrhage into the left thoracic and abdominal cavities. Death was caused by this single gunshot wound entering the victim from the posterior and was instantaneous.' That's it." Renee looked up.

"Pretty straightforward, eh? Let's move on." Hobey walked to the blackboard he'd set up and divided into two columns: THEFT and MURDER. "Renny?"

"OK, I know it feels like we're lookin' down a big, dark hole with a tiny little flashlight, but all we need," she began, sinking back into the chair, "is someone to connect everybody together."

"And everything."

"Everything, assuming they are connected," Renee agreed. "Come on, guys. City dicks would have this sewn up by now. What's stoppin' us?" For the next two hours she outlined everything they knew, with the chief and Jesse adding as they went along. Renee finished with, "And, of course, we have the letter from Betty without a postmark. It's frustrating tryin' to get ahold of Betty with her havin' no phone. The only thing I could do is leave a message with her friend and at the tribal office. I'm sure she didn't come here and deliver the letter. I suppose it's possible that Jed was out there, but that doesn't sound right. I think we'd have heard about it. So, my guess is someone else from the rez was there, saw Betty, and brought it back."

Hobey released a deep sigh. "Sounds reasonable."

"It's like," Renee started again, "we're looking right at the solution but it's the trickster, shapeshifter, and it keeps changing just enough to distort the message. Throw us off."

At 12:15 Bobbi came in to take orders for lunch. Waiting for her return, elbows on knees, Hobey, Jesse, and Renee crowded together like the town gossips. Renee reviewed: "On the theft, seems we agree the group musta had connections for selling everything. Finding the stuff last night from the caves, I think the article in the *People's Circle* might be important, plus what I heard on the radio. I double-checked the Browns Valley robbery, and they never caught anybody. Don't even have any good suspects anymore. The international conspiracy smell's sure gettin' stronger. I think this could be part of something like that." She paused.

"I called Dr. Laura Begay last night," Jesse began. "She lectured in a couple of classes I had at Arizona State. Navajo archeologist. She told me illegal looting of Indian sites has been on the rise the last five years because organizers of so-called artifact shows are getting bolder about what they sell and there's not much investigating going on. There's an organization called Native American Artifacts that has a show every year somewhere in the midwest. One of the biggest. Plus, there's dozens of private negotiations and sales between grave robbers and buyers from all over the world. She said that collectors in Germany and Japan are the most aggressive buyers right now. They occasionally negotiate directly with looters but mostly buy through a middle person. No questions asked."

"That's just what the article said," Renee added, "and that's where the Feds can help with their national and international connections. But it all starts same as here, probably. Some locals involved like Jed and whoever robbed the school. How about the car wreck guy, Peter Thompson? Looks likely he was at Jed's before the murder. Camel filter cigarettes in his pocket, one at Jed's, another one found at the murder site." Renee nodded to Jesse.

"Should hear from the BCA soon with a preliminary DNA blueprint on the cigarette butts," Jesse continued. "Their equipment is so sophisticated they can tell if he's what's called a salivator, and if he is, his ABO marking can be retrieved from both butts. These tests are designed to get more information from less and less. Once, fractions of an ounce were used; now, a millionth-millionth part of a gram is all they need. It's like looking at the moon with your naked eye and being able to see a mouse. Amazing stuff. And the gun, if we get lucky and find even one of Thompson's prints on it, that'll clinch it. The autopsy said he hadn't fired a gun recently, but the paraffin test on his hands is inconclusive after twelve hours. Thanks to Peterson's turtle attitude toward our investigations, checking twenty hours after doesn't help much. There's also one other thing. If the Walthers .9-mm. Mr. Leaper found is the gun he used, there wouldn't be any evidence on his hand that he fired a gun. A revolver spews gun residue out the back, and so it gets on the hands. But a semi-automatic has that mechanical slide motion which expels gases and particles out the barrel, so there'd be no evidence on his hands. Except if the gun's used by somebody who's not familiar with it—the slide action can snap back and cut your thumb. Thompson did have that cut on his left thumb." Jesse nodded to her boss.

Hobey beamed at his deputy as if he'd given birth to her. He sighed, relaxing his shoulders, and offered a quiet laugh. The chief had learned to be a patient man, understanding that patterns emerged as sure as the sun rising, and that these patterns told their own story. You only had to wait. He smiled at the two women sitting across from him. "We really have more than we think. The cigarettes. Fibers from Thompson's ripped T-shirt under Jed's fingernails. Tissue from the scratch on his neck. I'll bet the blood typing from the slide action on the gun'll match Thompson's. Plus we have imprints of his boots in the sand." He looked up. This pause was longer. "Looks like we're gonna have solid evidence Thompson's our killer. ARDS, the national tracking system, checked him for us. He really is a strange fellow. Among other things, Bernie from ARDS told me that Thompson was one of those recreational litigators. Filed over twenty-five lawsuits in the five years he was at Attica. Bernie said they were about everything from claiming he was forced to eat too fast, to not being able to get wheat dinner rolls, to not having the shoe style he liked."

"Hobey, puhleese. Gimme a break," Renee howled.

"I'm not kiddin'. Bernie said each lawsuit can cost the state as much as sixty thousand dollars and years of work. The guy had four pending when they let him out. All he did on one of 'em he filed was white-out the previous guy's name!"

"What's the point?"

"Boredom, I guess, or sometimes they do it to get travel time back and forth to court. Prison law libraries are better stocked now than a lot of lawyers' offices. Anyway, the report shows he's a small-time scammer, but they thought he'd cooled it on parole. It was a shock to them to hear he was out here."

The three sat quietly again for a long time, not moving until Hobey said, "'Course, with him dead, makes it very hard to find out the reason he killed Jed. So, let me see if this fits. We got three IDs on Billy Walking Bear's car at the school, so it looks like him, even though we still haven't found his old car, and at least one white guy committed that robbery. Don't have any idea about the caves. Everything ends up at Jed's. If Jed's the leader, he and others—maybe Thompson?—were selling what they got. Then the question is, Where? Jed's phone bill had some unusual calls. One was to a shipping company in Seattle. Several to a number in Palo Alto, California. I'd say not enough to make him the big cheese of this operation, but I've asked Boone at the BIA to follow up. They can do it easier than us. So maybe

Thompson and Jed argue about money and Thompson kills Jed. Doubt it was premeditated, though that might just be my prejudice. Only two on all the reservations in the country last year—it'd be an unusual kind of murder for us. Anyway, Thompson takes off and dies in the truck. Was it an accident? Probably. Was he alone? Probably. Did the two of them act alone? We know at least Billy Walking Bear's involved. And then, where does Blank come into all this? We can't forget about him."

"Somethin' is botherin' me," Ren interjected. "Isn't it strange that after he killed Jed he takes off in the opposite direction from Jed's house? He coulda gone over there and cleaned the place out before anyone even knew Jed was dead. Doesn't make sense." Renee paused, then added, "And what about Anderson and his lyin' about when he made the phone call on his truck? He's covering something. Maybe he knows Thompson and was called and warned that Thompson cracked it up. But who called him? And what about the report that his truck's been gone from his place since before Halloween?"

"That reminds me." Hobey moved the papers on his desk and picked up the piece on the bottom. "Larry Sam, Brenda Rogers, and Angie Blue were working in the ER the morning they brought Thompson in. Mrs. Effie tells me that Larry's a kid from the high school. Angie's a solid Red Earther—I know her parents. She went to nursing school and came back. Married a guy from Turtle Mountain. Brenda's a white woman, lives off the rez, and," the chief's pause was melodramatic, "her boyfriend is Mr. Lou Blank." Hobey glanced up smugly. "I talked to Larry and Angie. Both remember the morning. It was pretty quiet. Blank was hangin' around makin' his usual nasty remarks. All that was happenin' before the accident came in was a two-year-old with an ear infection, somebody from the mill broke an ankle when a log rolled off a truck onto it, and Theresa Bonner was in labor. Things got pretty hectic when they brought Thompson in 'cause, for about twenty minutes, they were tryin' to save his life. Neither saw Blank after that. I was thinkin' we could pick up Brenda and Blank. Talk to 'em separately, but let 'em each know the other is here. See what happens."

They were contemplating Hobey's suggestion when Bobbi and Mukwa arrived with lunch. The *ahnimoosh* leapt under Renee's outstretched hand. "Jeez, how'd I forget about *that*?" Renee exclaimed, then looked sheepishly from the chief to Jesse, who both sat staring at her. "The night before the murder, Mukwa was acting strange. Whined around the house. Restless. Couldn't wait to get outside. Soon as I let her out she tore off into the woods. Next mornin', she showed me a spot by the woodpile that'd been trampled by someone standin' around. Her runnin' in here now reminded me."

"Renny! You didn't remember to tell us this?" Jesse's voice rose an octave.

"Jesus, Mary, and Joseph, LaRoche." Hobey glared at her over his bag lunch.

"I know, I know. I forgot with everything goin' on. We've also had some hang-ups on the phone the last few days."

Just then the telephone rang, saving Renee from the hot seat. Bobbi peeked in moments later and whispered, "Suit on the phone, wants to know what time to come by."

"Why are you whispering?" Renee chuckled.

"I don't know. FBI, bogeyman—makes me a little nervous!"

"Me, too!" Renee and Jesse chimed in unison.

A 3:00 P.M. meeting with Lawton was planned. Hobey turned back to Renee. "This worries me, Renny. Thompson won't bother you anymore. We know that Jed can't. But what about whoever else's involved? The worst is, we don't know how to read all this." The chief's tone was decidedly fatherly. "You gotta think, girl. And for Chrissake, be careful!" The chief scowled at his friend. Then, reaching over, he patted her hand. "No offense, Renny."

"None taken, Chief."

A blanket of seriousness settled over the group. They sat in silence, picking at their lunches. Renee shared hers with Mukwa. Jesse was first to break the quiet. "I've been trying to track down Billy Walking Bear to question him about stealing the hospital equipment and ask him about what we found in Jed's shed. He's an elusive fellow. Seems to have disappeared. Nobody's laid eyes on him or his flashy new car since he left the tribal council meeting yesterday. Janice says she hasn't seen him either, and I don't think she's lying. Seems to really not know anything about any of it. 'Course, we know he's involved, I mean stealing formaldehyde! Can't get much for that on the open market."

"Yeah, even we don't drink *that* stuff," Renee offered sarcastically.

The mood lightened as their conversation eddied into the laughter of good friends. Hunched over, elbows on her knees, Renee said,

"It's frustrating to be so close to figuring this out. Somethin's still missing—about Thompson again, I think. It's really weird he didn't head back to Jed's to load up."

Hobey drummed his fingertips on the side of his cup.

Jesse's face clouded, her dark eyes gazing off in unfocused concentration.

Finally the chief said, "Only thing I can think of now is maybe he got turned around and went the wrong way."

A trip to the Cities raised life's tempo on the rez. Visiting friends and family. Big-city life and shopping for things you can't get in the north woods excited everybody. Ren wasn't surprised it took her art class of eight ten-year-olds, with enough energy to propel a steamboat down the Mississippi, a while to settle down that afternoon.

"Listen up, listen up, guys. We gotta agree on the sign for our table at the pow wow." After a few hours, their red-and-yellow sign declared the items for sale were made by teacher and students of Mis skwa Ahki Bema disid jig Ki we din Nodin/Red Earth People of the North Wind. Renee was proud, but even more important, the kids were. Her students liked Renee because she treated them with respect, combining the study of Ojibwa basket-making; field trips into the forest, prairies, and swamplands to gather materials; and designing and making baskets in class. And they respected her as a traditional artist, squealing when she finally agreed to display her awards in the classroom. She'd been embarrassed at first, but when she saw how excited her students got—thinking that they, too, could do award-winning beadwork and baskets—she let go of the feeling she was bragging and enjoyed the kids' enthusiasm.

Renee found a place to sell their artwork once a year, and this year they were going to the Twin Cities. They packed the finished baskets and beadwork into government commodity boxes from the cafeteria and loaded them into the school van. "That'll do it," Renee said to Susie, a favorite student of hers. Turning, she bumped into Melvin. "Jesus, Mel, where'd you come from? You're quiet as a breeze."

Melvin's gretting was his usual slight nod of a downcast head. The two stood in silence for several minutes until Renee said, "Say Mel, guess you heard 'bout Jed's murder, eh?" After another nod, Renee continued. "I've been helpin' the chief, that's why I was at your place yesterday." She paused, allowing time for that to sink in. "I was wonderin', in all your cruisin' the rez if you've seen anything unusual. Cars, people, activity?" His head came up quickly and he looked sharply at Renee. It took another twenty minutes but finally Melvin told her he'd seen recent activity at Jed's house. A new four-wheel-drive vehicle parked in the yard several days ago and a strange truck on Old Portage Road with a broken tail light. Renee figured the truck was the one Thompson was driving. But whose four-wheel-drive was it?

Returning to the classroom, Ren found Josh with the list of helpers for the pow wow table. The kids were off to the gym. She'd originally planned to take a couple of students with her in the van, but the recent developments in the investigation changed her mind.

The ringing phone greeted Renee as she walked in the door of the darkened cabin. "Damn," she exclaimed, tripping over the rocking chair.

"Renee LaRoche?" The voice caught Renee off-guard. She was expecting Samantha.

"Ah—that's me." She waited for the stranger to identify himself. When he offered nothing more she said, "Can I help you? You a friend of Jenny's?"

"No, no. I know you'll be in Minneapolis at the pow wow. Meet me at midnight out back of the Center. By the picnic tables. I got some information about the robbery."

"Why are you callin' me? Why don't you tell it to the police?"

"Take it or leave it." The man's words were angry, but his voice trembled.

"OK, I'll meet you. Midnight by the picnic tables. Say, have you called before? Have you been tryin' to get me?" She tried to be nonchalant, but the man hung up. "Damn!" Ren glared at the receiver.

She'd barely hung up when the ringing started again. "Hello!"

"Renee?"

"Yeah, it's—Sammy? Oh. Sorry, love. Hi."

"That's a little better. You OK?"

"I am now, hearing your voice."

After chatting with Samantha, Renee called Hobey to tell him about the earlier phone call and the meeting she'd set up in the Cities. He didn't like the idea. It was one thing to accept that cops occasionally got hurt in the line of duty. It was something else again to send Renee into an unknown, potentially dangerous situation. But he went along with it because they needed this—if it was what the guy promised—a chance to get some details on the robbery. Hobey agreed, only after he told her he thought she was a little reckless at times.

"By the way, Renny, the invoice you found at Jed's doesn't match Jed's handwriting. They used that variable light spectrum machine, and the laser, too. Still came up empty. Not even close, she told me. I also sent the note you guys found with the money in Jed's office down, and guess what? The note and the invoice are a match."

"Well, shit, that helps. Two notes that we have no idea who wrote are a match." Renee and the chief laughed. "Par for this course, I'd say."

"Don't forget, Renny. Come by the station and pick up Thomp–son's watchband. Let's hope some of the east coasters at the pow wow can give us an idea where he might've gotten it."

"Will do, Chief."

At bedtime, Renee suggested that she and her daughter sleep downstairs together. Jenny hauled her favorite pillow, blanket, and polar bear down and they snuggled in. Jenny, Renee, and Mukwa. "Frogs on a log, Auntie would call us," Renee said. "This is nice, just the three of us for a change, eh?"

"Yeah," Jenny responded wistfully.

"How are you and Sam doin', my girl?"

"Up and down, I guess. It's hard always havin' to explain stuff to her. The way we do things, I mean. But, she helps with basketball. Said she'd drive us to games and stuff."

"Her yearbook from Smith says she was a star forward. She must be pretty good, eh?"

"Yeah, but Smith, that's a rich girls' school."

"You don't think rich girls can play basketball?"

"Maybe. I don't know, but I don't wanna talk about it anymore."

"OK, baby. Jus' keep an open mind, eh?"

"Whatever. Night, Ma." J.J. fell asleep quickly. For Renee, sleep was longer in coming. Thoughts trickled through her mind. First she worried about Sam and Jenny. Then she mulled over this fact, that clue. Finally, her eyes closed on the day. Surrounded by all that love, she fell asleep.

11

The birds twittered and chirped their thrill to be up. Emerging from the evergreens next to the van in a sunburst flash, a goldfinch flock rose up over the Leaper cabin and rolled into their wavy flight pattern heading south. "See ya next year," Renee called. "Have a nice trip." She knew she'd see them again on their return flight, probably back to Canada, since they held to strict flight patterns. Renee had been up since 6:00 A.M. She and Walter Leaper stepped on to the trail he'd been on when he found the gun. Two white-tails greeted them rounding a curve downwind in the foggy bottom. Walter had pointed out the hoofed tracks earlier, so Ren was expecting them. Her grandfather taught her you could walk up almost on top of a deer if you were downwind of it. If not, they could smell you a mile away.

"Time was, squirrels could climb a tree in Maine and not have to come down till they hit the Mississippi. Be nice to see that, eh?" Walter was referring to the massive destruction of the forest in the short time since Europeans had come to North America. From more than eight hundred million acres of virgin forest in the area known as the United States, to less than three million today.

"Who's been arrested for the murder of all those trees, Walter?"

"Creator tends to that. We tend to our responsibilities," the old man replied. "That's why the Elder Center has tree-planting weekends, started by your auntie."

The silence on this stretch of Old Bridge Road was interrupted in the early morning only by the peeling paint on the county road signs. A musky odor from the peat bog just beyond the aspen stand permeated the heavy air. The sky was changing to the color of carbon steel. This time of year that always foretold of a coming snow. Walter stopped at the top of the next rise and nodded at the water-filled gully below. "This it?" Ren queried.

Nodding, the Ojibwa elder repeated how he found the .9-mm. pistol two mornings before. In response to her question about anything else he might've noticed, Walter stood quietly. "Forgot this till now," he said. "Later I heard a rifle. Toward the river. Someone ran up the road, half a minute's worth. Got into a four-wheel drive and left by way of that ol' wagon trail down from Goodbears."

"Four-wheel drive?"

"Down-shifted."

"Left on the wagon trail?"

"Sound of the tires. Didn't come by here and didn't go back on the gravel over the bridge."

Renee then inquired, "It was a man?"

"*Chimook.* He had jackhammers for feet. Long strides. Left a funny smell, too. On top of the oil and gas. Chemical smell."

This pause was longer. Finally, Renee asked, "Ever smell formaldehyde?"

Forty minutes later at the hospital Renee stopped outside the lab to call Jenny. Walter's loud *harrump* behind her, uncharacteristic of the usually quiet man, told Renee his response to her question. When she got off the phone, Walter confirmed the smell was as she suspected—formaldehyde.

Gram and Auntie—wearing her green accountant's visor— pulled in just after Renee. They were there to deliver Jenny's shawl, "spruced up for dancin' with them downtown Indians," as Auntie called relatives who moved to the city.

Lydia never went more than fifteen red dirt miles off the reservation after coming home from boarding school seventy years ago. She remembered too well her dread as a little girl when the Coon family returned their young Nigi oday Ikkwe back to school. The family stayed on for a week, camping across the lake with others, burning the sacred fire at bedtime so the little ones wouldn't be so afraid. Then they had to return home: it was wild ricing time. Nuns at Holy Rosary Mission School did their best to "beat the heathen" out of Otter Heart Woman and the other little Ojibwa children. After all, the U.S. House Committee on Indian Affairs had made it clear: "In the present state of our country, one of two things seems to be necessary—that those sons of the forest should either be moralized or exterminated." Ten years later when the youngest Coon girl came home for good, on the surface she seemed a little like her new name. Lydia. Her hair was short, and the beatings for talking Indian had taken their toll. But Nigi oday's Anishanabe spirit remained. Once home, she had no desire to ever leave again.

"I heard 'bout the other night," Auntie began, adjusting her green bingo visor a little lower on her forehead as she took Renee aside. "And I wanna tell ya somethin'. Takin' Gram over ta Thunder Lake yesterday there he was, Billy Walking Bear, his ol' drunkin' self sittin' in a fancy new car. He asked all kindsa questions 'bout what you was doin' on the robbery and if you was goin' to the pow wow. I told him he looked bad, troubled. Didn't look like he's been sleepin'. Tol' 'em you were goin' to the pow wow and you were a good listener. Then, when I tol' him his gram was worried 'bout his drinkin' and carryin' on, he got in a big snit an' tore off. An' Renny, his drivin' was, well—" Auntie clucked her tongue. Renee chuckled at the thought of Auntie criticizing anyone else's driving. Lydia went on to tell Renee she'd seen what she thought was Billy's old car in the ravine on the north side of the Chippewa County dump during her latest pilgrimage to the dump, "lookin' at all the fancy stuff those white folks throw away." Renee gave her aunt a big hug and they returned to Gram and Jenny.

Harold LaFleur was waiting on young Larry Blue when Renee went into the trading post to pay for gas on their way out of town. The little one handed Harold a note and two dollars, pressing his face against the glass candy case. It was the same case Renny saw the first time she came into the store with her Daddy and Ben. Benny's initials, *B.L.*, were still in the right corner where he'd carved them that day that seemed like a hundred years ago. The three shelves held what Renny thought must have been all the candy in the world. Larry, too, was having a hard time with the choices, but finally pointed to a bag of Gummy Bears. Harold pulled them out and smiled at Renee, unhurriedly tending to the boy. The Blue boy scrabbled up the change and a generic pack of cigarettes before heading for the door. "Don't you be smokin' any of those cigarettes, Larry. They'll stunt your growth and make your teeth yellow," Harold called.

Larry's eyes got big at the thought.

"That's right," Harold winked at Renee. "Then the Little People'll come and take you to live with them," he added, referring to Ojibwa belief that little people with magical powers lived in the forest, appearing especially to the children.

"I won', I won't smoke, Mr. Harold, promise. Bye." Larry turned and ran out, banging the door against the wall in his rush. Harold laughed, sliding his left hand into the bib overalls to rest on his massive belly. Auntie said bibs were the only kind of pants he could get to stay up anymore.

The LaFleurs' trading post was the cracker-barrel of Rice Lake. They'd only moved the store once, thirty years ago, changing from its original log longhouse to the larger wooden and brick structure they were in now. The mahogany ceiling fan installed after the move ran continuously, summer and winter. Open every day from dawn to sundown, the LaFleurs sold everything from fish bait to perfume. Beer was the big seller until the tribal council banned its sale on the reservation in 1985. Though bootlegging had always been part of the reservation underbelly, it flourished after that, and today booties could make forty dollars a case for beer and up to fifty-five dollars on liquor. Short Step LaFleur, Harold's older brother and a drinking pal of Renee's father, had been one of the earliest booties, taking up the profession after catching his right pants leg in the slaughterhouse sausage grinder and tearing up his knee.

"Headin' down to the pow wow?" LaFleur asked, ringing up Renee's gas.

"Yep."

"Well, I hear you're helping the chief with Jed's murder and the robbery. You be careful, eh. Mary'd be mighty sad if you didn't come back to class!" Harold smiled. "You're her favorite teacher."

Harold's nine-year-old granddaughter was a student of Renee's. She was so quiet, she often got lost amidst the noise of the others. "She's a talented girl, Mr. LaFleur. I'm bringing three of her baskets. Someone at home a basketmaker?" Ren picked up some window washer for the van and was standing again at the counter.

"Her grandmother. You should see her baskets!" Harold reddened as he bragged about his wife.

On the way to the highway, Renee passed the tribe's wetland revitalization project running along both sides of County Road 3. Esther and Lydia walked this stretch every morning, and last spring they had noticed a drop in the number of whooping cranes. As the wetland's sentinel, if cranes aren't healthy and multiplying, the wetland isn't vital either. The tribe's natural resources unit investigated and discovered that insecticides were killing one level of the food chain, endangering all the others. They started a reclamation project, and Renee was comforted knowing that next spring the whooping cranes would be on their way back, guttural purrs in full voice, to hop and skip their mating dance. All thanks to the wisdom of our elders, she thought. *Every time we lose an elder it's like white folks losing a library.* She glanced in the mirror at Jenny and Jody in the back and was deeply grateful that her daughter was living near the elders of her family.

Turning onto Highway 7, Renee headed south. The earlier threat of snow was keeping its promise now as sleet began to drum on the van's window. She didn't know when the highway had been given its nickname, the Yellow Brick Road, but Red Earthers got the meaning. For those growing up on the rez, hopelessness lay over everything like an early spring fog; reality became what was right in front of you. The Yellow Brick Road bordering the reservation led to magical places, or so everyone thought until they'd been down the highway one too many times seeking, but never finding, the promised rainbow. Passing Aspen Cove, with the last mowed grass drying in windrows before baling, Renee broke into song. "Weee're off to see the wizard, the wonderful wizard of Oz—"

"Ma, puhleese," came the predictable response from Jenny.

"Come on. You guys know about the yellow brick road." She looked at the girls in her rearview mirror.

"Yes, Mother. We know. It's your singing we can do without," she moaned.

"Hey now, gimme some respect. I used to sing in that world-famous Calliope Women's Chorus when we lived in Minneapolis," Renee responded with mock indignation.

"I thought they only let you in 'cause you had friends in the chorus!" The two girls howled at Jenny's comeback. "OK, OK," Jenny added, leaning forward and whispering to Mukwa, "plug your ears,

Mukie. She's gettin' ready to wail her favorite 'goin' down the highway' song. Come on, Ma. Let's get it over with."

Renee jumped enthusiastically on the first word—"Freee-dum." Mukwa sat up and looked sleepily at the three singing the freedom song at the top of their lungs. With the last line, the *ahnimoosh* raised her head and howled a contribution.

They settled in for the long drive, and Renee began reconstructing what Jesse had told them about DNA testing, particularly about the most accurate of the tests, the RFLP.

"First, they do a blood typing," Jesse had explained. "Then they take out the white cells, which have a lot of DNA. The white cells are treated with a special chemical combination. The DNA floats free as kind of a sticky bundle. Then they cut the DNA into smaller pieces using some kind of protein called, I think, restriction enzymes. They act like molecular scissors. The chopped up DNA is marked with a colored dye and put in tiny wells at the end of a sheet of gel. There's an electric terminal at each end of the tray. Under ultra-violet light you can watch the negatively charged fragments being drawn through the gel to the positive end at the top. The smaller strands move quickly and the long ones drag behind. The genetic profile develops in bands. After a radioactive probe is added to the gel, patterns are revealed in the bands—the full DNA profile of the person. What used to take six weeks for some of these tests can now be done in six days, thanks to the FBI's latest invention in this field."

Renee marveled at the smarts Jesse brought to her job and just how far forensic science had come in the last ten years. Criminals were definitely at a disadvantage nowadays. Especially on the rez with the new ace female deputy. Renee liked Jesse and believed the Red Earth tribal police was a much better department with her on board. She definitely was an essential team member on cases like the one they were working on.

Getting off the freeway and making the final turn on to Franklin Avenue four hours later, Renee was flooded with memories. The Ave.—the urban reservation's main street—was the area of Minneapolis she used to call home. Ben was killed just off the Ave., down by the railroad tracks. Jenny was conceived in a house half a block from Franklin. It was the Ave. that encouraged her descent into drugs and alcohol. And where she got the support to find her way back.

Renee turned into Alice and Mollie's driveway, switched off the motor, and leaned back. "Here at last. Sure be glad when you can drive, J.J. Let Mukie out, will ya? I gotta sit here for a second."

"Anybody here?" Jenny asked, opening the door for the *ahnimoosh.*

"Nope. Both at work."

Renee listened to the sounds of the city. Sounds of busy lives. The freeway hum in the distance, a dog barking, somebody honking their horn. Kids were yelling to each other at the corner bus stop. Another horn. Far off, an airplane. It always amazed her: you could sit so long in the city and not hear a bird or the sound of the wind. Soon, restless and a little cramped, she got out of the van and walked the half block back to Franklin Avenue.

To move along the Ave. today was to be confronted by change. A neighborhood coalition had closed down the liquor store at the busiest intersection, turning it into a pow wow grounds. Six months ago, a Tobacco Ceremony celebrated the planting of the last bush. That store closing followed on the heels of a victory over the porn theater, which now housed Four Winds, a Native art store. Parasite businesses had been hounded by the coalition. The last ones to be "run outta Dodge" were the bars. "Too much hassle from the goody two-moccasins," a white bar owner was overheard declaring as he loaded the remaining cases of whiskey in his truck and drove off.

The third largest urban Indian population in the country was a neighborhood in transition, but still as poor as the western suburbs were rich. This end of Franklin had never been the fancy part of town. The transition here had been from working class to poor to poorer still. The Gothic structures—turrets and gables painted one of the authentic period colors authorized by the Minnesota Historic Renovation Commission—stopped seven blocks west, and didn't take up again until they lined both sides of the Mississippi River, a mile and a half to the east of the Indian Center. Mercedes diesels and Saab turbos wouldn't be seen creeping along this one-mile stretch until the prowling time of night, stopping momentarily to ferret out companions of the two-legged, or powder-in-a-baggy variety, for a brief encounter before returning to their plusher worlds.

Mollie and Alice came home just as the Red Earthers were leaving for the pow wow. Mukwa, resigned to staying behind, snoozed on the blue-and-white wide-striped couch under the front bay window. It was what she must endure in order to make the trip, so she didn't protest.

"Hey, ya buncha redskins!" Mollie called, coming around the corner. "Another successful skip down the yellow brick road, eh?" She laughed, holding her high school friend's face between her hands. They'd finally shared their secrets a year out of school, spending nights sitting by Gi sina Nibi Lake, laughing and teasing about the things they'd endured to cover their queerness. Best of friends, but never lovers. When Mollie had fallen madly in love with Alice seven years ago, and worried about getting involved with a white woman, Renee was the first person she'd called. Renee returned the honor six years later.

"Just headin' out," Renee said. "Have to set up before the hordes come."

"You look especially beautiful tonight, my dear. Yellow's a good color on you. New ribbon shirt? I've never seen this black bear silhouette in the red shield here on the back before. Did you make it?" Mollie teased.

"Very funny," Renee poked her friend. "You know I can't sew. Gram made it," she said, shooing the girls out the door in front of her. "See you for Grand Entry?"

"You got it. And I wanna talk to you LaRoche. You know I've been talkin' to Sammy about what's happening on the rez."

Samantha showed up as they hauled the last box of baskets into the pow wow. She was wearing the blue-and-white beaded tipi-style earrings and multiple-strand liquid silver necklace interspersed with pieces of turquoise Renee had given her for an anniversary present. Her melon gabardine suit jacket strained across her back and full breasts, much to her lover's delight. The suit contrasted sharply with Sam's short, tousled hair and little-girl face.

"Boozho." Renee waved to get her attention in the growing crowd. Sam's long-limbed, loose-jointed stride was so Sam-like, Ren could recognize it anywhere. The spicy smell of Indian tacos filled the gym, and soon after her arrival Samantha headed off to beat the hunger wave guaranteed to explode after Grand Entry. She returned thrilled because Lorraine Jamison, a recent Red Earth transplant to the city, recognized her.

After they'd settled in with their tacos to wait for Grand Entry, Renee said, "Sammy, I have to meet a guy at midnight."

"Jeez, Renny. I wasn't gone that long!"

"It's about the robbery, goofy. He called last night saying he had information. But not to worry, Hobey's sending Jesse down to hang around in case I need back up." Renee looked at Samantha, squinting her eyes. She knew this wasn't going over too well when she heard Sam suck in her breath.

"Don't worry? In case you need back up?" Samantha's words squeezed out between clenched teeth, popping full force into the air like whipping cream from an aerosol can. "Who is it?"

Renee shrugged. "Couldn't tell. Think it was one of us, though. You know, he had that reservation, clipped, slide the word out way of talking."

"But you *don't* know. It could be anyone with a little gun, a big one, a whole damn army, Renee."

"I know it's someone who wants to help. I could tell by what he said and the tone of his voice," Renee offered plaintively. Samantha offered no reply. "It sounds worse to you than it is, Sammy. Really." Renee wore her long-suffering look, but the pause grew. Finally she looked over at her partner.

"I'm going with you," Samantha said evenly.

"I feel perfectly safe, Sammy. That self-defense series I took helped a lot. I've been doin' those exercises every day." Renee's babbling trailed off, having had no obvious effect. Next she tried, "How about you go with Jesse, wherever she's watching from. OK?"

It was another long wait before Sam responded, "Don't think for one minute I'm happy about this, Renee LaRoche!"

"I would never think such a foolish thing," Renee answered. Then she caught her lover's eyes, played with them a little, and finally let them go as the drum started announcing Grand Entry. Standing, Ren squeezed Sam's hand, whose flush began at her neck and exploded up to her hairline like a flash prairie fire.

12

" T he first rule in criminal investigation is don't assume anything," Renee reminded herself as she prepared to meet the mystery man. "Sure hope he's not a no-show." She turned to Samantha and crossed her fingers.

"I hope he is," Samantha growled, her frown expressing her unhappiness.

The parking apron along the west side of the Center was still almost full of cars, vans, and trucks declaring which part of Indian Country they'd come from. "One of these days we'll ban smoking like we did drugs and alcohol at these things." Renee coughed, clearing her throat as the door closed behind her.

Out front, the Indian Center's blinking sign offered a surreal announcement of current events. She walked slowly up the alley bordering the parking lot. Her boots crunching on the gravel seemed unusually loud. The wind eddied around the northwest corner of the Center, carrying the trash of the transient and poor. Old newspapers, Land O' Lakes milk cartons, flattened cardboard boxes, Four Roses wine bottles, empty Spam cans, apple cores. She walked back along the sidewalk. It was 12:15 and still no sign of the mystery man, so she moved through the picnic area and sat on the last bench. To her right she heard someone mumbling, "God Bless the molecules I'm swallowing and breathing. God Bless—" She turned, thinking the man was talking to her. Renee could feel his thoughts swirling between them, but could tell by the look in his eyes there'd be no connecting with any of them. Then he drifted off down the street.

The street runners and alley dwellers had taken over the Ave. despite the chilly temperature, and people leaving the pow wow gave them a wide berth as they hurried to their vehicles. A cold spot between her shoulders caught Ren by surprise. Someone suddenly came up behind her. "Don't turn around," the male voice said. "He's in the Wagon Wheel. Says to meet him in there."

Renee felt like she was operating her body from somewhere out in the stratosphere. Her voice cracked, but she steadied herself and said, "How'll I know who he is?" She strained to hear herself, her voice sounding like it was under water, her lips moving in slow motion.

"Sit at the bar. He'll find ya." And the voice was gone.

"Breathe, LaRoche," she said to herself. She rallied and stood, carefully testing her legs. Just inside the door Renee stopped and surveyed the people in the Wagon Wheel, the last liquor-selling holdout at this end of the Ave. The bar crowd tonight seemed to be the regulars: transients able to beg enough loose change off pow wow-goers for a beer or two; hard-core neighborhood drinkers who couldn't stop even for one night to attend the chemically free event next door, and the ever-present pool hustlers found in bars across the country. The music was loud enough to jump-start even the most pickled heart. It reminded Ren of her own mind-numbing days on the Ave. She sat on an empty stool at the end of the bar to take advantage of the occasional wave of fresh air rolling in when the door was opened. The smoke hazing the air matched the booze haze in people's brains. Soon she was being entertained by the mating dance of a pair of two-legged reality escapees on the bar's tiny dance floor. Photo negatives coming together posing and prancing, mimicking the mime, they strutted around each other until they stumbled into a booth, one on top of the other as the dance ended.

Someone sat down to her right. The last stool by the wall. Renee continued staring straight ahead, but caught a glimpse of the hands on the bar. An Indian male. She looked up at the bartender, who was smiling familiarly at the man next to her. All at once she knew who it was, but she waited to let him make the first move. Finally he spoke.

"Renee, I'm Billy Walking Bear."

Sensing that this guy spooked easily, Renee just nodded. She didn't want him to cut and run. Billy's dark eyes were cold and distant, as if he'd separated himself from any feelings threatening to humanize the moment.

"I know some stuff that'll help the police," he began, "but I don't wanna get in any more trouble. I gotta kid, and me and Janice, we were just gettin' on track. Now this. Janice gets so nervous about..." Renee glanced up. Billy was lost in a memory only he could see.

When she was certain he was waiting to hear from her she declared, "The sooner we clear this up, the sooner we can all get on with our lives." Billy's shoulders relaxed a little. He obviously wanted and needed to trust someone.

Then he said, "I've been tryin' to talk to you. Get up my courage."

"You been at my house? Callin' me on the phone?"

Billy nodded sheepishly. "Sorry if it scared you or anything. I been wantin' to tell ya somethin'. Saw you at Jed's and almost did it then, but that new cop came."

"You mean when we found the stuff in the shed?"

"Yeah. Then I saw your auntie and she said you'd be here. I'm havin' these dreams. I've heard you know about this stuff." When his pause was met with silence he continued. "One of 'em is about Jed chasin' me. We're runnin' along the river and I fall over this cat. I get up and try to run again, but the cat grabs my pant leg and I'm like paralyzed. It's jus' a little bitty cat, but I can't move. Jus' when Jed gets to me, I wake up."

Renee was feeling a deep sadness for this man sitting next to her with his long black hair pulled back in a single braid. He certainly didn't do that himself, she observed, distracted by the beauty of the young Indian's hair. Someone took time and care on that braid, maybe the one outside that gave me the message. She hoped whoever it was took the same care with Billy's heart. He was obviously in way over his head and now was being terrorized by internal demons. Renee could see that tonight he'd gotten some of his courage from the bottle. Growing up on the rez and learning to drink was as normal as growing up in Grosse Point, Michigan and getting ready for college.

Renee could have told Billy what the dream meant: That to dream about the cat is to dream about suspicion, anger, violence. That wanting too much of what others have creates confusion. But it wasn't her dream to interpret. It was something Billy Walking Bear had to come to understand himself.

"Billy, do you know the story of Wabemee, the pigeon with the beautiful song?" she offered. "Always tryin' to make his song sound like everyone else's so he could declare he was the best singer on Mother Earth. He'd listen to others and imitate 'em. Nanaboozho tried to convince him to be satisfied with his own beautiful song, but Wabemee wouldn't listen. He was causing confusion in the village and fighting amongst other birds but nothin' anyone said would stop him. Nanaboozho asked Creator for help but was told, 'I know of Wabemee's jealousy, but greed will do him in. Tell the other birds to be patient.' One day Wabemee heard another song he wanted to copy. He started to sing but one note was too high. He kept forcing his voice until it got dry and sore. After stopping to take a drink he tried again but only low, moaning sounds came out. And from then on, Wabemee's only sound was a low moan."

Billy sat, still as a gray wolf in hunt. After a long time he said, "Wantin' everything he got nothin'?" Renee let the silence answer as Billy's history passed quickly through her mind. She left him with his own thoughts for several minutes. Muttering, "Yeah, I get it," he ordered another beer for himself and a Coke for Renee. He peeled the money off a wad of bills before realizing the contradiction between doing that and Renee's story. He put the money away, embarrassed. Whatever he'd been up to, he was being paid well for it. They talked back and forth for a while. Ren chose her words carefully, knowing this might be her only chance to bring him over. And she maintained a respectful emotional distance, letting Billy tell his story.

He told of a man he didn't know and never saw who called the shots. "He was headin' it up from the jump. Sounds like a white guy. You know, his voice." He stole equipment from the hospital per instructions from Mr. X., who seemed to know quite a bit about medical supplies. After the first theft Billy claimed, "They had me. From then on I had to go along, they threatened to turn me in." Billy and a guy named Sam did the robbery at the school, but he said it was the *chimooks* that emptied the caves. "I tol' 'em I couldn't do the caves," he said, shaking his head. "Tol' 'em they could kill me, I didn't care, I wasn't doin' it."

Sam and Dave were the first names of the two white guys, but Billy admitted he didn't know if they were real. He also didn't know who killed Jed. After oversleeping the day of the murder, Billy hurried to Jed's, where he was supposed to meet Jed and Sam, but by the time he got there they were gone. The plan was to pack up everything in the shed, then call a contact number in Minneapolis. The contact was arranging delivery out west somewhere. Billy said everybody was getting nervous. Things were taking longer than expected, and Mr. X. was pressuring them to move everything off the rez. He didn't know why Jed would be down at the river but admitted he was the one who had called in the body, finding him there on his way back from Morriseau's. Hearing that Jed Morriseau and Billy were the only Indians involved in the plan helped Renee understand why Billy now feared for his life.

"How did you miss the accident by Goodbears' then?" Ren queried.

"I went back out on Portage 'cause there's a pay phone across The Narrows." Billy said he went home after the phone call to try and think what to do next.

"My Aunt Lydia said she saw you in Thunder Lake."

"I've got this phone number. It's a phone in town there, a contact for Mr. X. I thought if I hung around I'd see somebody. Or something."

"What would you've done if you saw someone you thought might be your mystery man?"

"Insurance for my life, I guess," Billy shrugged. "I know they'd kill me in a heartbeat for any little reason."

"The day of the murder, someone on the road smelled formaldehyde coming from a truck, or a jeep, maybe. And they heard a shotgun blast. Any ideas?"

"Formaldehyde's used in the lab, the morgue. A little in the OR."

"Speaking of the morgue, what were you talking to Lou Blank about the night of the robbery?"

"Blank? I, I don't remember. I was pretty drunk. Somethin' about a truck, I think."

"Is Blank involved in this?" Renee asked in a hushed voice.

Billy shrugged indifferently. "Couldn't tell ya. Only one I knew for sure was Jed."

"Damn," she muttered.

"I think Creator kept me away from Jed's for a reason that morning. I wanna make it right," Billy mumbled, still lost in his own problems.

Renee looked piercingly into Billy's eyes, trying to hold his attention and penetrate the liquored veneer. She wanted to leave him with a connection to her.

"I don't know you except for this past hour, but I believe you want to make things right. You're Anishanabe. You came to me. I respect you for that and the people will too." She pulled a folded piece of red felt from her bag and set it on the bar in front of Billy. He raised his head and unfolded the felt. Renee heard him inhale sharply. His hands shook as he picked up the feather nestled between the folds. Renee could sense he wanted to give it back but knew he wouldn't dishonor her.

"Migizi *migwan*," Billy whispered in a choked voice.

"Gram says when Eagle flies out of the crack between light and darkness, she's going to talk to Creator to ask for understanding for our foolishness. We owe our lives to Migizi. I wouldn't usually bring an eagle feather around alcohol but I think Creator understands this once." She laid a hand on his arm and squeezed. Again, Ojibwa silence filled the space.

Billy refused to talk with Jesse or go back to the rez with her, but he promised to stay in touch. "We need you to ID these guys, Billy. I'll take your promise and wait to hear from you," she said, knowing she was taking a risk letting him go. But trust was more important now, so she slid off the stool and left the bar.

Renee stepped around the corner and collapsed against the wall of the building. She took a deep breath of clean air, so emotionally exhausted she wasn't sure she could move. All but a few cars had left the parking lot. The Heart of the Nation van and Sam's car sat next to each other by the door. "One of these must be Jesse's," Renee figured, looking around for her friends. Then she saw him. A man, sitting in a late-model car halfway down the alley in the darkness, or at least she thought it was a man. Turning back to the bar she found the door locked. Renee's watch said 1:30. Moments later, Jesse and Samantha appeared around the corner and stood next to her. "Jeez, am I glad to see you guys." She grabbed Sam's hand. "There's a guy sittin' in the alley in a car, about halfway down."

Jesse stepped around the corner of the building, and Samantha tightened her hold on Renee. "Nobody there, Renny," Jesse said, returning a few minutes later.

"Oh," Renee giggled, embarrassed. "Guess I was gettin' into a little cloak and dagger stuff. Probably someone just leaving." Arm in arm they walked across the parking lot to their cars.

A car pulled up to the stop sign a block away and slowly drove off down Franklin Avenue as the women's retreating forms disappeared into the darkness. A faded sticker on the back bumper read, *Anderson & Sons Excavation—We Dig Your Desires.*

Renee slouched on the couch, next to Jenny, leaning her head back just as Mukwa jumped in her lap. *You shoulda had me out there, niji,* she said, licking Ren's lips. Renee began her story as everyone listened spellbound. After half an hour, though, the girls tired of the conversation and retreated to the back bedroom they'd staked out as theirs.

"It's so great to see you guys again," Renee said to her friends. "Let's talk about us for a while. Too long between visits. When you gonna come up and see us in God's country?"

"Soon," Mollie said. "We gotta finish the upstairs, then we'll have a little more time to travel."

Buying the house as part of a revitalization of the Phillips neighborhood had been a great deal, but it wasn't without twists. The house needed a lot of work. After gutting most of the downstairs and turning what was three small rooms into one large expanse, they added the fireplace, in front of which the four women now lounged. They had a city-size but grassy backyard bordered with annuals and perennials in a riot of colors. A vegetable garden grew in the far corner of the lot, and on the side of the house was one of those little screen porches that make summer evenings lazy and pleasant.

"I don't know about this city livin', you guys. We can't even eat our veggies this year now that they built that polluting garbage burner downtown. Environmentalists say anything grown within a six-mile radius is contaminated," Mollie moaned.

Although Mollie and Alice had been together for seven years, their description of how they met still had distinct differences. To hear Mollie tell it, it was all Alice—maneuvering her on to the dance floor, dancing until Buffalo Springfield's "For What It's Worth" ended, and then, Mollie swore, Alice leaning over, boldly kissing her, and whispering, "I know what's happenin' here. I want you!" Over raucous laughter Alice protested her innocence once again, claiming that if truth be told, it was Mollie who asked for the first dance and then proceeded to charm her way into Alice's heart. Round and round they went, trying to out-banter each other, one of their favorite endearing games.

The four women relaxed and enjoyed their time together.

An hour later Renee and Sam stepped out of the shower into the silence of the house, streaming water like a couple of river otters. Muffled giggles could be heard until Sam raised a finger to Renee's lips, following it with her mouth. She stared at Renee, passion pouring out of her eyes as Ren leaned into her. Renee felt like she'd just returned from a long and painful journey into hostile territory. The sensation of being safe raised tears in her eyes. "It's good to be home, *saiagi iwed.*" She stood shyly while Samantha's fluffy-toweled hands gently rubbed down her cinnamon limbs.

Sam smiled invitingly, helping Renee into her nightshirt, then draping the white towel around her shoulders. She kissed Ren's neck seductively. "Time for bed, my sweets," Sam murmured, shrugging into her nightgown before leading her lover out of the bathroom with the towel. They fell on the bed side by side, Samantha groaning at the sight of Renee in her oversized men's pajama top opened to expose her neck and shoulders. She ran her fingers along Renee's collarbone and down between her breasts, unbuttoning as she went. Ren trembled under her lover's touch. When the space between them began to feel like a great canyon she drew Samantha urgently to her, kissing her neck, her ear, until Sam turned her mouth to meet Renee's.

Slipping out of her top Renee revealed broad shoulders. "I love these beautiful brown melons," Samantha cooed, cupping Renee's breasts and circling the nipples with her lips. "Renny," she gasped for air, face flushed, desire exploding in her pelvis. "I want you, Renny. God, how I want you." Sam had on the red flannel nightgown that had become a favorite of Ren's.

Surges of longing washed over Renee, too. Undressing Sam quickly, then rolling onto her, her lips lingered first on the softness of her lover's belly. "Remember we're not alone in the house, you'll have to curb your vocalizations. We wouldn't want anyone to think I was killing you, love." Renee blew into Sam's ear, running her tongue along the edge to the earlobe, Sam's most sensitive spot. She wrapped Sam in a big bear hug, cradling her head on her shoulder. Her hands moved over the soft contours of Sam's back, over the gentle rise of her belly, and up under her breasts. Renee's body pulsed with a surge of energy. She felt she could run a marathon—uphill. "God, I love you." Renee pressed her cheek against her lover's forehead and squeezed tight. Samantha brushed Ren's lips with her own. Then they kissed, a long, lingering meeting of two passions joined in the vulnerability of love. All differences, all doubt faded. It was a moment so good, so complete, that Renee thought if she died now she would die a fulfilled woman. She relaxed into her partner's arms, confident after a year of lovemaking of Sam's ability to satisfy her.

Sam looked intently into Renee's eyes. She could always count on them to reflect Ren's feelings, if you knew how to read the signs: the little wrinkles at the corners, more pronounced when she was worried; the shine they took on when she was holding back a smile; or the deep pools of blackness they became in anger. Now, they returned Sam's loving gaze. "My beautiful Indian Two-Spirit," Sam whispered. And Renee melted into Sam like she was the liquid metal and Sam the mold. Sam's fingernails skating up the inside of her thighs started the shudder in her toes and Ren's passion filled her consciousness.

Later, as they lay in each other's arms, tranquil and content, Renee ran her finger along her partner's belly. "We're so good together...doesn't matter how. We can get crazy and orgasmic or just lay here. Making love with you is all I need." She brushed the damp hair off Samantha's forehead.

The professor, head nestled in the curve of Renee's arm, moaned, "I couldn't run out of a burning building right now." A long pause followed. "Did you mention being quiet earlier?" Sam rolled up on her side and rested an arm on Renee's chest as she played with her lips.

"Uh-huh."

"Well?" She pinched Ren's lips out.

"Well, other than the crystal you shattered down the block, I don't think we bothered anybody!"

Samantha threw her head back and howled, and Renee, never able to resist a laugh, joined in. Then they looked at each other, fingers to lips. Ren dove under the covers giggling uncontrollably. Peeking her head out like a wary turtle she whispered, "Is it safe? Any of the Christian Right out there patrolling for anyone, anywhere, who might be having fun?"

A miasma of love scents wafted above, finally seducing them

into thoughts of sleep. Tousle-haired, eyes brimming love, Samantha stretched for her discarded nightgown. Renee felt Sam's smile in the dark next to her, and she reached over for her hand. They lay quietly. The quarter moon peeked in over the cafe-curtained windows.

"See how close together those three stars are?" she whispered.

"Mm."

"Gonna be a cold fall. They're huddled to keep warm." Unconsciously, they both slid a little further under the covers.

"I love your stories, Renny. Tell me that one."

"OK. At one time our whole area was a huge glacier. We never had summer. But life went on. One day Nanaboozho—you know, our great *manido,* our spirit-being—came by to visit and asked, 'How're you gonna keep living on this ice and snow? There has to be something we can do to make the area better for all living things.' Nanaboozho got everybody excited about the idea so they met, offered sacrifices, fasted, and prayed to Gitchie Manitou. Nothing happened, so another meeting was called and they invited Nanaboozho to a feast. After a lot of talking the wisest elder said, 'Only one thing to do. We'll have a feast of *manomin* and wild roots and invite North Wind. After he's enjoyed our wild rice meal we'll plead our plight to him and ask him to blow in another direction for a while so South Wind can breathe her warmth on us.' And so it happened. North Wind pitied the shivering life of the North and said, 'Watch the sky. When the three stars begin to huddle you'll know I'm coming back. When they move away you'll know I've turned my face. Use the time wisely, to plant and prepare, because after seven fullnesses of Nokomis Moon I will always come back.'

Renee could feel the relaxed body beside her. Sam was drifting off to sleep, and now, so did Ren. In each other's arms, they promised to rise early despite the 4:00 A.M. glowing out of the darkness from the bedside stand.

13

Humanity rose from the items lined up for sale around the edge of the pow wow. Beaded headbands and key rings, uniquely designed earrings, ribbon shirts, dreamcatchers, baskets, and watchbands all made by the creative hands of people from around Indian Country. Sometimes you could find the artist's name on the piece, or an accompanying explanation. Lottie, Hazel, Wilbur, Harold—names from a generation past, designing and sharing pieces of their hearts. Renee, Susie, John, Ben, Mary—names from today proving the cry, Original People live on.

Mollie and Renee were sitting at the Red Earth table Saturday afternoon. Ren held up a hand, feigning innocence. "Me? I'm not ignoring anybody."

Mollie scowled. "Oh, and their complaints to me are the wailings of mad women, eh?"

Renee looked embarrassed. "I've been busy," she muttered.

Mollie groaned. "Goddamnit, LaRoche. Look at the writing on the outhouse wall. I just think you've done enough now. Let somebody else take it from here, risk their neck on this." Mollie threw up her arms, her face filled with exasperation.

"Mollie, you know I can't do that. Auntie asked me, now I'm into it. You remember how it goes with elders, eh? And," she mumbled under her breath, "I get off on it."

"Mm, and you think all those drunks and wife beaters on the rez remember the traditions?" Mollie said derisively. "You think they're gonna thank you after this, Renny, or keep on snickering behind your back 'cause you're a lezzie, and with a white woman at that! Flip 'em a digit my friend, and move on."

"Come on, Mollie. It's not like that. We don't have any trouble on the rez. Some folks are actually starting to take to Sammy. You just like sayin' outrageous things to keep people on tilt, Gardener," Renee added, poking her friend in the ribs. "At least we have traditions about folks like us. More'n you can say for *chimooks* and their Christian-nuclear-family-missionary-position-boy-girl view of sex and relationships."

"True enough, but our traditions aren't so pure anymore, Renny."

"No, but they're comin' back. Anyone hassles me I jus' send 'em to Gram and Auntie's circle. Those elder *ikkwe* set 'em straight."

"Yeah, you're lucky, LaRoche. You got that generation to hold on to. All mine are dead."

"Oh, boo-hoo, Gardener. You know any one of those old ladies'd take you under their wing. If you weren't too goddamn pig-headed to ask."

"You always did see the world through rose-colored glasses, LaRoche. Guess some things never change."

"Oh, lookee there, she dropped the subject!" Renee laughed, giving Mollie a push. "Enough already. I want to talk about this watchband Thompson had on at the time of the accident." Renee laid the band on the table. They'd just come back from walking the sales area of the pow wow, hoping someone could identify the style of the beaded band.

"Well, my sister, your hunch was right about the beads used on the band, eh? They are the Hungarian ones those east coast Indians like. Does that help at all?"

"What'd help more is if we could find out where he bought it. Might lead us to someone who'd recognize the band."

"Was interesting what the guy from Onondaga said about the turtle design on the band being Mohawk. Do you think there's any way you can track it?" Mollie was turning the band over and over in her hand. "Sure is a beautiful job."

"We'd need a break, I'm afraid. This Thompson guy seemed to get around. He coulda even bought it in prison. Attica's practically right in the middle of Mohawk country. They don't do much for

Native brothers in prison, but they've gotta provide time for cultural stuff." Renee shrugged.

"Wasn't it Dostoevsky who said, 'A country's civilization can be seen in its prisons'? Or somethin' like that," Mollie asked. "Wonder what he'd think of this so-called civilization, eh?" Their laughter was without humor.

"Ya know, Mollie, I just thought of somethin'. We've been focusing on the band. What about the watch? Lemme see that a second." Renee slipped the pins out and took the watch off.

Mollie picked the band up. "Alvin Minton, artist of beaded watchbands." She grinned broadly, holding up the band.

"What?"

Mollie pointed to a name burned into the leather of the watch bed.

"Oh my God, look at that, right under the watch. Looks like a wood-burning stamp or somethin'," Renee said excitedly. "Maybe that means he does a lot of this work. Way to go, Gardener. Let's go check with that Onondaga guy."

"Hobey? Renee here. I think we got somethin'." She gave Chief Bulieau Alvin Minton's name and phone number. "He's Mohawk. Goes back and forth between Akwesasne and Syracuse. Pretty well known, I guess. Mollie found his name on the watchband and then we located someone here who knows him. Jesse has a person she can contact at Akwesasne to go and talk to him."

Hobey agreed and told them to send the watchband through registered overnight mail to Jesse's friend.

"How 'bout callin' Betty? Maybe she could help," Renee suggested as an afterthought.

"No, I don't wanna bother her, not with something that might belong to her brother's killer," the chief said, "but let's hope things start fittin' a little better into one puzzle. Seems like we've been to this dance before. I've got so many slips of paper with bits of evidence on 'em, I look like one of those Alzheimer folks at the Elder Center."

Jesse got on the phone. "Chief, Billy called Renee this morning, and she's talking to him one more time before we head home. If he doesn't agree to come back voluntarily, I'll have to arrest him, but we want to keep him feeling he's part of the team rather than a prisoner.

I'll call in when I get back."

Jesse hung up and leaned against the wall next to the phone, giving in for a moment to her fatigue. She closed her eyes and listened to the pow wow sounds reverberate throughout the gym, watching as the tiny-tot group got ready for their exhibition dance, prancing and high-stepping, twirling and dipping even before the drum started. "Someday a little one of mine will be out there," she sighed. There was a yearning in that thought that surprised her.

Billy showed up at the pow wow early Saturday evening. "Here he comes. Billy Walking Bear," Renee whispered, "the skinny guy with the leather jacket comin' this way. Look at him, Sammy. I know the Indian Fat Readers in Mexico say everyone's body grows to the size it needs for survival, but look at him." Renee shook her head. "If it only takes a feather or a soft breeze to knock you over, you have to wonder. Survival seems iffy at best."

Renee introduced Billy to Samantha. "Yeah, I've seen her 'round the rez," he muttered, eyes downcast.

"How'd it go last night, Billy? Get any rest?" Ren asked, noticing how jittery he seemed.

"OK."

On closer examination, Renee could see that he was sober. She figured his jumpiness was probably from that. "Wanna get something to eat?" she offered.

"OK." His discomfort was becoming painful to watch.

Half an hour later, Renee fell into the folding chair behind the table. "Oh, God! That boy is a handful. Do you know he's only eighteen years old? Mr. X. has him so scared he's ready to boot-scoot for Canada. I think if it wasn't for the baby and Janice he'd be long gone. He's on the verge of becomin' one of those people who walk around yellin' at cracks in the sidewalk, but I hooked him up with Jesse and they're gonna head back." Renee kissed Sam's hand. "Sure glad you're normal...sort of," she giggled.

Samantha, in measured nonchalance, rested her arm on the back of Renee's chair. Affection in public still threatened her a little, especially at Indian events. Leaning over, she whispered, "I've been dreaming about last night. Mm, what you do to me and what thinking about it makes me want to do to you!"

"Ooh, is my little blue-blood talkin' dirty?" Renee smiled, then stole a quick kiss. "Let's dance, eh?" Taking the girls' shawls, Renee and Samantha moved out into the circle of intertribal dancers. The song was being played by the Montreal Four Winds drum group.

Jenny and Jody left with Sam the next day, and Renee and Mollie headed for one of their favorite Minneapolis hiking spots. Parking the van at the top and following Mukwa's lead, they headed down the long wooden steps on the west side of the Mississippi River. The trees still held on to a few leaves this far south, and a spattering of yellows and oranges brightened the fall sky. Honeysuckle vines clumped like groups of chatting friends along the river trail. "Mol, ya know it's weird. This guy Thompson's maybe been to Akwesasne. With Betty livin' there and all, what a spooky connection, eh? Betty's gonna be shocked when she finds out. I keep worrying about how she feels about Jed's death, but I can't get ahold of her. She doesn't have a phone." Renee offered a brief smile. "Left one message at the tribal office and one with a neighbor but no luck yet."

"Hope she's all right."

"I keep remembering somethin' she said to Bobbi about bein' sure she'd hear from me soon." Renee laid an arm across her friend's shoulders.

They moved through the woods like a gentle breeze, barely lifting the leaves covering the trail along the western shore of the Mississippi. A mile downstream they stopped to watch a barge moving through Lock and Dam #4 before they returned to the lower trail and headed to the van. The wind came up, blowing Renee's hair straight up into the air. "Ya look like a porcupine, LaRoche," Mollie giggled, tousling her old friend's hair. "Wish I had a camera."

After dropping Mollie off, Renee settled back in the van seat for the long drive home and began replaying the weekend. Continuing gaps in the evidence frustrated her, but she felt they were at least creeping along now, not standing still anymore. *Why did Thompson come all the way from New York?* Jesse's friend at Akwesasne talked to Minton this morning. He acknowledged the watchband was his but didn't remember Thompson. The band was a new creation sold out of a shop on the rez. *So what brought Thompson to the rez recently?* Neither Jesse's friend nor Minton knew of any thefts or grave robberies similar to what Thompson was suspected of being involved with at Red Earth. Jesse's friend checked with *Akwesasne Notes,* but the newspaper editor told her they hadn't had any trouble with grave robbers in that part of Indian Country for at least seven years. And it still nagged Renee why Thompson didn't return to Jed's to retrieve stolen items worth in the hundreds of thousands in the underground market. Not very smart for a supposed international thief. *Maybe it was just too big of a scam for him.* Ren glanced over at her *niji*.

Then there's John Anderson, victim extraordinaire. Renee's smile was without warmth. Talking with Mike Swensen before leaving Minneapolis, all she'd learned about was Anderson's two DWI arrests, though Mike did say he hadn't given up checking. It didn't sound promising, but Renee conceded that at this point, she'd look into anything with even the tiniest chance of success.

White-fringed gray clouds, scouts of a storm forecast to arrive by nightfall, moved eastward, pushed by the wind. There was an icy crusted hoar frost on the countryside, left by a sudden rise in morning temperature. It spread a surreal veil on the world speeding by. Renee wondered why farmers had started plowing up their old plants before winter. She knew when she was small no one plowed until spring, saving what was left of the season's crops as erosion protection from winter's strong north winds. Some fields even lay fallow year-round now, farmers taking subsidies from the government to not plant. It was another thing she didn't get—there were so many starving people in the world.

With the whine of the tires as her mantra, Renee cruised down the highway, past the remaining red sumac lining the forest's edge looking like flaming sentinels flying by. She hummed the last song she'd heard at the pow wow to quiet her mind. It had been disappointing to discover that the women's drum group wasn't there. After talking with two of the women singers about how they'd gotten spiritual direction from an elder *ikkwe* but resistance from some of the male drum groups, she could see the problems they were up against. A feminist artists group had provided funding for their album released just three months ago, and the women were happy with all the support from the women's community. They were disappointed with the lack of support from parts of the Indian community, though. Men are men are men, Renee thought.

Her mind drifted back to the crimes. *Mr. X., who in hell are you?* Last night she'd really grilled Billy, trying to dislodge something, anything that might be a clue. Mr. X. had done a good job of protecting his identity. There were a few things she'd picked up nonetheless. The guy knew hospitals, what kinds of supplies they had, and generally where they were kept. *You'd have to be some kind of medical person to know about things like OR packs or cooling blankets.* Mr. X. also seemed to know his way around Thunder Lake. The chief's check on the phone number Billy had been given connected it to a phone booth on the corner of Smith and Lake Boulevard. *I wonder about Blank, or his* girlfriend, Renee mused. *The coroner's office is in that town, and Blank never did give a good explanation about what he was doin' at the school parking lot the night of the robbery. Plus, there's that business with him and Peterson near the caves.*

On a whim, Renee took the Thunder Lake exit. Turning right onto Lake Boulevard, her pulse quickened. *This might be the piece of the puzzle the rest are hooked to. I'd love to pin this on Blank and send him up the river.* She passed the park with the statue honoring seven men from the area killed in World War II. Nowhere on the plaque was there mention of the nine Red Earth Ojibwa who had died in the same war. *Goddamn uppity white folks. Even after our vets asked that the names be added they refused.* Renee glared at the statue as she and Mukwa passed by. The beautiful northern red oak in the southeast corner of the park came into view. A hundred feet plus in height with a six-foot diameter was a record for northern Minnesota red oak, and the park had been built around the tree.

Renee remembered coming into this town and Granite Rock as a kid, hearing the hoots and mocking "Hows" from the townspeople, thinking at first that folks were just being friendly. She was five when the first rock followed their hoots. Her drunken father was no help in explaining what had happened. Renny was left to her own tears after catching the rock in her back as she was dragged along the street by her long-striding father. That day, the bus from town to the rez broke down halfway home. They walked until Short Step came by in his old Chevy pick-up, then rode in the box the last few miles, her sore back banging the side the whole way.

Main Street's historical pink granite courthouse sat next to the only Frank Lloyd Wright-designed gas station in the country. With its windswept roof, the station's distinct design attracted even folks who didn't have a clue about its history. The county coroner's office was on the other side of the maple tree-lined boulevard. Dr. Peterson boldly ran a private medical practice next door. *He's been coroner so long he just moved his practice down the street.* Renee scowled. *Smug asshole.*

Sunday afternoon found few people in town. During the week, diagonal parking along the sidewalks filled up early and people parked down the middle of the wide street, one behind the other as if lining up for a parade. Today she found a spot right in front of the bank. The phone booth stood between the bank and Raleigh's Variety Store. Killing the motor, Renee felt the quiet of Sunday afternoon in small-town Minnesota drop over her. Not like Minneapolis, she thought, as she leaned back. Mukwa stretched and stood up on the seat, anxious to get out now that they'd stopped. "You lazy ol' rez dog. About time you woke up." Ren chuckled as the *ahnimoosh* leaned over with a wet kiss.

Renee walked around the bank corner to the grassy boulevard, then sat on the curb. A half hour passed before she stood and walked to the corner. After another ten minutes of nothing happening she sauntered over to the phone booth. Ren lifted the receiver and pretended to make a call in case someone was watching. She studied the booth. Any directories that had been there were long gone. She passed over the usual *BL + JM* hearts, *The Only Good Indian Is A Dead Indian,* and *MJ Sucks Best.* Then, just below the phone on the edge of the shelf, she noticed a number newly scratched into the metal. It was a 415 area code. Ren scratched her head and dialed the number.

"The Hoover Scholastic Institute is closed on Sunday. Dr. Lawrence Toole can be reached Monday through Friday from..."

Renee hung up and tucked the scrap of paper she'd written 415-723-2864 on into her pocket, not confident anything would come of it, but, once again, not wanting to overlook anything. As she drove by the coroner's office she wished she could have seen Blank peeking out from behind the curtain at the front window. Then she warned herself not to get too focused on Blank. Too delicious to even contemplate, the Ojibwa told herself.

Flashes of lightning on the evening horizon grew brighter as Renee headed north. The strangeness of fall lightning returned her to reality, to the natural world. A world of wonder and spontaneity, as the storm sky now demonstrated. Soon, rain mixed with sleet was coming down in sheets and Renee reluctantly rolled up her window. She hated giving up the odors of a rainstorm, the metallic ozone smell mixed with dust and the faint sour smell of damp, dead leaves. Ren continued the last fifty miles to Red Earth past the now-leafless stag horn sumac and speckled alder. "One of our favorite spots in the fall, eh Mukie?" She yawned, stretching the kinks out of her back. As she turned off Highway 7 onto County Road 3, past the *You Are Now Entering Red Earth Reservation* sign, the Spirit's campfires faded on the clearing western horizon and darkness invaded the reservation. Renee felt herself relax. *"Boozho,"* she muttered. "It's good to be home."

14

Aunt Lydia had aged hard. The years criss-crossed her face in irregular patterns and her shoulders sloped with the weight of a life lived surrounded by prejudice. But her walk told another story. She moved with direction, each step showing purpose and determination. Her stride bespoke years of getting from here to there on what were still young legs, and people noticed, as Renee did now, seeing Lydia coming out of Nora's Red Owl late Monday morning.

"Hey, Auntie."

"Hey to you too, my girl. How was the pow wow?"

"Great. Exhausting. Saw Billy Walking Bear."

"That boy's got more troubles than Custer had standin' on that hill." Lydia clucked her tongue. "Ya know, Renny, Billy was a good little boy. Playful, but always helpin' the ol' folks. He wasn't like some of the kids nowadays thinkin' the ol' ways are too hard, that they don't make no sense anymore. Not Billy. His grandfather taught him right. I remember your gramps and his talkin' one day 'bout Billy. Grampy—that's what Billy called him—had big plans for his grandson. Billy was set for his vision quest when his Grampy died. Sent Billy into a tailspin. Jus' too much for the boy. Only eleven, you know, at the time. Sensitive boy, Billy, and he couldn't understand what happened, why Grampy was taken. Blamed Creator."

"Never been in trouble with the law or anything before?"

"Little stuff, I guess, after that. Never satisfied. From then on always wantin' more'n he's got. Makes him one crazy Indian sometimes."

"He was drinkin' a lot in town." Renee leaned against the fender of her jeep.

"Lately. His gramma's been worried. She found him smokin' weed a couple weeks back. Got her hoppin' mad, I'll say."

"Billy's back on the rez and he's got some mean people after him, Auntie. We need a place to hide him." The remark brought a long silence.

"I'll talk to the ladies," Lydia said finally. Renee knew that meant the Elder Circle, and prayed they'd agree to help. Non-Indians would never find Billy in one of the spots where the women held their ceremonies. They looked like any other clump of trees or rise on a hill. The Circle's secrecy came from having to hide ceremonies after the Federals declared them illegal seventy-five years ago. The elders had little enthusiasm for sharing these important ceremonies with outsiders, even today.

Renee walked into Hobey's office an hour later. "Jus' came from talkin' to Aunt Lydia. Think she'll get us a place to hide Billy. How're you?"

"Nerves. Bound up as a rusty tractor. This case's startin' to get to me, Renny. Got the BCA ballistics' report on the pistol though." He handed it to Renee who read:

> The Walthers .9-mm. semiautomatic slide-action pistol recovered and labeled with evidence #2173 is determined to be the murder weapon after test firing and matching the fired bullet with the one recovered at the murder scene. According to the autopsy report the bullet hit the victim straight on between the scapulas and began tumbling in a downward path. As it advanced it nicked the aorta, and after lacerating the liver, exited the body at the lower right quadrant of the abdomen. The fatal bullet was recovered buried in the sand five feet east of the body which was found lying in a north-south position facing east. The cartridge was found fifteen feet to the north. Primary and secondary feed marks matched the rifling and breech characteristics of the recovered .9-mm Walthers. The sample fired bullet duplicated the markings of the fatal bullet recovered at the scene.

Renee held up the report. "Thank the Great Spirit and Walter Leaper's turtles."

"That's the truth. So, now we know that the prelim DNA on the cigarette butt matches Thompson, boot tracks match his, and the skin scraping under Jed's fingernails do come from Thompson. We placed him at Jed's beforehand with the cigarette and his prints on the coffee cup. The blood on the gun's slide action is Thompson's type, and he's got that cut on his left thumb. Josh found his prints on the phone, too." Hobey paused, retrieved a piece of ginger root from his drawer, and popped it in his mouth, chewing slowly. "Sour stomach," he said, responding to Renee's puzzled look before adding, "Think we've got 'em, don't you?"

"I'd say he's our murderer. Let's wake him up and ask him why he did it." Renee laughed.

"Oh yeah. Lawton called D.C. after I talked to him last Thursday. The good ol' boy came through for us. Did it in a friendly manner, too, which surprised me even more."

Within minutes of being brought up to date on the events at Red Earth the previous Thursday, Agent Lawton had made contact with a technician in the FBI's building in Washington, D.C., who in turn fed the information about what tribal artifacts were available for sale into a globe-circling satellite system. A half hour later the phone rang in the chief's office. They discovered buyers of paleo-Indian and Ojibwa artifacts waiting in Japan and Hong Kong. Waiting, apparently, for a phone call from a yet-to-be-identified middle man on the west coast. "I called the number that came off the wire," Hobey explained, "but the place was closed. Place called the Hoover Scholastic Institute."

"The Hoover Scholastic Institute? You've gotta be kiddin'!" Renee let out a self-satisfied squeal. "Well, well, here's somethin' might interest you." She dug through her purse, then dropped the phone number she'd found in the chief's hand. "From the phone booth in Thunder Lake. Didn't think it'd be anything, but it was fairly newly scratched so I wrote it down just in case."

"That Billy's phone booth? OK, I like that. You're right, LaRoche, we're inchin' along here. Maybe I'll call Lawton, see what the ol' boy thinks we should do about this." Hobey spread his arms and shrugged his shoulders in response to Renee's wider-than-usual grin. "Jus' feelin' a little friendlier now," he winked.

"Go for it, Chief."

"Phone for you Renny," Bobbi called from the front office. Renee lifted the receiver on the chief's desk. *"Boozho."*

"Renee?"

"Billy. You OK?" After a few minutes Renee hung up and turned to the chief. "He thinks someone might be watching him. Told him to switch cars. That Pontiac of his is like drivin' somethin' with bells and whistles. If he's sure he's not bein' followed, he'll head for Sucker Creek and wait to hear from us. Hope you don't mind—I gave him the cell phone earlier."

"Sounds like we're making a little progress?" Jesse said, coming into the office. "Finally. I mean, how many times do you get a case where the murderer dies right after in a car wreck? Rubbed out. This is too weird an investigation. It's like smudging out some of the dots from 'Girl on a Swing' and then trying to recreate it."

The other two Ojibwa stared, first at each other and then at Jesse.

"Well, sort of like that. You know, the painting? By Monet?"

The silence was pregnant.

"OK. OK. So it's a stretch. Happened to be looking through my art history books today," Jesse giggled, her embarrassment growing.

Their laughter began as a soft breeze. By the time it circled the group it'd taken on gale force. "Oh, right. 'Girl on a Swing.' Of course, how silly of me. Dot to dot," Renee howled. Tears streamed down her face. Eventually they all slumped in their chairs exhausted. Ren leaned over and gave Jesse a hug. "Thanks, we needed that."

"Uh, Chief? Mrs. Effie's here for your meeting?"

"Oh. Come in, come in, Mrs. Effie. Excuse us." Hobey stood. "Relieving a little tension."

"Good for you. It's healthy to laugh, you know. Everyone should have one good belly laugh a day, keeps your immune system healthy. And, I should add, it causes the release of something called endorphins which improve your short-term memory, your concentration, and your alertness. So, I'm lucky, really. You just finished a good laugh. Now what I tell you will be taken in by very receptive brains." That elicited another hearty laugh from everyone as the gray-headed woman took the seat offered next to Renee.

Renee smiled at Mrs. Effie, pulling the chair up. Elder women, she thought, no matter what color, they feel like your grandma.

"It was important for me to talk to you in person about the gossip going around the hospital," Mrs. Effie began. The silence encouraged her to continue. "At first I paid no attention, but after you were in with that fellow Anderson I couldn't get him out of my mind. Could've sworn I'd seen him before. Later that day, Barb—the assistant head nurse in the emergency room—asked me what he was doing at the hospital again." The Red Earthers in the room exchanged a quizzical look. "That was my response, too," the older woman nodded. "Barb said he'd been in trying to find someone but she couldn't remember who, so I started checking around. You know about Billy's firing and sudden windfall of money? That's one piece of gossip gets everybody stirred up—money. That and sex." Mrs. Effie paused, embarrassed by what she'd just said. Blotches of red began appearing on her neck. "Anyway, when Lou Blank also started throwing money around, of course everyone got curious. Started noticing him more. Several staff told me Anderson had come looking for Lou Blank."

"Lou Blank!" Hobey and Renee reacted simultaneously. Renee said, "I've been wondering more and more about that guy. He's been turnin' up everywhere: at the school, in the ER at the time they brought Thompson in. And the formaldehyde Walter smelled, maybe that was him too. Anybody know what kind of car he drives? And if he has a rifle?"

"No, but we can find out easy enough," Jesse said.

"Any bets that it's some kind of four-wheel drive?" Renee was feeling almost giddy with the dizzying turn of events.

Mrs. Effie stood to leave. "Oh, I almost forgot. Attica faxed the hospital Mr. Thompson's medical records." She held a packet out to the chief. "Nothing much of interest. Curious thing...well, you'll see, Thompson's mother's name was Anderson. All of a sudden all these Scandinavian names here on the rez," the nurse laughed.

Renee smiled at the assimilation of this white grandmother to the Indian way of thinking.

Gram leaned forward and reached for the pipe laying in its red cloth. At the same moment Lydia stood and retrieved tobacco off the mantel, all in silence but with the sureness of a lifetime of repetition. "We've been waiting for you," Gram said. "Come, sit here." She motioned with her lips to the floor on her left. Gram began as Renee sat down. *"Boozho, Gitchie Manitou, aw Ikkwe Ondjishkaosse..."*

After finishing the prayer the elder started telling stories about Anishanabe experiences—crystals revealing messages from the past. Since Creator's breath into the *megis* shell, Anishanabe *ikkwe* knew what the Great Spirit expected from them. They, too, were crystals. Bearers of messages from the past, teachers and healers. The women of the Circle understood their power and took care of it. It was Creator's gift to them; what they did with it, their gift back to Creator. Not even many Red Earthers knew about the Circle. But although few people knew, all benefited from the Circle's prayers.

During her next prayer, Woman Who Walks Against The Wind felt a cold hand on her shoulder holding her back, but Gram willed it away, replacing it with the childhood vision of her mother hiding the leader of the Benay Clan, spirit-keepers of the tribe. "At the beginning of time we organized by studying nature. That's who was in our world, and they were our teachers," the elder continued. "We lived unchanging, like nature, and the traditional ways of ancestors became our ways. No matter how deep archeologists dig they've never found jails, prisons, mental institutions, nursing homes. Until 1492, when everything changed."

Renee settled back. Stories from the elders took a while. She was antsy to get to Billy, but she knew she couldn't rush Gram.

"With the coming of the *chimook* we were told, No, no, you cannot live like this. They forced us to live a different way. But nature continues the old way. We watch the loons, the beavers, still living that thousands-of-years-old way, the way Creator gave them at time's beginning. Trees, plants still live that way. The circle of life—with beginnings, without end. We are working our way back and it is good, but some days I wonder if our biggest enemy isn't ourselves. We will help this young man Billy and pray that through example he will turn his life back to the Red Road. Finding our sacred pipe before it left us was a good sign. *Nojishe*'s dream about the pipe worried me, but the spirits led her to it in time. So now we pray for our young warrior, that we've been led to him in time."

Following the Tobacco Ceremony, Renee spent the next hour with the elders answering questions about Billy and assuring them he wasn't part of Jed's murder. As they were nearing the end of their conversation, Billy called and Renee left. Twenty minutes later, at the confluence of Crooked and Sucker Creeks, Ren pulled her jeep in behind the only car in the dirt turnaround. Billy stepped out of the woods. "Where'dya find that car? Steal it from the Feebees?" she laughed.

He managed a weak smile. Billy looked ragged. His eyes were even more frightened than the last time she saw him.

"I've got supplies and a spot only the spirits and the elders *ikkwe* know about." She glanced hopefully at the young man, wishing she'd see a flicker of lightness in his terrified eyes.

Billy barely nodded.

"OK. Well, follow me." Just before Little Moss Lake at Pine's Row, Renee slowed and turned into the ancient, no longer used, St. Mary's Cemetery. It was dark enough for lights under the canopy, but Ren resisted. She drove around the newer section, pulling up to a gate in the back, the only part of the fence separating the two sections still standing. Behind the gate stood the wooden grave coverings of *midewiwin* members Auntie'd told her to look for. *Midewiwin* houses, built over the graves of the tribe's most sacred order, were three feet high with peaked roofs running the length of the grave. At the west end of each house was a small platform to hold offerings of food to sustain the spirit on its journey to the spirit world. West was the direction of the Path of Souls. None of the graves were marked after all these years, but Red Earthers knew they held the tribe's ancient spiritual leaders. The original markers were intended to last only as long as people's personal memories of the one who died.

Gathering the supplies from Renee's jeep, they started off north-northwest of the last *midewiwin* grave, the trail visible only to someone looking for it. Just across the meadow, Renee stopped. "Auntie said at the woodpecker tree go left, and here it is. See the wood chips here at the bottom? They're making a new nest up there." After following the trail over one rise and across Sucker Creek, Renee found the sugarbush she was looking for. "We're here," she declared, squatting next to a red maple tree and leaning back. Billy seemed almost serene now as he returned Renee's smile. It took Ren a few minutes to locate the eastern white pine Auntie had described. She crawled under and through its long, drooping branches to the other side and, finding the opening she'd been told about, she called to Billy.

Entering the lodge, Ren imagined this must be how dark the Black Hole in the universe was. It had a texture to it. Only when she looked back out the entrance could she see a faint glow of light. The smell of sage, sweetgrass, and cedar permeated everything; it was in every pore of the lodge after decades of ceremonies. She felt the place's sacredness, holding memories of songs and prayers like it was holding orphaned bear cubs in its arms. Billy Walking Bear would be safe here and, shining the flashlight just below his chin, she could see he felt it, too.

After promising to return as soon as she could, Renee walked back to the cars, circling the area first to reassure herself no one had spotted them. Satisfied they'd gone undetected, she moved the brown Chevy down the path behind a thick stand of mixed pine, then brushed the grasses back up to cover the tracks. Looking out over the *midewiwin* grave houses, across the meadow, and into the darkened woods reassured her that anyone walking along would have no idea there was a lodge further back, wrapping its protection around a very frightened young man. She smiled as she remembered the first thing Billy had pulled out of his pack—the eagle feather.

Renee drove to Cedar Street in Granite Rock in a record forty minutes. It wasn't difficult to locate the student housing area in this college town. The structures were small, clapboard, single-family next to double bungalows and duplexes. Unkempt yards, cracked sidewalks, sagging sheds and garages seemed to be the decorative style of choice. Lou Blank's house fit right in. And they accuse us of not caring how we live, she thought, stepping carefully out of her jeep and around a broken beer bottle. She was beginning to feel a sense of urgency. Things were finally moving. If they could maintain the pace and keep the pressure on, it wouldn't be long before they could wrap up this whole mess.

Lou Blank came to the door after several loud knocks, looking like he'd just gotten out of bed. His Granite Rock College athletic shorts and sweatshirt revealed a well-muscled body, something he worked hard at, judging from the array of weights and barbells stacked in a corner of his living room. Reluctantly, he invited Renee in.

The interior of his house had the look of someone outgrowing their surroundings. A mountain bike leaned against the west wall. Racing shoes, gloves, and a helmet lay on the floor under it. Rollerblades and a football occupied the swivel chair Blank offered to Renee. "Have a seat." He nodded, making no move to clean it off. "I'll be a minute. Change my clothes," he added over his shoulder.

Renee glanced at her watch. Four-fifteen. Must be workin' the night shift, she thought. Under several books on the lamp table next to her chair she noticed a file folder. The edge of a newspaper article was sticking out. Renee peered down the hall, then slid the article out: "Archeologists Discover Browns Valley Man Remains." It was the same one she'd found at the library. Renee was standing so still she could feel the blood coursing through the veins in her body.

There was another article underneath the one she had pulled. "Local Excavating Company Uncovers Indian Camp." The body of the Minneapolis newspaper article detailed Anderson & Son Excavation Company's accidental uncovering of Indian campsites a year before, fifteen miles northwest of Minneapolis. The contractor had to go to court to try and obtain the rights to continue the housing subdivision excavation. Following an order from the court to involve both the Minnesota Indian Affairs Council and the University of Minnesota Archeology Department in an investigation of the site, the area was determined to be another camp of the Paleo-Indians of the upper midwest, "An important find since so little is known about this culture now believed to have inhabited this area of the United States up into Canada, as long as ten to twelve thousand years ago." The article went on to report that after a six-month inquiry, the section uncovered was identified as a dugout canoe building area. It ended with a quote from the senior Anderson complaining about how far behind schedule they were: "Why do we care so much for this old Indian stuff? Gives me the willys. Think they'll care two thousand years from now when they dig up one of our parks and find old Coke and beer cans or hot dog wrappers?" Renee memorized the date on the Anderson clipping, gave the rest of the file a quick perusal, then slid it all back into the folder.

Blank came out toweling his hair and sat opposite Renee in the one remaining chair in the room.

"We'd like you to come to the station," she began, her pulse pounding in her temple.

Dr. Peterson's assistant slouched in the chair, legs spread, hands resting on his inner thighs, the kind of unconscious sexual aggressiveness Renee had come to expect from white men. "Well, well. Now Chief How Not To Do It has the local leezbeenn doing his grunt work. I've always wondered, Renee, why a handsome woman like you'd become a muff diver?"

"With you the alternative?" she replied curtly. Renee stood up.

"Chief Bulieau has a few more questions for you about the night you were at the high school."

"Why didn't he just call me up?" Blank responded tersely.

Renee moved toward the door. "You're not an easy guy to find. You want to come with me or drive your own car?"

"I'll meet you there."

"Oh, that's all right. I can wait. I'll follow you." She paused, then offered, "Do you know the cockroach can run at ninety-three miles an hour when it's trying to get away?"

"What the hell does that mean?"

Renee shrugged her shoulders, standing patiently at the front door. She had no intention of losing sight of him now after all the trouble they'd had getting him to cooperate. Hobey hadn't been worried, though. He was certain Blank wouldn't go anywhere, at least without the police hearing rumors beforehand. He figured that by leaving Blank on the loose he might hang himself.

Lou Blank continued to sit like a defiant child. He finally jumped up, grabbed his car keys, and angrily brushed past Renee. "Let's get it over with then," he snarled. Smiling, Renee closed the door behind her. She liked him pissed off. More likely to make mistakes in that frame of mind.

15

Brenda Rogers fidgeted in her chair. "Can I get you something to drink, Brenda?" Bobbi inquired. "The chief should only be another minute."

"No thanks, I'm fine. Do you know why he wants to talk to me?"

The question had barely been asked when Chief Bulieau came into the interrogation room. "Good afternoon, Ms. Rogers. Thanks for coming. I heard your question so I'll get right to it. I'm interested in your relationship with Mr. Lou Blank."

"Oh, OK," the young woman responded perkily. "Well, we're seeing each other. Engaged, actually." She proudly held out her left hand, displaying a larger-than-average diamond ring. "Louie just gave it to me last night."

"Well, congratulations. It's very nice. I hope you don't think I'm being too personal now, Ms. Rogers, but do you and Mr. Blank share a residence?" Embarrassed to ask the question, when the young woman shook her head Hobey quickly moved on. "Can you tell me, has Mr. Blank been unusually busy recently? Working late? Things like that."

"I don't pay that much attention to tell you the truth. We see a lot of each other with work and everything. Louie comes and goes a lot without telling me. He plays a lot of sports. Then, sometimes either me or Lou's working the evening or night shift so we see each other during the day."

"Is he out late at night?" The chief couldn't believe how easy this was. The girl was so forthcoming—apparently Brenda couldn't imagine anyone being otherwise. He felt a little guilty not being more up front with her.

"Sometimes he calls late at night," she shrugged, "after he gets in."

Hobey's smile was polite and friendly. "Known him long?"

"Since the first day I started at the hospital. I was in orientation and we stopped at the morgue. Lou and Dr. Peterson were there doing an autopsy. Then, I saw him later in the cafeteria. He asked me out for a bike ride after work and we've been dating ever since. Three or four nights a week at least, except lately." Her voice trailed off.

"You from around here?"

Brenda shook her head. "My family—three sisters, two brothers—lives in Duluth. Just off North Shore Drive on Woodland Avenue."

"What brings you here, eh, so far from home?"

"Three years ago when I graduated nursing school—St. Scholastica, best nursing school around—" she grinned proudly, "there weren't any hospital jobs in any of the bigger towns on the Range, and I didn't want to go down to the Cities. It was either a nursing home or moving to a smaller place. This seemed interesting, and I'm only two hours from home."

"I guess you know how Mr. Blank feels about us here on the reservation?" Hobey watched the woman carefully.

"Well, yes," she paused, a flush beginning to rise on her neck. "I don't know why. You people seem very nice to me. I've made friends here on Red Earth, and some of you are even Catholics," she added enthusiastically. Hobey smiled inwardly. *Northern racism. It's like uncle's phantom-limb pain: nothing seems to be there, but something hurts like hell.*

The chief offered a friendly smile and continued. "Has Lou been spending a lot of money the last couple of months?"

"Well," she hesitated, looking down at her hands and fidgeting with her ring. "I really shouldn't, but, I guess it'd be OK to tell you. An uncle of his died and left him almost a hundred thousand dollars. He doesn't want anyone to know about it, though. Says everyone'll be after him with ideas on how to spend it."

"No kidding! A hundred thousand dollars. What luck, eh?" Hobey glanced up and saw Renee coming down the hall with Lou

Blank. Stepping to the door he said rather loudly, "Excuse me, Ms. Rogers. I'll be right back."

Blank's head shot up, and he glared at the chief.

"Well, Mr. Blank, finally you grace our doors. How nice of you to drop by," Hobey chided.

"Did I hear you say Brenda's here?" he whispered as Hobey came down the hall.

"Ms. Rogers? Why, yes she is. Right down there."

The coroner's assistant blanched noticeably as Renee directed him into the room adjacent to Brenda's. A room where he could see Brenda but she couldn't see him. Hobey returned to the young nurse. To his question about whether she knew John Anderson, Brenda replied, "I met him a few weeks ago." Then she added, "Mr. Anderson was in a big hurry. He didn't talk to me. Between you and me, Chief Bulieau, I think he's kinda rude, but Louie says he needs him for the antique business they're starting so I'm nice to him." Hobey had a hard time imagining Brenda Rogers being mean to anyone, and after another twenty minutes he was more than satisfied the young naive nurse from Duluth knew nothing of the robbery and murder. He walked her out, smiling to himself at what Blank must be thinking as he watched them.

"Think we've made him wait long enough, Renny?" The chief sat on the edge of Bobbi's desk.

"I'd say so. He's probably in there eating his fingers by now. By the way, know what kind of car Blank drives? A new Ford Ranger, four-wheel drive. With a big old gun rack in the back window, I might add. I knew it, I just knew it." Ren raised both fists in the air. "Made my day when he drove out of his garage." Her eyes snapped and she grinned broadly.

Hobey winked at Renee before opening the door. Then he went into the interrogation room, where he found Blank pacing back and forth. "Sit down, Mr. Blank," he said curtly.

"Why, what's this all—"

"Sit down, Mr. Blank. There, did you hear me that time?" Hobey stood toe to toe with the suspect.

"OK, OK." Blank moved to the chair and, with affected casualness, sat down, propping his feet up on the table. "I'm a busy man, Chief. Let's get to it then. I don't have all night."

"Quit your damn whining and settle in. You're gonna be here a while," the chief said as his foot came up and unceremoniously pushed Blank's off the table. "Show a little respect," he hissed. "First off, Mr. Smartass, someone saw you down by the river the morning of Jed's murder. Why don't you tell us about that."

"Oh, who?"

"Why were you down there, Mr. Blank?"

"OK, OK. I was down there to check on the truck accident, all right. But I wasn't at the river. I was over at the curve where he went off the road."

"You didn't come over the bridge?"

"I took the shortcut over by the lake." The sweat was beginning to soak Lou Blank's shirt. They had been at it for the better part of an hour and the room was not designed for comfort. A fluorescent ceiling light hummed like an insect. Something the experts would probably call a subliminal irritant. The chairs around the gun-metal gray table were the metal folding type, stiff and unfriendly. Gray-blue walls that began to feel oppressively close after about twenty minutes and, with the weather this time of year changing almost hourly from warm to cool, the room was never the right temperature. Today it was unusually hot. Renee and Hobey had planned their strategy well and it was starting to pay off. "I'll do the talkin', Renny. You observe the guy closely. I'd guess he's damn slippery when cornered and you're good with all that body language stuff. I'll find some reason to stop after about an hour so then we can talk," Hobey had instructed. Now, taking that break, they were smiling broadly at the state of their suspect. It was an adrenaline-pumping experience. Renee was surprised at how much she liked cornering this guy.

"You've got him on the ropes, Chief. No doubt he's involved. He flinched when you mentioned Billy Walking Bear, and I thought he'd lose his lunch when you dropped John Anderson's name. He's really not a very good liar, not nearly as cagey as he wants us to believe. I don't think he's Mr. X., Chief. Not near smart enough. But I'll bet he knows who the guy is, even though I doubt he'll give him up. Should we cut Blank loose and follow him? If we can shake him up enough, he might lead us to the head man."

"He was pretty defensive when you mentioned his gun rack and where all the guns were," Hobey said. "Let's work on that a little more. Then I'll tell him we're close to tracking down Mr. X. Give him a chance to roll over. If he doesn't, we'll give him a little rope." The chief shrugged. "Hopefully just enough to lead us to the big guy, assuming he knows who he is. Remember, Renny, the first rule in interrogatin' is to make the prisoner think you know everything. Even when you don't."

"Got it." Renee grinned.

Back with the suspect, the chief began, "So, Lou, I'm not gonna mess around anymore. I think it's about time we read you your rights."

"Read me my rights? What the hell you talkin' about? For what?"

"How about attempted murder and robbery for starters." Hobey leaned over and glared at Blank, whose hostile expression was fast becoming one of panic. Renee could see his left eye twitching from across the table.

"I don't know what you're talking about." Blank's words tumbled out, tripping over each other.

"Yes, Mr. Blank, you do." Chief Bulieau paused, then proceeded to read the coroner's assistant his rights. Blank sat slack-mouthed. What color he did have drained down into his yuppie socks. Renee had a fleeting moment of pity for the guy.

"Now, wait...wait just a minute," he stuttered.

"No, you wait. We've been wastin' our time with you this last hour. You haven't made one honest statement since you came in the door. So here's the deal, wise guy. I want you to tell me about the rifles you usually carry around in your truck and when you fired them last. And depending on your answer, I'll reconsider my attitude toward you." The chief offered a fleeting smile, enticement of happier times if Blank cooperated.

Silence filled the space before Blank finally said quietly, "I had a 30/06, but my brother took it a couple days ago. He went hunting in Montana. Left yesterday."

Hobey ceremoniously picked up his pen and began writing. "Don't want to miss any of this...bullshit," he snarled, glaring at the suspect. He stood and stormed out. Renee looked pityingly at Blank, spread her hands as if she was offering a blessing, and shrugged before following the chief.

"Let's let 'em go," Hobey sighed, "and we'll stick to him like a June beetle on a screen door till he gives us something."

Renee nodded.

Lou Blank's nervous system was rapidly changing to that of an amoeba. He sat staring at the empty wall, barely responding when the two Ojibwa returned to the room. The chief told him he could go as long as he did not leave Chippewa County, but Blank continued to sit immobilized. Several minutes later, some synapse having occurred, the coroner's assistant got up, glanced at the two Red Earthers, and shuffled through the door.

Twenty-five minutes after Blank walked out of the building Hobey and Renee, in separate cars, sat waiting for him to leave the parking lot. At first Ren thought the guy wasn't going to budge: he sat slouched over the steering wheel for so long. Then he appeared to pull himself together. She could see him use his cell phone to make a call, then slowly move out onto Anishanabe Circle. He sat, once again motionless, at the stop sign at County Road 3 for what seemed like an eternity. Renee wondered if he'd lost consciousness, but finally he rolled forward, turned left, and headed in the direction of Rice Lake. Hobey pulled out, and Renee took up the rear in the Toyota Samantha'd been generous enough to leave at the station on her way out of town with Jenny's field trip to Bemidji.

The coroner's assistant drove slowly through Rice Lake. Hobey suddenly turned into the angle parking in front of the post office. Renee followed. A minute later, Blank drove by, having made a U-turn at the end of town. The two Ojibwa pulled out and the tandem continued. Blank made three more turns before heading back out County Road 3 toward Highway 7. He obviously had enough wits about him to try and avoid being followed. Renee only hoped they hadn't been spotted. There weren't many cars on the road, and the Red Earth police weren't called upon to put tails on many suspects. They had to hope for the best. Maybe Blank would only lose one of them.

There were two cars between her and Hobey, and one between the chief and Blank about a mile out County 3. Suddenly, a pair of bright lights appeared in Renee's rearview mirror, approaching rapidly, then swung out and roared by without a sideways glance. The high-rider truck wedged its way in behind the chief, and an alarm went off in Renee's head. It wasn't because of the wildness of the driver: reservation cowboys often drove crazy on this stretch. It was the glimpse she'd caught of the guy's face as he flew by. Even in the near-darkness with a cap pulled down over his eyes, she could see the determined set of the *chimook*'s jaw. It was just enough to raise the hair on the back of Renee's neck.

The truck began ramming the back of Hobey's Ford Escort almost immediately. The crunch of metal hung in the air over the wetlands. When the two vehicles between Renee and the truck turned off, Renee killed her lights and slowed down. With the next crunch Hobey's car fishtailed fifty yards. He'd barely recovered control when another battering jolted him. Renee could see the chief struggling with the wheel. He pulled it sharply to the right just as the truck hit him for the fifth time. Hobey's correction was too much, and the Escort swerved, plummeting into the swampy wetlands off the right side of County 3. The truck slowed momentarily, then thundered off, careening wildly into the now-darkened countryside. Renee stopped and jumped from her car, noticing at the same time the truck brake a couple hundred yards up the road. Hobey had banged open his door and was standing up to his knees in water and wetland grasses. "I'm OK. Don't lose him," he called. "I'll get Harry to pull me outta here."

"You sure?"

"I'm sure. Lookit, down the road. Whoever that was he's a friend of Blank's. That's gotta be them up there. Get his plates and call me. But don't lose Blank, this is our best chance, Renny. Keep in touch."

"The truck's plates are Minnesota 531 AEF. I'll call in where I am."

Renee hurried back to her car. She waited until the two up ahead started off again, then set a comfortable pace behind the double sets of taillights. Her headlights were still off. She thanked the Great Spirit that she knew this road so well. At Highway 7 the truck turned left. Renee called his direction in to the chief before she turned right, hit her lights, and followed Blank at about fifty yards down the Yellow Brick Road. Thirty minutes later Blank took the Thunder Lake exit with Renee behind him. She pulled off Lake Boulevard on to Squaw Lake Road and watched Blank turn into the county coroner's drive. He stopped, and then disappeared behind the electronic garage door.

16

Billy Walking Bear emerged into a dark and chilly forest, leaning against the giant oak tree on the edge of the clearing. Browsing deer rustled the dry leaves, the sound carrying far in the still night air. The spirits' campfires filtered in through the trees, barely penetrating the dense growth around Billy. A few crickets not yet ready to give in to the changing season welcomed the young man.

Ancestors' land stretched in all directions. It was full of memories and meanings, some of which Billy knew, some forgotten by the People, and some that only the highest order of *midewiwin* members passed down amongst themselves. Off to the west Billy thought he could see what was, no doubt, the last rainstorm of the year. A bank of gray was moving toward him as though someone was slowly pulling a giant blanket over the sky. Then he heard another rustling. Turning only his eyes, Billy saw the elusive, secretive timber wolf, once a fairly common sight in northern Minnesota, now seen only by the spirits and those two-leggeds communing with them. As Billy watched, the wolf caught his smell and dropped into his aggressive stance, the hair on his back and tail standing straight up. Their eyes met. Billy whispered, *"Boozho,"* and averted his gaze quickly so the wolf wouldn't think he was issuing a challenge. The *maingan* paused. Just before he loped off Billy glanced up to see him lay the hair on his back and tail down. The young man grinned broadly.

Billy didn't like to dwell on his part in the crimes he was now in hiding because of. The shame was too much. He did think a lot lately, though, about his place in the universe. He'd let his life spin out of control and now he was up to his eyeballs in shit. His own, mostly, and Janice's, but he couldn't get mad at her. Even after she got pregnant when she'd promised she was on the pill. Oh well, he thought, I promised to stop smokin' weed, too, so... He stretched. Trying to say evening prayers after so long was harder than he thought it would be. The too-familiar stomach cramps and sweats were starting. He needed the prayers now more than ever if he was gonna stick to his commitment to Janice: a new beginning off the booze and weed. "I'm sick of our life, Janny," he whispered to the approaching night. "We've been lickin' broken glass and we're runnin' outta luck." Billy walked out to the clearing, praying as he went. He stood for a time watching the mist settle on the meadow.

Finishing all the prayers he could manage for one day, the young Ojibwa turned back. He knew he was being tested, tested like he'd been when his Grampy died. This was not a human test. This was straight from the spirit world. From the ancestors. And what was at risk was the worst kind of loss to a traditional Ahnishanabe—loss of respect and identity as a Red Earther, the ultimate in banishment. Billy fought off the shame and fear that threatened to consume him and lead him straight back to the bottle. It wouldn't do any good now. Making it right, clearing up the mess he'd helped create, that's what it would take. His last prayer was that he'd be up to it.

"I hope Renee doesn't leave me here too long," he mumbled, banging his head on a pine limb on his way into the lodge. "This alone thing is goddamned hard." Billy dreamed he was on his vision quest that night, with Grampy waiting at the support camp.

Luckily it didn't take Josh long to get to Renee's stakeout spot on Squaw Lake Road, the side street adjacent to the coroner's office. "Got a clear view of the front door and garage entrance, Josh," she reported. "Blank's in there, but I don't know if Peterson is. The chief and I'll be back soon's he gets the search warrant," she called as she started to drive off. "If Blank leaves, Hobey said to follow him and call in, OK? He should be back on line shortly in the squad car."

The chief decided on a search warrant of the coroner's office after Blank led Renee there. Blank's attempt to throw them off his trail, including his accomplice's ramming of Hobey's car, as well as his be-havior during interrogation, made the chief believe it was time to move in. Showing their hand with the search warrant was, he knew, a gamble. He still didn't have the kingpin. But Billy's cooperation and Blank's beginning to show his hand gave Hobey enough to take the risk.

The call came just after Renee got back to the tribal police station. With orange juice and a doughnut in her hands she had to clear a spot on the desk before she could pick up the phone. Things were moving so fast she almost didn't answer. She wanted to be ready when Hobey arrived to head back to Thunder Lake and relieve Josh.

"Shall I begin?" The young male voice on the other end sounded irritated.

"Ah, begin? Excuse—"

"You called, right?"

"Yeah. OK. Sorry, things are kinda hectic. Who is this?"

"I'm calling from FBI headquarters. Responding to request number 73424 from the Red Earth Reservation," the voice said irritably, "dated November 8. We have the following information on what's called the Hoover Scholarly Institute. They are a conservative think tank, self-described as the "institute that sets the political agenda rather than responds to it." Their yearly budget is $18 million, with 98 resident scholars, 25 miles of climate-controlled archive storage shelves, and 1.6 million books."

Renee listened intently. Apparently the chief had made the call to Lawton to check up on the Institute. "Located on the Stanford University campus," the man continued, "they have been at odds with the university administration of late. Stanford has been returning Native American artifacts to the appropriate tribes, and the Hoover Institute is vehemently opposed to the practice because it is very lengthy and not cost-effective. Dr. Lawrence Toole, resident scholar, wrote a paper opposed to the Smithsonian Institution's announced plan to build a new museum on the Mall in Washington, D.C. devoted exclusively to America's Indians. Apparently he opposes all of these types of things. His article was quite pointed, saying the Smithsonian's plan was "ill-advised sloppy sentimentalism toward Indian tribes' insatiable appetites for trinkets from their past." Dr. Lawrence Toole oversees the intern program that conducts everything from weekend intensives to year-long study programs graduating Institute Diplomats. He's also an authority on the social and political structures of pre-Columbus America. Bureau sources describe Dr. Toole as arrogant and self-serving. For a long time now there have been suspicions about his trafficking in illegally gotten artifacts, but operatives have been unable to gather enough evidence to indict him." The anonymous voice paused.

"You're kidding!" Renee exclaimed excitedly.

"No, ma'am. We don't kid," came the solemn reply.

"No, s'pose not. OK, well, is that it then?" Renee queried. She had a feeling the person connected to the voice might be new. He was giving her much more information than the Feds usually divulged without a lot of prodding. "Anything else you've got would really help us. You guys are the experts, you know," she added, massaging his ego a little.

"Well, I guess. OK. There's three phone calls in the last three months from a number in Rice Lake, four from Thunder Lake, and...wait, six from another number in Thunder Lake." Ren quickly took down the numbers. The first one she recognized as Jed's office, and the last six were from the pay phone. The most recent call to Dr. Toole was earlier that night at 6:04 P.M. from the one number she didn't recognize.

"How long was the last call?"

"Twenty-seven seconds."

"Paid by?"

"The number in Thunder Lake."

"You'll fax us a report, eh?"

"That would be protocol, yes, ma'am."

"OK. Anything else?"

"I had ham and cheese for an early lunch. Haven't eaten since and it's almost nine o'clock."

"Hah. Well, well, Mr. FBI. Very good. Didn't think you guys had a sense of humor. *Meg*...thanks a—" The phone went dead. Renee stood looking at the receiver, shook her head, then dialed the one unfamiliar number.

"You have reached the Chippewa County Coroner's Office. Our hours are 8:00 A.M. to 5:00 P.M. Monday through Friday. If this is an emergency, call Thunder Lake Memorial Hospital at—" Ren hung up and sat down all in one motion. She heard herself suck in a breath. "Holy shit. Where's Hobey? We gotta get over there."

Renee called and caught the chief just as he was leaving the judge's house. She arranged to meet him in Thunder Lake instead of at the station. Heading out County 3 she prayed that the events about to unfold would fall their way, offering as many bargains to Creator as she could think of. Thirty minutes later she careened off Highway 7 on to Lake Boulevard, cutting her lights just before she turned left on Squaw Lake Boulevard and pulled in behind the squad car.

Hobey was waiting where she had left Josh.

"What in almighty hell, LaRoche. You musta drove like a bat outta *chimook* heaven. I just got here myself."

"Jeez, Chief. What were ya doin', takin' a Sunday drive? You had a twenty-mile head start on me."

"Tryin' not to kill myself, I guess," Hobey laughed. "So, what ya got?"

"Where's Josh?"

"Well, Josh was just bringin' me up to speed when the garage door went up and Blank drove out, headin' for seven. Josh's following him, seeing what he's up to, then he's gonna pick him up."

Renee nodded.

"Josh said Peterson's in his office so I guess this warrant's either gonna get us what we need on Blank, on Mr. X., or...." The chief spread his arms questioningly. "Whadya got?"

Renee briefed Chief Bulieau on the phone call from the FBI, finishing with the information that someone in the coroner's office was making phone calls to Toole and the Hoover Scholastic Institute. "Do you think that means Peterson's involved, or that Blank's been usin' the office as a front?"

"Chrissake, I don't know, Renee," Hobey mumbled. "This case is so weird, we'll probably find out that it's Peterson's wife behind it all."

"You know, I can't imagine Blank's smart enough to pull this off himself," Renee began, "and we know how much Peterson hates us, but he doesn't have the guts to do this. Does he?"

Hobey shrugged. "Well, let's go have a chat with the good doctor and see. I bet if we ask him, he'll tell us, eh?" Hobey winked, then grinned. "You ready?"

"It'll be my pleasure," Renee exclaimed. The sharp wind swirled in dervishes down the boulevard, raising up the trash of the day. "By the feel of this wind Billy's gonna be happy to see us tomorrow. I hope this really is the end of it," she called to Hobey. They drew up at the front door, each taking a deep breath. The chief was surprised to find the door unlocked. "Think he's waiting for someone?" he whispered. "Maybe Blank's supposed to be comin' back. Won't he be surprised when his assistant shows up cuffed to Josh." Once inside the waiting room Hobey called Dr. Peterson's name.

The inner door opened. "You made it back fast, John. Let's get going, we don't have much time. I tried to call—" Peterson stopped abruptly as he was coming through the door, shrugging into his jacket. "What in hell are you two doing here?"

"Dr. Peterson. Sorry to disappoint you. John's not here, but we'd like to ask you a few questions," Hobey said, using his most official voice.

Peterson pursed his pinched mouth even smaller. "An outside image of the guy's heart," Lydia would say. Renee smiled at the thought, studying the doctor's face.

"Questions? About what?" Peterson responded icily, with a voice croaking after too many years of two-pack-a-day smoking.

Another example of what a fool he is, Renee thought.

"For starters, the autopsy." The chief scowled.

"The autopsy? What about it? You got the report."

"We got it. This is just to fill in some holes." Hobey had decided to start with the autopsy because it wasn't really what he was after. Peterson's report, while at odds with a few things the BCA told him, as well as his own observations—like the time of death—was complete enough. The questions were a diversion.

"All right. Come in, but make it quick. I'm a busy man." Renee chuckled at Peterson's irritation. Right on schedule, she thought.

Once in the coroner's inner office the chief said, "You don't mind if we tape this, eh? Routine. Do it all the time." He was speaking to Peterson's back as the doctor stood impatiently looking out the window.

"Couldn't care less," he responded with his typical cockiness.

Too cool. Ren studied him. *He thinks he's talking to a couple of dumb Indians.* She smiled. *Good. That means he may let his guard down.*

Hobey, operating on his cardinal rule for interrogating suspects, began his questioning by pointing out the coroner's errors on the autopsy: time of death at 6:30 rather than 8:30 A.M., the debris under Jed's fingernails was human skin rather than random environmental. "Oh, and by the way, if you'd checked Thompson's left hand, you'd have noticed an injury on his thumb—consistent with an injury from firing a slide-action pistol." A flicker of emotion ran across the doctor's face, too quickly for Renee to get a read on it. Hobey moved on to questions about who'd handled the body, how much Peterson himself had done. Suddenly, he asked, "Is it true that a few weeks ago you told one of the hospital staff that Indians didn't deserve to keep their artifacts because they'd just rebury them and what good would that do?" A piece of gossip from Mrs. Effie he'd been saving for just such a moment as this.

With that question the sharpness faded from Peterson's pale blue eyes as if he'd pulled the shade. "That's an inquiry about the autopsy?" he spit out angrily. "What's going on here?"

Renee was chilled by the steeliness of his voice. She felt like she was in the presence of evil.

"Very good, Peterson. Very good. You're paying attention. You are absolutely right, that is not a question about the autopsy," Hobey replied.

Renee watched the chief with deep respect. Nothing Peterson was doing or saying was shaking him. "Since you're having some trouble answering questions, why don't you sit down and relax and let us tell you a story," the chief continued. To Renee's surprise, Peterson allowed the chief to direct him to the leather couch against the wall.

"Let's start with Billy Walking Bear, eh?" Hobey drew in a breath as Peterson glared at him. He'd been observing the man closely, and his growing discomfort reminded the chief of the look on Peterson's face at the river when Hobey had suggested maybe the doctor was the one that killed Jed Morrisseau. He also felt an increasing suspicion of Peterson's mistake on the time of death. Two hours off on a relatively simple calculation now seemed a little more than carelessness to Hobey. As did the doctor's failure to mention the injury to Thompson's thumb and his statement that Jed's fingernail scrapings were nothing more than environmental debris. Peterson always played it fast and loose with reservation investigations, but what if these mistakes were deliberate? And what about his bizarre sighting at the caves on Halloween? The chief had quickly dismissed Peterson's statement to Father Murphy that he and Blank were just out driving around after a long, hard day at the hospital. He knew Peterson hadn't been at the Red Earth Hospital that day.

The chief made a quick decision to play it like Peterson was Mr. X. Couldn't hurt. If he wasn't, they could still go for Blank or whomever. He turned angrily to face the doctor, his heart pounding.

"Billy Walking Bear. Yes sir, you pick your wounded prey well, don't you, doctor?" The chief's voice hardened. "It was easy for you to con young Billy and get him to steal for you from the hospital. I suppose after that first time blackmail was a strong motivator for the boy. All Jed had to do was threaten that he'd lose his job and Billy did exactly what he was told. Except for the caves. Even your threats and filthy money wouldn't get him to do that. Is that why you were there on Halloween? To supervise the cleaning out of the caves? You didn't figure that Billy'd get caught though, eh? Then fired and, of all things, develop a conscience?"

Hobey's taking the offensive was having an effect. The coroner's anger was clamped to his thin lips, and as the chief talked, the line disappeared completely. Peterson was beginning to get rattled.

Renee scanned the room. Peterson's walls boasted his position in the community. Plaques honoring him from the Rotary, Jaycees, Masons—a WASP in good standing. He obviously cast a long shadow in the white community of Chippewa County. Only one small photograph of his children and wife sat on his desk, but around the room Peterson egotistically displayed pictures of himself in the act of destroying various other living things: walleye, deer, bear. One even showed him big game hunting out west, though Renee knew that Big Game Lodge—where it said the picture was taken—catered to hunters who liked the comfort of cushioned four-wheel-drive vehicles while shooting game through the window. Much like the early days when white hunters from back East rode across the plains in trains hunting buffalo. There were magazines and catalogs on the bookshelf: the *Encyclopedia of Revenge: How To Do Anything To Anybody* and several military/police mail order catalogs. Opening one of these, the *Survivalist*, she read the letter to customers from the company's president. His final words were: "In purchasing from us we are required by law to ask you to promise not to break any laws with any of your purchases. We are certain your only interest is to protect your family and property." The catalog advertised pepper guns, ballistic mace, riot-buster smoke grenades, pipe bomb kits, homemade fragmentation devices, and survivalist clothes, books, and videos. *Some way to protect your family.* Renee scowled, dropping it back on the shelf as if it had suddenly caught fire.

Peterson's eyes were bulging. His face burst into a rainbow of reds and purples. As he rubbed his thumb and forefinger together in a nervous reflex, the doctor's voice sliced through Ren's distraction. "You have no proof of what you're saying. Now get out of here before I call the sheriff and have you arrested for harassment." He glared from one to the other through watery, vacant eyes.

"Ah, but now you see, you've jumped to a conclusion here," Hobey offered sarcastically. "You've left a trail clearer than a sand crab. We do have proof. Let me ask you about a colleague of yours." The chief paused, picking up a brochure he'd noticed earlier off the eight-foot oak desk. "Here, at the Hoover Scholastic Institute. Dr. Lawrence Toole, I believe his name is?"

The feral smirk slowly evaporated from the doctor's face. "He's not a colleague of mine. I got that brochure in the mail."

"Doctor, how can you fix your lips around a statement like that?" Renee asked.

"Show me your proof," Peterson yelled in reply. "If you were so goddamned sure, we wouldn't be standing here. You'd have already arrested me. You're a couple of hicks playing cops and robbers. Tryin' to make a name for yourselves by accusing a respected member of the community. Well, it's not gonna work. I'm not as stupid as you'd hoped." The pollution off his words filled the air, making it hard for Renee to breathe.

He hates having to answer to us for anything, Renee thought, enjoying every minute of the interaction. She had picked up on the chief's direction of questioning with Peterson right away and had offered a silent prayer that it would lead somewhere. It seemed that Hobey was on to something very big.

"Maybe, Dr. Peterson, you should call the sheriff," Renee heard the chief say. "It'll save me havin' to do it. Meantime, we'll just wait here for your friend—John did you say?—to show up. You know, the one you thought we were when we came in?" Hobey sat down behind Peterson's desk.

Just then the phone rang and the coroner jumped. The chief stood. "Go ahead and get it, doctor. We'll give you some privacy." He motioned to Renee, and the two Red Earthers left the office, closing the door behind them. Renee went straight to the phone and lifted the receiver on the receptionist's desk, holding down the button while she unscrewed the mouthpiece.

"Jesus Christ, listen to me. I'm tellin' you they're on to it," she heard Peterson whisper.

"Don't blow it, Peterson. They've got to be bluffing. Two hicks from Red Earth couldn't know anything. We've been too careful—haven't you?" he added in a menacing tone.

"Yes, yes, of course. I'm sure, except for Blank. He was here earlier tonight in a panic because they interrogated him for a couple hours. Claims he didn't give them anything, but why are they here now then? And, they've hidden the Indian kid somewhere. That's why I was trying to call you earlier."

"Find him and shut him up."

"We've been looking. No luck, but don't worry, John found his car today. We'll find him."

"We've got to cover the paper trail. Just in case they get lucky and trace sales out here."

"I don't know, I think it may be too late. I'll call you back so stay by the phone. I might need one of your connections to take a little trip. I better go. You know those Indians, limited attention spans." Peterson gave a short laugh.

"You listen to me, Peterson. This will not go over well either here or on the other coast. You swore you could pull this off. If you can't you won't be welcome here and, I must say, you'll need protection for your own life. There'll be no tickets available for you."

Peterson sucked in his breath before answering, "Yeah. OK, OK. I hear you."

The caller hung up without further comment.

Renee replaced the receiver and turned to Hobey, eyes snapping. "Got him." She could barely control her excitement. "Didn't say who he was talkin' to, but I'm sure it was Toole—threatened him if things fell apart," she whispered. "He's off the phone."

Hobey nodded, opening the front door as Josh and a handcuffed Lou Blank came up the walk. "Jesse picked up John Anderson about ten minutes ago. He was driving the truck," Josh said. "She's taking him in."

The chief smiled, knocking on the inner door. "All done?" he asked. The entire group reentered the doctor's office.

"If it's any business of yours." Peterson spit the words out before he noticed Blank. "Lou, what in hell are you doing here?" He gaped at the handcuffs. Blank continued to stare intently at the design in the carpet as Peterson came around the desk to stand within an intimidating foot of his assistant.

Hobey backed Blank up, guiding him by his handcuffed hands to a chair. "Oh, and by the way, Dr. Peterson, John Anderson won't be coming by tonight. He's been arrested for attempted vehicular homicide and reckless endangerment. Tomorrow we'll add to those charges."

Peterson's head jerked up from Blank and glowered at the chief.

"Now, Dr. Peterson, let me finish telling you what else we've learned about your little group. Or should I call you Mr. X.? Your main contact for selling what you steal is Dr. Lawrence Toole at the Hoover Scholastic Institute on the Stanford University campus in Palo Alto, California. You have buyers waiting for what we found at Jed's place in Hong Kong and Japan." Hobey's pause was short for Ojibwa. For white folks it was way beyond their comfort zone, and both Peterson and Blank began to fidget.

The tribal police knew they had to get Peterson to go with them voluntarily or they'd have to enlist the help of the county sheriff's office. That was not something Hobey wanted to get into at this time of night. He continued. "Mr. Blank here's been very helpful." He winked at the coroner's assistant and proceeded to outline a plan to transport the stolen goods. It was not anything Blank had told them, but he wanted Peterson to think it was his assistant who'd given it up.

"Yes," Renee interjected, getting into the swing of things, "I bet Dr. Lawrence Toole is not going to be a happy camper when he's visited later tonight." She was a little ashamed at how good it felt to stick the knife in Peterson and twist it.

Peterson came up into Blank's face and stared at him. It was fascinating to observe the nonverbal interaction between the two. Renee could see Peterson's philosophy at work: humiliate someone long enough and self-doubt creeps in and sits on their heart like an incurable infection. It obviously had worked on his assistant.

"Boss, now wait a second, I—"

"Mr. Blank, if I were you I wouldn't say any more." Ren interrupted the man before he could contradict Hobey's story. "Right now you're on our good side, but..." She shrugged her shoulders.

Muttering, Peterson turned on his heels and strode to the window. "I don't know why this Toole's name keeps coming up. I don't have anything to do with the guy. Never heard of him, though I'm sure I'd rather have a conversation with him than with any of you people."

"I think your phone records will show an interesting list of conversations you've had with the good doctor—doctor," Renee said with a great deal of satisfaction.

Peterson turned and fixed his gaze on Renee, his face taking on a horrified expression. He stood for a long time looking from one to the other in the room. Renee watched his jaw slacken, his eyes empty of emotion. He walked from the window to his desk. She heard the sound of a drawer opening, then a moan like a wounded animal. In a single motion, Dr. Peterson took a revolver from his desk, stuck the barrel in his mouth, and pulled the trigger.

The sharp smell of gunsmoke followed quickly on the sound from the .38 caliber pistol. The coppery odor of warm blood flooded Renee's nostrils as she stared into the face of a man who'd rather die swiftly and violently now, at his own hand, than suffer the humiliation of losing his reputation and respect slowly in the courtroom. His eyes held a look of shock, with just a hint of regret. Dreams of outrageous wealth gone in a millisecond. Eyelids fluttering as pain washed over him, he convulsed in an almost poetic wave starting at his shoulders, moving through his abdomen and circling his hips, slipping down his thighs and over his knees, until he rolled up on his toes and took a final bow. All life had drained from his eyes by the time the slow motion pirouette ended with Peterson's body crumpled on the floor. With a silencer on the barrel, the shot sounded like a snapped rubber band, but the consequences had been deadly: what had been the back of the doctor's head was spattered over the English fern growing so elegantly next to his desk.

Everyone in the room stared in horrified silence. Renee and Josh rushed to Peterson's side, checking for life they both knew had flown out the back of his head along with part of his brain. The chief was trying to calm Blank, who was writhing on the floor hysterically, tearing up his wrists with the handcuffs. Renee could barely hear the 911 operator as she tried to direct the paramedics to the scene.

In his out-of-body state, Blank began to babble, as though his co-conspirator had been murdered by some outside force that was going to get him too if he didn't confess, and do so immediately. And his first admission was that he had been the one who took the shot at the chief by the river. "I was just tryin' to scare you. I never would have killed you," he mumbled.

An article Renee had read recently flashed in her mind. It was about prosecution not being the only thing you had to fear if you were a thief of Indian artifacts. The article reported a curse by the ancient ones put on those who stole from them. It talked about a man who signed his letter "Sleepless In Tulsa," describing his life as "the pits" since he dug a stone out of the ruins of Mesa Verde National Park. "Nothing but bad things have happened to me, my family, and my dog, ever since. I have to return it," he wrote. He'd told his story, he said, to a Pawnee Indian who warned him it was the revenge of the Anasazis, the cliff dwellers who inhabited Mesa Verde one thousand years ago. "He told me to return the rock because a spirit is attached to it," the man wrote. The article went on to quote a park official: "Every year a dozen or so people who've stolen bits of flint or chunks of stone send them back apologizing and telling tales of woe."

Renee believed she was seeing firsthand what it meant to make the spirits angry. The coroner's assistant stared at Peterson like he was watching his world shrink before his eyes. He couldn't breathe—all his dreams of riches were choking him. Blank dropped to his knees and began retching. Embracing himself, the young man rocked back and forth, moaning, "Oh God, it's all done. It's over, it's over, it's over."

After the removal of Peterson's body Josh left with Blank, still mumbling "it's over," for jail. Unfortunately for Peterson's accomplices, the suicide opened his office to broader inspection than the search warrant the chief had obtained allowed, and Hobey and Renee wanted to cover as much ground as possible before the county sheriff's office showed up.

"Here's something interesting," Renee said, pulling a piece of paper from a file folder on Peterson's desk. "It's an article on the downfall of communism by none other than Dr. Lawrence Toole. This guy sounds like a real piece of work. Him and his think tank. I wonder how they'll take to the publicity he's about to generate?" She smiled broadly. Halfway through her comment the door opened and in stormed the Chippewa County Sheriff's Department. "There goes our peace and quiet," Ren murmured.

Leaving Hobey to explain to the deputies why they weren't called earlier, Ren proceeded methodically through Peterson's office. She found a file containing newspaper articles about various excavations around the country. Another file held articles on the discovery of the Browns Valley Man area west of Red Earth: a local article from the *Thunder Lake Bulletin* and one from the Minneapolis paper on the discovery of the Red Earth caves. Both of these quoted Gram and Renee.

The deputies joined the search of the office, and in the bottom drawer of the desk one of them retrieved a rubber mask of Custer. "Musta been tryin' to revenge the ole guy, huh?"

The deputies' laugh was cut short by Renee's response. "Had about as much success, too, eh?"

Her sharp retort hung in the air, then seemed to break the ice for the four people from such different worlds. The rest of the evening continued in a much lighter vein, and as time went on they discovered there were things they had in common. Halfway through their investigation of the office, one of the deputies went out for Cokes and pizza. The irony of Indians and *chimooks* coming to understand and even to like each other a little better in Peterson's office was not lost on either the Ojibwa woman or the others. It turned out that Deputy Ewald was dating a Red Earther and had just received a belt buckle from her, made by Renee, for his birthday.

Earlier in the evening, Renee had noticed an Eagle kachina sitting on a wall shelf. There was something about the beautiful piece that seemed damaged, the right leg bent at an unusual angle at the ankle. On inspection she found the kachina lifted off the base, leaving the right foot attached. The leg had been hollowed and inside she found two pieces of paper rolled tightly together. On the first was a list of Indian artifacts: a Cheyenne lance, umbilical fetishes, leather beaded bags sewn as turtles and lizards, Navajo rain sticks, Tlinget prayer sticks. Beside each item were two prices under the headings BOUGHT and SOLD. *So they do buy some of the things, eh? But they're still selling them illegally because I'm sure these are museum pieces.* The second sheet listed only one item, including its description: a Zuni clown kachina mask with its black-and-white stripes, beaked nose, and tuft of corn silk hair. It listed the buyer as a Professor Arlene Baxter, but there was no address or phone number. She remembered the article in the *People's Circle* about the Zuni recovery, and that the only item not returned was a kachina mask believed to date back to the 1500s. Renee placed the kachina and notes in an evidence bag with a notation about the *Circle* article. She included a comment that she would contact Agent Lawton regarding the mask's possible whereabouts.

The last thing they found before leaving Peterson's office was a telegram dated October 29: ARRIVE MINNEAPOLIS 12:15PM TODAY. STOP. LEAVING IMMEDIATELY FOR YOUR AREA. STOP. ANDERSON'S TRUCK. STOP. MEET AT THE FISHING HOLE GRANITE ROCK 7PM AS YOU INSTRUCT. STOP. The telegram was addressed to Lou Blank. It was from Peter Thompson.

17

"Dr. Begay? *Megwetch* for calling back. It must be only eight in the morning there." Renee had been up and out the door at sunrise. Now she was wishing she'd taken the time to run. She'd just been too antsy to finish up the case.

"I'm an early riser, no problem."

Renee spent twenty minutes bringing the Navajo archeologist up to date on events of the last few days. "You can probably guess my next question. We're trying to pinpoint all national and international fashionable art markets that are hooked into our situation, so I wondered if you might have any ideas." Renee paused. "We've got Toole on the West Coast, but there's been some evidence someone on the East Coast is also involved."

"Well, Renee," the Navajo scholar began, "the markets of Paris, Tokyo, Hong Kong, and Germany claim thousands of artifacts a year. There are no laws to protect archaeological ruins except the one passed in 1979 making it illegal to buy, sell, or transport items of, quote, 'interest that were wrongly obtained, such as relics taken by trespassers.'" Begay hesitated, then with a hint of sarcasm said, "Grave robbers, in other words. Sites are at the mercy of property owners and developers who excavate for shopping malls and housing developments—as your friend Mr. Anderson tried to do—even though they're required by this same law to notify authorities when they accidentally discover a site. If they don't believe in the law or the principles involved, they hide what they find. Sometimes a worker will report them, sometimes not."

"Mm, my friend Anderson you say? I don't think so," Renee sneered.

"No, I suppose not," the doctor laughed. "Your case is especially close to my heart right now, Renee, because we just finished saving the Sinagua ruins near Cornville, just north of here. We were able to mobilize Hopi, Apache, Yavapai, some white folks, and the Heard Museum people in Phoenix to protest the excavation. The houses they were going to build would have destroyed a site believed to be home to 500 people before it was abandoned for unknown reasons around 1425, and the artifacts found there would have gone into the international fashionable art market and been lost to us forever." Begay stopped, then added, "We have another problem out here you might watch for. People who come on the reservation as teachers, medical people, or whatever, and befriend us. Worm their way into our lives and our trust, then begin stealing artifacts. It's so easy to sell these stolen items. You could almost advertise them in some of the trade papers."

"With more and more digs going on in this part of the country," Renee commented, "I wouldn't be surprised if we don't start having the same problems."

"How do white folks say it, 'Better to be safe than sorry'? Anyway, about the names, there's a few I can give you that are almost always mentioned in conjunction with this market. After I got your first message I called an archaeologist colleague at Georgetown University and asked him if he'd heard any rumors about Minnesota. He called me back with a couple of leads, but cautioned me they were only rumors about someone getting ready to flood the market with pretty incredible artifacts, including thousands of year old skeletons and a one of a kind rattle. First, your guy Toole from the Hoover Scholastic Institute seems to be a key player on the West Coast, he said, and a Professor Arlene Baxter at Columbia University in New York. My contact did say he'd heard the deal had gotten a little messy and then stalled for some reason. There's also a dealer's newsletter, comes out six times a year, and lists legal items available for sale. On the back page they have a regular column on stolen artifacts and their value. Of course, they don't identify them as stolen. It's a sneaky way of letting buyers know what's out there. If you have the right contacts, you can usually track down what you want to buy."

"Gotten a little messy—that's an understatement, eh? Three people dead. Don't these guys care about the lives at the other end of the deals? This is a situation of the heart for us, not the head or pocketbook. Our people are hurting, especially our elders. My gram and auntie and their buddies don't deserve this. They've been through enough already in their lives." Renee stopped and took a deep breath, overcome with feelings she'd been holding in for a long time in order to work on the crimes. "I'm sorry, I didn't mean to go on like that. I—"

"Hey, it's OK. I understand. Like I said, we've just been through it. Not the murders, but worrying about losing more of our history. I know the feeling. They've already stolen our land, as much of our identity as they could, our ceremonies. Can't they leave us be now? First they tell us and the world our cultures are worthless and must give way to their way of life, then they bust their butts to find—steal—and sell examples of that culture for millions of dollars. White man's logic. Guess we just can't understand that complicated way of thinking." The two women's friendly, silvery-laced laughter floated over the phone lines. It felt good to Renee, very good.

"By the way, you mentioned Professor Arlene Baxter. I found her name connected to buying what I think is the missing Zuni kachina mask. It was on a slip of paper in a hollowed-out Eagle kachina leg in Dr. Peterson's office."

"Wow, that's a significant find, Renee. That Zuni mask has been central to every celebration of the Zunis since, I think, the 1500s. They'll be thrilled to know it's been located." Renee could feel Dr. Begay's excitement.

"We hope it's the one. Agent Lawton's checking as we speak. Maybe you could give them a call over at Zuni and share the news?"

"You wouldn't mind? It's your find, Renee."

"Nope, not at all."

"I'd love to be the one, for once, that's the bearer of good news. Thanks, you've given me a wonderful gift."

"Least I can do for all you've done for us."

Renee hung up and leaned back. She liked this woman she'd never met. They would have to send her a gift for all her help.

Reeling from the last couple of days, Renee had hardly eaten, let alone been home or had time to reflect on anything. Samantha had called from Bemidji last night, catching her just as she'd rolled in after midnight—a more than welcome distraction. The field trip with Jenny's class was going well, and Renee was extremely grateful that Sam had been willing to take it on. She would have gone if she had to, but finishing up the investigation was her first choice.

"You owe me, girlfriend," Samantha said into the phone. Renee could tell by the sound of Sam's voice that she wasn't having such a bad time, though, and it made her smile to think of the two of them off together being mother and daughter. With her family due back tomorrow Ren was determined the final pegs would be in place so she could relax with them for the first time in many days. She and Sam were starting to click again, and she didn't want to mess it up.

Her thoughts lingered on Samantha and their last lovemaking. She propped her feet up on Bobbi's desk and closed her eyes. Fifteen minutes later Renee startled out of a dream involving k.d. lang in a red silk slip, black garter belt, and thigh-high white leather boots, just as k.d. raised the slip over her head. "Get back to it, LaRoche. Shame on you," she admonished herself. "It's almost over and then there'll be time for that."

There still was one piece Renee wasn't satisfied with—Jed's murder. Finding out Thompson's mother and Anderson's mother were sisters made more sense of that connection, even though Anderson was still denying everything. But Jed. Why was he killed? Why was he killed when and where he was? All of Thompson's accomplices claimed to be shocked about the murder. Hobey wanted to leave it at an argument between two crooks, but Renee worried on it. It was distracting her like sand chiggers around her ankles.

She was alone at the station for the moment with everybody at the council meeting planning reburial of the bones and other articles from the cave. It was important that it happen as soon as possible. Despite the turmoil, the council had called an emergency meeting to make the arrangements they would implement as soon as the FBI released the evidence. *The murder. Was it a fight between two crooks for any one of the dozens of reasons crooks fight? Why? Why?*

It took a few minutes because Ren had never been to the storage room before. Now, turning the knob on the door downstairs, she prayed she'd find something to close this final gap in the mystery. Thompson's personal effects were in a plastic box, his name taped to the front. It was the last box in the row, next to Jed Morriseau, who was next to Eddie Juneau who was next to Karen Lambert—two teens killed in a one-car crash out on Porcupine Road three months ago. They'd been to an all-night party at the Crooked Lake dam. The police figured Eddie either fell asleep or passed out, leaving the car to find its own way down the road for fifty yards, weaving and skidding before hitting the railroad abutment at about eighty miles an hour. Next to Karen's plastic box was Tchibing Wenowin, an elder who people estimated was about 104 years old when he was found dead from natural causes last June by Swamp Lake. Winks With The Eyes' fishing pole was still in his hand, resting on his leg, his *ahnimoosh* Matilda standing watch next to his lawn chair. Renee wondered if they'd used this system for people's personal effects thirty-five years ago when her mother was found frozen to death halfway between Trader Jack's—her favorite Rice Lake bar—and home. The report on her death said the only thing not frozen on Marie LaRoche was the half pint of Four Roses in her pocket. A low moan escaped involuntarily from Renee, stirring Mukwa, who came and lay next to her two-legged's thigh.

Renee lifted Thompson's box out of the row and sat back down on the floor. There wasn't much in it. The beaded watchband, a cigarette lighter and near-empty pack of Camel cigarettes, four quarters, and a belt. She stared intently at the contents and narrowed into the moment. Tunnel vision. *Think, LaRoche. Think.* The acoustic tile ceiling absorbed the sounds of her and Mukwa's breathing. She examined the lighter. Pulling the guts out of the tin case advertising the B & E Bait Shop. Nothing. *OK. Don't give up.* She took the cigarette pack out and examined it carefully. Nothing. She'd already studied the watch and band. With a fair amount of success I might add, she thought proudly. Her last hope was the belt. Ren nudged Mukwa over and laid it out on the floor in front of her, staring at it like it was a poisonous snake. Obviously homemade. By Thompson in prison, maybe. The belt carried the burned-in message: *Rehabilitation Is For Sissies.* "Cute, Thompson," she said to Mukwa. "No wonder you made it so far in life." She picked up the buckle, turning it over and over. Nothing. Then she ran her fingers along the belt. She was just about to forget the whole thing when, near the buckle end, she felt a small bulge on the inside. A flap. Lifting it revealed a pocket. A money belt. One of those belts travelers use. She felt her pulse quicken. In the pocket she found a folded piece of paper with a phone number on it.

The 315 area code seemed familiar. She held it in her hand as if it might be the answer to life itself, watching it for a long time. A sick feeling was starting in her gut. "Is this something I really want to follow to the end?" she whispered, so quietly she barely heard it herself.

Ren returned to the front desk, grateful she had this time uninterrupted by the phone. She repeated the 315 number scribbled on the paper she held and looked at her watch. Eleven-ten. "Be about noon there." She tapped a pencil slowly on Bobbi's desk, then stood and went to the window. Mukwa lifted a sleepy eye to watch her two-legged pace back and forth in front of the window. *Somethin's worryin' her mind,* Mukwa frowned. *I better stick close. These last few days have been hard on her.*

Outside, the sun angled its fall shadows first one way, then another. A cold mist still levitated along the ravines and gullies, reluctant to give way to the day's warming. *Ahnimoosh* and their two-leggeds romped in the park. The children were learning the moccasin game as part of this week's history lesson. Renee was proud of the school's indigenous-centered curriculum, reversing the Eurocentric teaching done in neighboring schools. Giggles rose and fell from the park as even the teenage teachers' aides let go of pretense and posturing long enough to join in the fun. The enthusiasm of the little ones was contagious.

With the flurry of artistic explosion in this last gasp of summer, it was as if every living thing was bursting to have just one more colorful dance before settling in. Even the browns had a depth not visible in winter. "Must be why they call it Indian Summer, eh Mukie?" Soon just the memories of these days would be left, with people saying, "Remember how warm it was that day in the park when the kids were..." Stories would be repeated around the rez as the below-zero blizzard days became daily occurrences.

Renee stepped out into the sunshine, walking along the outskirts of the park, Mukwa at her heels. She let her mind wander. Soon she was transported to maneuvering through a section of the Journey River white water, heading straight for two chutes. Which one to choose? Along the river's edge evergreens and willows shared space with the rocky shoreline, sisters of the boulders creating all the foam and spray in the middle of the river. Ren picked the nearly hidden chute at the last second and her canoe flew between the curls and out the other side just as she made her final turn circling the park. She returned to the station, sat down at Bobbi's desk, and picked up the phone.

Two rings. Three.

"Hello?" a hesitant voice said.

"Hello. My name is Renee LaRoche. I'm calling from—"

"*Boozho*, Renny. I've been expecting your call."

"Who's—Betty? Oh no...it *is* you."

"It's me, Renny. It's me."

The day had flown by after that. Renee hoped Billy wasn't going crazy waiting for them. The sun's slanting light was about to disappear into a bank of dark and threatening clouds, and by the smell in the air, Ren knew it wouldn't be long now before the first big snowfall. Turning on to The Narrows, the river bluffs' aura after millions of years standing sentinel on this part of Mother Earth hit them full force. The beauty of Red Earth's little corner of the world never failed to thrill Renee. "Cemeteries dark as night no matter what time you come," she murmured to Hobey as they pulled up next to the *midewiwin* houses fifteen minutes later. The going had been slow without the use of her headlights, but she knew even a flashlight's glow traveled in an open countryside and she didn't want anyone with unfriendly thoughts to come investigating. Getting out of her jeep, Renee looked at Hobey and nodded toward the meadow. "Beautiful, isn't it? Nice to look at after the last few days we've had, eh? Some turn of events. Who'd of figured Peterson?"

Renee offered a prayer to her gramps as the spirits' campfires colored the western edge of the storm clouds a soft glowing orange. Lifting her face to the sky she felt big, wet flakes beginning to drift slowly down. She stepped around the houses into the open meadow. Renee wondered how long it would take someone to start robbing from these graves, sneaking around in the middle of the night, stealing another part of Ahnishanabe history. As Hobey and Renee approached the woods the faint odor of burning wood, topped by the distinct smell of sweetgrass, cedar, and sage, drifted across the field. *Maybe Billy's found a way besides booze and weed to soothe his spirit*, she spoke into the silence. They'd made the trip without talking, each seeming to sense in the other a need to reflect on their own thoughts. Renee hadn't told anyone about her phone call. She'd left it up to

Betty to decide what to do. But now Renee was anxious to share this next experience. Walking along the path she'd traveled with Billy just a few days before, she pointed out all the markings to the chief.

In camp, Billy couldn't believe how clear his head was starting to feel. It'd been almost a week since his last drink and four days since his last toke on weed. The fact that he'd remembered the different parts of evening prayer, and that he could stay with it without drifting off, amazed him. Sitting before a small fire in the lodge he fanned the sage he'd dropped on the fire using his eagle feather. Then he heard the three-sound call of the white-throated sparrow. Once. Again. He crawled out of the lodge, recognizing it as their agreed-upon signal. Billy saw them approaching as he walked to his little clearing's edge. When Renee and Hobey ducked under the oak branches, the young Ojibwa was sitting by the fire he'd quickly started in the clearing for them.

"*Boozho.*"

Ren noticed the change in Billy's voice immediately. It sounded calm and peaceful, no longer full of suspicion and anger.

"How's it been going?" she asked, hoping to confirm the change.

"Very good. It's been very good. I'm almost ready for a sweat. Do you think the elders would let me?" Billy asked with an enthusiasm Renee'd never heard before.

She smiled. "If you want we'll take some tobacco to them and make a request."

For the first time Billy's smile lit up his face. "I'd like that a lot. *Megwetch.*"

"You still have some charges to answer to, young man. You've behaved very stupidly." The chief glowered in the flickering firelight. Ren knew he was sounding especially firm because he wanted Billy to take this seriously enough to turn his life around.

Billy avoided the chief's dark eyes. "I know." He acknowledged the accusation quietly, and by the pained expression on his face Renee knew he meant it.

The two older Ojibwa sat quietly, respecting the magnitude of this moment for the young man. Sober and standing face to face with his life, he was not looking away. Renee felt almost a mother's pride.

Finally, Hobey pulled a manila envelope out of his pack. "Billy, we brought some pictures we want you to take a look at. See if you can identify any of them as your accom—as the men you got involved with." The chief spread the pictures out in front of him.

Billy stared at them for a long time. He was glad Renee was here. He'd come to trust her. She was a dreamer, and dreamers saw past the first layer, even the second and third. Into the center of the soul. She'd helped him with his dream about the cat, and the running, the terror. After their talk he'd stopped having the dream. Stopped, he believed, because he understood his motives. His greed and selfishness. And he determined to change. He'd talked to her about his life with Janice and told her things he'd never said to anyone. Looking at these pictures was important to Renee. He wanted to do right by her, not identify the wrong guys.

Renee noticed Billy's hands start to shake. "Take your time," she said, laying a hand on his. "This light isn't too good, so if there's no one there you recognize, it's OK."

Billy turned his face to hers and smiled. When he looked back down at the pictures they were in better focus. Eight separate eight-by-ten photos lined up in two rows on the spongy forest floor stared back at him. His eyes scanned from left to right and back across them all. "This is the one who called himself Sam," he said, pointing at Peter Thompson. "And this one is Dave." He identified John Anderson.

Renee and Hobey looked at each other, then grinned broadly. "*Megwetch*, Billy," the chief said. "We needed this to firm it up on Anderson. He's been denying everything. This is the link that'll do it on the guy."

Renee put her hand on Billy's shoulder. She knew this was an important step for him. Part of his road back. As he'd said in the bar that night, the Great Spirit keeping him from Jed's place that morning woke him up to what he was doing. Woke him up to wanting something different in his life. Ren knew Billy saw this as another payback to the people he'd betrayed.

The chilly air pushed a hefty breeze across the meadow, swirling it into the woods and under the oak trees surrounding the enclosure where the three two-leggeds and Mukwa sat. They grabbed for their jackets, pulling them up under their chins and huddling closer next to the fire. Billy set another log on. Renee's back was leaned up against a black walnut, watching the few remaining leaves on the quaking aspen across from her tremble and fall to the ground in the wind. Come next spring this and other stands of hardwood would be cleaned of twigs and foliage by browsing deer and elk.

A half hour later Billy finished cleaning out the lodge, sweeping the floor with a pine bough. Ren hung the sweetgrass braid she'd brought as a gift on the wigwam wall, and the three Ojibwa and Mukwa prepared to leave. Renee eyed the area closely as they walked toward the meadow, wanting to remove any signs of human life around the lodge. It was important they respect the elders' choice for secrecy.

When they reached his car Renee put an arm across Billy's shoulders and smiled warmly. "Janice and your little one'll be happy to see you. I stopped by to tell her how things were going and that you'd be home soon. She can't wait to see your handsome face again." Ren gave his face a loving pat. "You take care and don't worry. You're all safe now."

"See you in court, son," Hobey growled, then let loose with a hearty laugh.

Billy's first reaction was to tense up with fear. He relaxed visibly, hearing the laugh. "You got it, Chief. I'll be there."

The cellular phone was ringing in the jeep. It was Bobbi with a message for the chief. Betty Atori had called and wanted him to call her back.

Renee smiled to herself.

ACKNOWLEDGMENTS

Megwetch to Zoe, Janet, and Kate Lynn, who gave me honest, loving, valuable feedback and held my hand through my first book jitters. *Megwetch* to all the Ojibwa elders who helped me, as an adult, find the essence of who I am. And *megwetch* to my family—Nancy, Susan, Mary, dog Mishi, cats Squeaker and Bo, and especially my daughter Theresa, who loved me through it all and called me a writer, even early on when I know they didn't really believe it. I love you all.

AFTERWORD

Theresa Lafavor

It has been twenty years since my mother's novel *Along the Journey River* was first published. After finishing its sequel, *Evil Dead Center*, she toured the country reading from her books and dreamt many other stories that unfortunately did not find their way to print. Carole laFavor died in 2011. While I would have been pleased to write this piece for her republished stories regardless, given her death I am more motivated, dedicated, and inspired to help bring her ideas to life once again.

My mother was an avid reader, conversationalist, and storyteller. She often became teary during television dramas, comedies, and even commercials, and it was her genuine and deeply rooted compassion for all living creatures that inspired her waterworks and her stories. I remember as a child watching with mixed embarrassment and awe as she cried. I couldn't imagine being so moved by a greeting card advertisement or an after school special. I did know that she truly felt the joy, pain, frustration, and confusion of characters and countless animals that paraded across the screen or came to life in the pages of a magazine or newspaper. At some point in my teen years, I stopped going to movies with her: I was too concerned about what other people thought of her frequent guffaws, gulps, and gasps to enjoy the films. I was impressed and relieved when she formed a middle-age women's matinee movie club with two of her closest friends, and I imagined them sitting front and center, oblivious to the other filmgoers. Luckily for me, I got over myself after my teens, and my mother warmly welcomed me to join her again at the movies. Experiencing the world through my mother's eyes was remarkable—and often emotionally exhausting.

My mother was an eternal optimist, which seemed counterintuitive to me when I was young, given her willingness to fight for her beliefs. As I matured, I understood that her optimism was the inspiration for her activism. She believed social change was possible and that we owed it *to* each other to work our hardest *for* each other. I learned early that it was not enough to think positively about each other; you had to stand up and take part.

The same compassion, interest in others, optimism, commitment to address challenge, injustice, and adversity, and wholehearted acceptance of our individuality drew my mother to write stories like *Along the Journey River* and *Evil Dead Center*. Before she wrote about protecting the rights of others, she fought for them. She stood on the front lines of countless marches, protests, and picket lines. Her voice was strong and her convictions were unbending. She vehemently opposed war and the destruction of our planet. She believed in the equality of all living things. She spoke out for the elderly, disabled, abused, disenfranchised, and oppressed. She was confident that writing, even fiction, could be big-hearted activist work, that it could bring people together and illuminate ideas. And she was overjoyed to find out that people believed that *her* writing did just that. She rated publishing her two novels high on her list of accomplishments, but maybe more importantly these books gave her hope that people were still interested in learning about each other.

My mother's novels were unique when they were first published in the 1990s, and they continue to be their own unique genre twenty years later. She skillfully and artistically wove together two mysteries about a Native American lesbian mother living on a rural reservation in an interracial partnership. She brought to life crime and abuse that are all too common in our society but rarely discussed. She gave a voice to people largely underrepresented in published literature: women, lesbians, Native Americans. My mother chose a feminist publisher, Firebrand Books, to publish her novels because she wanted to support female entrepreneurs and small businesses. She would be honored that the University of Minnesota Press is republishing her novels today and would be excited that her writing will reach a new and expanded audience.

My mother was introverted and deeply private. How then did she convince herself to travel the country, visiting feminist bookstores from coast to coast, reading her personal thoughts, ideas, and creative musings in front of rooms full of people she didn't know? She questioned her choices on many occasions, choices that left her feeling fatigued and exposed. But each time she peeked around a corner and saw a room of many eager and excited people she mustered the courage to put one foot in front of the other and take the stage. Although she collapsed exhausted after every reading, she was equal parts exhilarated, inspired, and grateful to share her stories.

Along the Journey River and *Evil Dead Center* are works of fiction, but that does not mean they do not reflect real struggles, personalities and characters, and complex landscapes. There are many parallels throughout both stories to my mother's life, my family, the communities where I grew up, and our people's history. I have no doubt that Renee LaRoche personified the values and ideals my mother held dear. Renee's voice is so familiar to me, and I recognize my mother in her love for her daughter, her unending energy for her animal companions, her shy and slightly reserved nature, her passion for conversation and communication, and her curiosity for knowledge, connection, and belonging.

The lessons imparted by Renee LaRoche's adventures are more relevant now than ever before. We are at another important crossroads in history, where we have the choice to burrow back into our comfort zones or stand up and fight for each other's rights, like my mother did. We have the opportunity to use our voices for good, to unite people. I am comforted knowing my mother believed there was hope in the world and that words can bring people together. I look forward to a new generation of readers discovering her calm way with words and the deep sentiments that *Along the Journey River* and *Evil Dead Center* express.

Carole laFavor (1948–2011), a Two-Spirit Ojibwa from Minnesota, was a novelist, a nurse, and an activist. She was a founding member of Positively Native, an organization committed to helping Native Americans with HIV and AIDS, and was appointed to the first Presidential Advisory Council on HIV/AIDS in 1995. She also wrote *Evil Dead Center* (Minnesota, 2017).

Lisa Tatonetti is professor of English at Kansas State University. She is the author of *The Queerness of Native American Literature* (Minnesota, 2014) and coeditor of *Sovereign Erotics: A Collection of Contemporary Two-Spirit Literature*.

Theresa Lafavor is a professor of psychology at Pacific University in Oregon. She is the daughter of Carole laFavor.